"What is the use of a book," thought Alice,

"Without pictures or conversations?"

- Lewis Carroll, *Alice in Wonderland*

Printed by Createspace
A DBA of On-Demand Publishing LLC
Charleston, SC
2013 Print On Demand Edition

Copyright © 2013 Rick Griffin

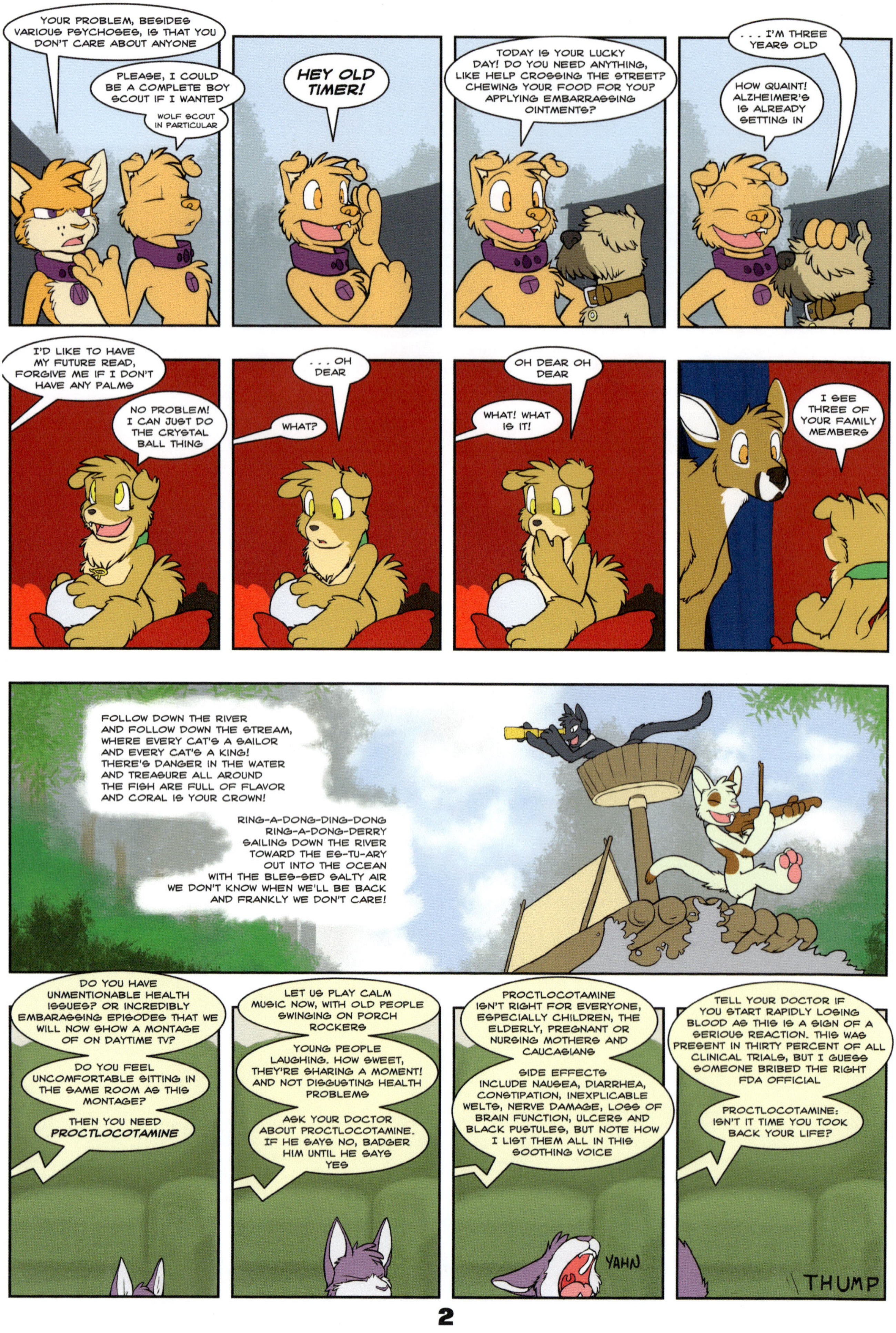

YOUR PROBLEM, BESIDES VARIOUS PSYCHOSES, IS THAT YOU DON'T CARE ABOUT ANYONE
PLEASE, I COULD BE A COMPLETE BOY SCOUT IF I WANTED
WOLF SCOUT IN PARTICULAR
HEY OLD TIMER!
TODAY IS YOUR LUCKY DAY! DO YOU NEED ANYTHING, LIKE HELP CROSSING THE STREET? CHEWING YOUR FOOD FOR YOU? APPLYING EMBARRASSING OINTMENTS?
. . . I'M THREE YEARS OLD
HOW QUAINT! ALZHEIMER'S IS ALREADY SETTING IN
I'D LIKE TO HAVE MY FUTURE READ, FORGIVE ME IF I DON'T HAVE ANY PALMS
NO PROBLEM! I CAN JUST DO THE CRYSTAL BALL THING
. . . OH DEAR
WHAT?
OH DEAR OH DEAR
WHAT! WHAT IS IT!
I SEE THREE OF YOUR FAMILY MEMBERS
FOLLOW DOWN THE RIVER AND FOLLOW DOWN THE STREAM, WHERE EVERY CAT'S A SAILOR AND EVERY CAT'S A KING! THERE'S DANGER IN THE WATER AND TREASURE ALL AROUND THE FISH ARE FULL OF FLAVOR AND CORAL IS YOUR CROWN!
RING-A-DONG-DING-DONG RING-A-DONG-DERRY SAILING DOWN THE RIVER TOWARD THE ES-TU-ARY OUT INTO THE OCEAN WITH THE BLES-SED SALTY AIR WE DON'T KNOW WHEN WE'LL BE BACK AND FRANKLY WE DON'T CARE!
DO YOU HAVE UNMENTIONABLE HEALTH ISSUES? OR INCREDIBLY EMBARASSING EPISODES THAT WE WILL NOW SHOW A MONTAGE OF ON DAYTIME TV?
DO YOU FEEL UNCOMFORTABLE SITTING IN THE SAME ROOM AS THIS MONTAGE?
THEN YOU NEED PROCTLOCOTAMINE
LET US PLAY CALM MUSIC NOW, WITH OLD PEOPLE SWINGING ON PORCH ROCKERS
YOUNG PEOPLE LAUGHING. HOW SWEET, THEY'RE SHARING A MOMENT! AND NOT DISGUSTING HEALTH PROBLEMS
ASK YOUR DOCTOR ABOUT PROCTLOCOTAMINE. IF HE SAYS NO, BADGER HIM UNTIL HE SAYS YES
PROCTLOCOTAMINE ISN'T RIGHT FOR EVERYONE, ESPECIALLY CHILDREN, THE ELDERLY, PREGNANT OR NURSING MOTHERS AND CAUCASIANS
SIDE EFFECTS INCLUDE NAUSEA, DIARRHEA, CONSTIPATION, INEXPLICABLE WELTS, NERVE DAMAGE, LOSS OF BRAIN FUNCTION, ULCERS AND BLACK PUSTULES, BUT NOTE HOW I LIST THEM ALL IN THIS SOOTHING VOICE
YAHN
TELL YOUR DOCTOR IF YOU START RAPIDLY LOSING BLOOD AS THIS IS A SIGN OF A SERIOUS REACTION. THIS WAS PRESENT IN THIRTY PERCENT OF ALL CLINICAL TRIALS, BUT I GUESS SOMEONE BRIBED THE RIGHT FDA OFFICIAL
PROCTLOCOTAMINE: ISN'T IT TIME YOU TOOK BACK YOUR LIFE?
THUMP

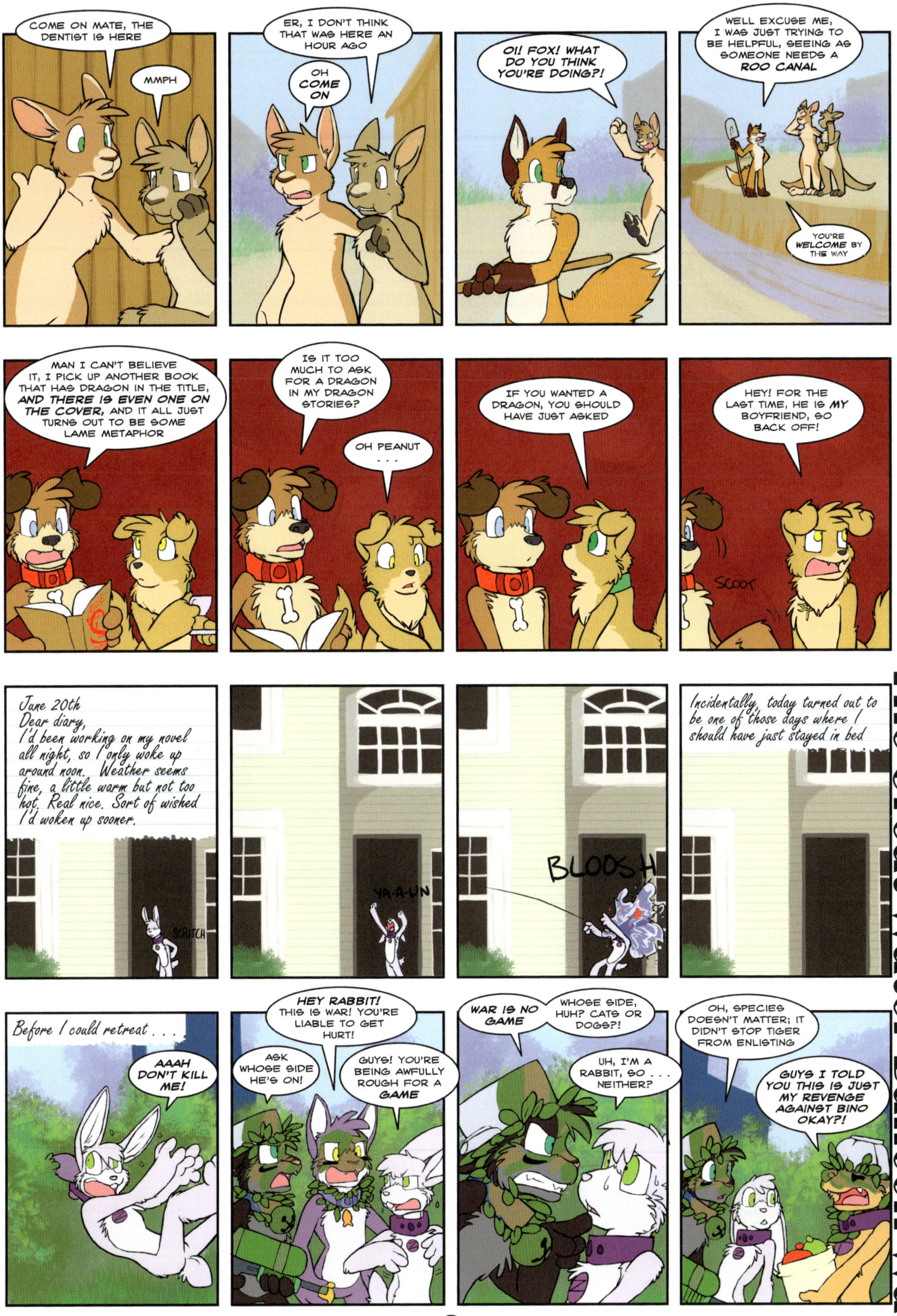
COME ON MATE, THE DENTIST IS HERE
MMPH
ER, I DON'T THINK THAT WAS HERE AN HOUR AGO
OH COME ON
OI! FOX! WHAT DO YOU THINK YOU'RE DOING?!
WELL EXCUSE ME, I WAS JUST TRYING TO BE HELPFUL, SEEING AS SOMEONE NEEDS A ROO CANAL
YOU'RE WELCOME BY THE WAY
MAN I CAN'T BELIEVE IT, I PICK UP ANOTHER BOOK THAT HAS DRAGON IN THE TITLE, AND THERE IS EVEN ONE ON THE COVER, AND IT ALL JUST TURNS OUT TO BE SOME LAME METAPHOR
IS IT TOO MUCH TO ASK FOR A DRAGON IN MY DRAGON STORIES?
OH PEANUT . . .
IF YOU WANTED A DRAGON, YOU SHOULD HAVE JUST ASKED
HEY! FOR THE LAST TIME, HE IS MY BOYFRIEND, SO BACK OFF!
SCOOT
June 20th
Dear diary,
I'd been working on my novel all night, so I only woke up around noon. Weather seems fine, a little warm but not too hot. Real nice. Sort of wished I'd woken up sooner.
SCRITCH
YA-A-WN
BLOOSH
Incidentally, today turned out to be one of those days where I should have just stayed in bed
Before I could retreat . . .
AAAH DON'T KILL ME!
HEY RABBIT! THIS IS WAR! YOU'RE LIABLE TO GET HURT!
ASK WHOSE SIDE HE'S ON!
GUYS! YOU'RE BEING AWFULLY ROUGH FOR A GAME
WAR IS NO GAME
WHOSE SIDE, HUH? CATS OR DOGS?!
UH, I'M A RABBIT, SO . . . NEITHER?
OH, SPECIES DOESN'T MATTER; IT DIDN'T STOP TIGER FROM ENLISTING
GUYS I TOLD YOU THIS IS JUST MY REVENGE AGAINST BINO OKAY?!

The Great Water Balloon War

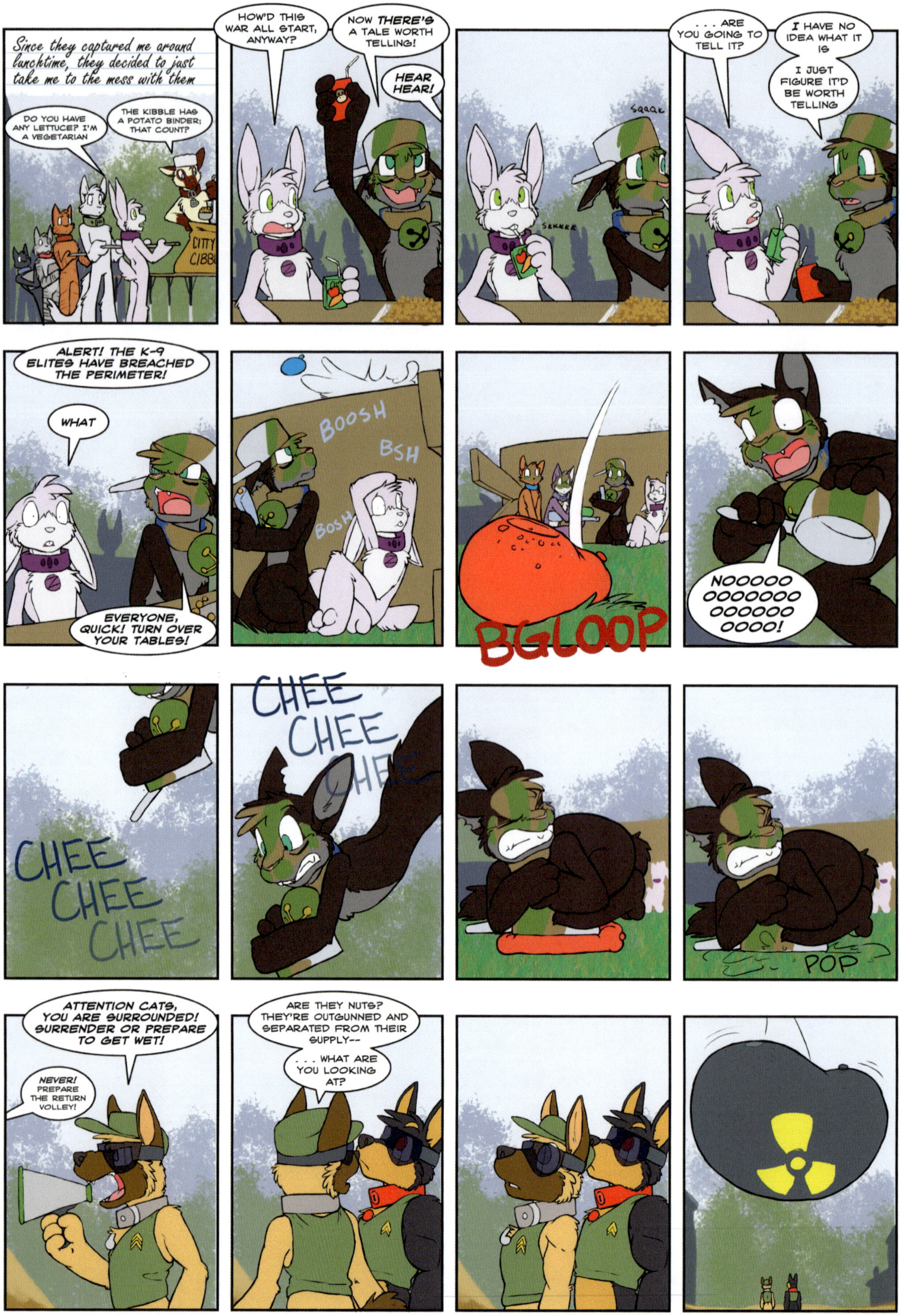
Since they captured me around lunchtime, they decided to just take me to the mess with them
DO YOU HAVE ANY LETTUCE? I'M A VEGETARIAN
THE KIBBLE HAS A POTATO BINDER; THAT COUNT?
CITY CIBB
HOW'D THIS WAR ALL START, ANYWAY?
NOW THERE'S A TALE WORTH TELLING!
HEAR HEAR!
SQRQK
SKKKKK
. . . ARE YOU GOING TO TELL IT?
I HAVE NO IDEA WHAT IT IS
I JUST FIGURE IT'D BE WORTH TELLING
ALERT! THE K-9 ELITES HAVE BREACHED THE PERIMETER!
WHAT
EVERYONE, QUICK! TURN OVER YOUR TABLES!
BOOSH
BSH
BOSH
BGLOOP
NOOOOOOOOOOOOOOOOOOOOO!
CHEE CHEE CHEE
CHEE CHEE CHEE
POP
ATTENTION CATS, YOU ARE SURROUNDED! SURRENDER OR PREPARE TO GET WET!
NEVER! PREPARE THE RETURN VOLLEY!
ARE THEY NUTS? THEY'RE OUTGUNNED AND SEPARATED FROM THEIR SUPPLY--
. . . WHAT ARE YOU LOOKING AT?

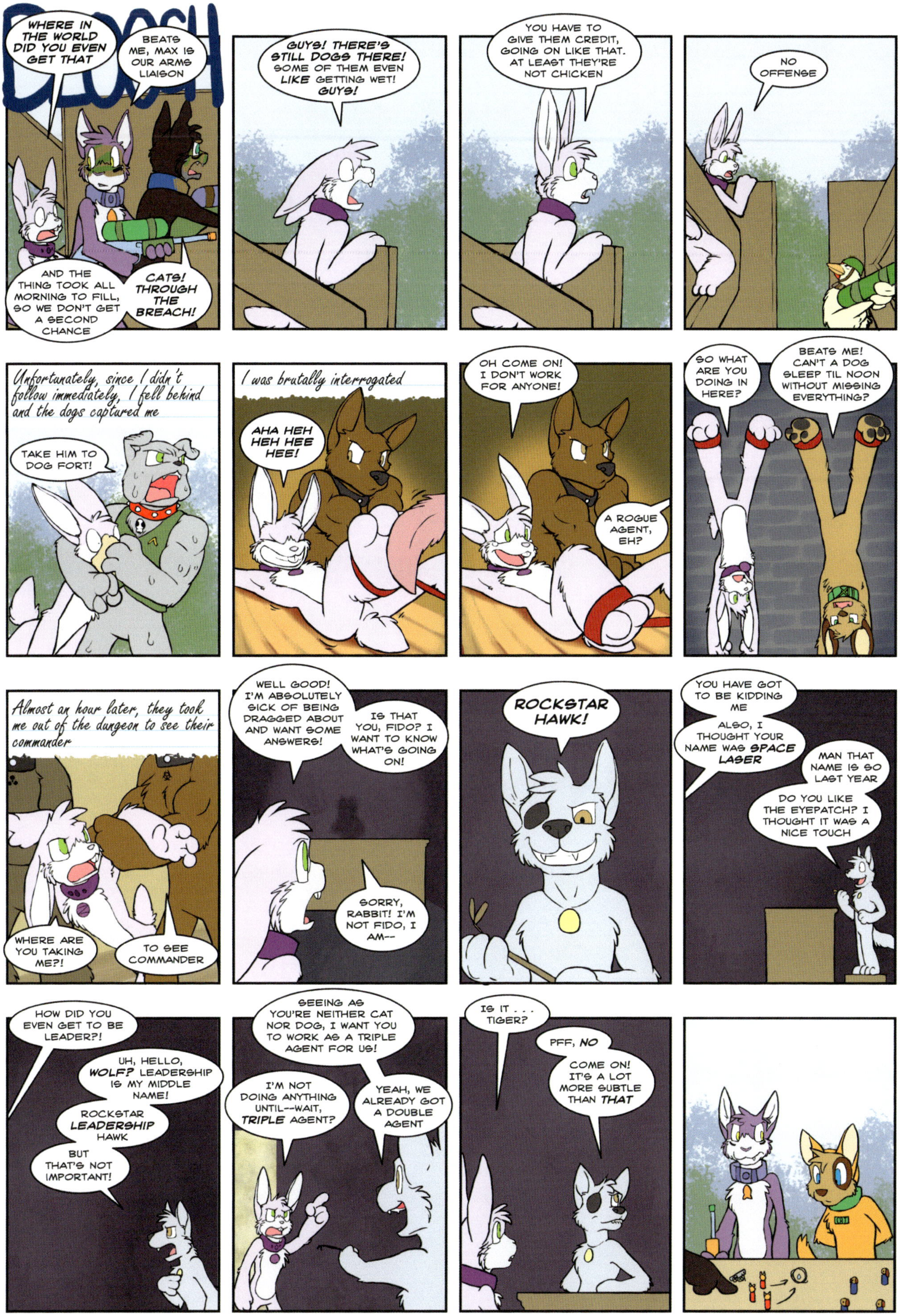
BLOOSH
WHERE IN THE WORLD DID YOU EVEN GET THAT
BEATS ME, MAX IS OUR ARMS LIAISON
AND THE THING TOOK ALL MORNING TO FILL, SO WE DON'T GET A SECOND CHANCE
CATS! THROUGH THE BREACH!
GUYS! THERE'S STILL DOGS THERE! SOME OF THEM EVEN LIKE GETTING WET! GUYS!
YOU HAVE TO GIVE THEM CREDIT, GOING ON LIKE THAT. AT LEAST THEY'RE NOT CHICKEN
NO OFFENSE
Unfortunately, since I didn't follow immediately, I fell behind and the dogs captured me
TAKE HIM TO DOG FORT!
I was brutally interrogated
AHA HEH HEH HEE HEE!
OH COME ON! I DON'T WORK FOR ANYONE!
A ROGUE AGENT, EH?
SO WHAT ARE YOU DOING IN HERE?
BEATS ME! CAN'T A DOG SLEEP TIL NOON WITHOUT MISSING EVERYTHING?
Almost an hour later, they took me out of the dungeon to see their commander
WHERE ARE YOU TAKING ME?!
TO SEE COMMANDER
WELL GOOD! I'M ABSOLUTELY SICK OF BEING DRAGGED ABOUT AND WANT SOME ANSWERS!
IS THAT YOU, FIDO? I WANT TO KNOW WHAT'S GOING ON!
SORRY, RABBIT! I'M NOT FIDO, I AM--
ROCKSTAR HAWK!
YOU HAVE GOT TO BE KIDDING ME
ALSO, I THOUGHT YOUR NAME WAS SPACE LASER
MAN THAT NAME IS SO LAST YEAR
DO YOU LIKE THE EYEPATCH? I THOUGHT IT WAS A NICE TOUCH
HOW DID YOU EVEN GET TO BE LEADER?!
UH, HELLO, WOLF? LEADERSHIP IS MY MIDDLE NAME!
ROCKSTAR LEADERSHIP HAWK
BUT THAT'S NOT IMPORTANT!
SEEING AS YOU'RE NEITHER CAT NOR DOG, I WANT YOU TO WORK AS A TRIPLE AGENT FOR US!
I'M NOT DOING ANYTHING UNTIL--WAIT, TRIPLE AGENT?
YEAH, WE ALREADY GOT A DOUBLE AGENT
IS IT . . . TIGER?
PFF, NO
COME ON! IT'S A LOT MORE SUBTLE THAN THAT

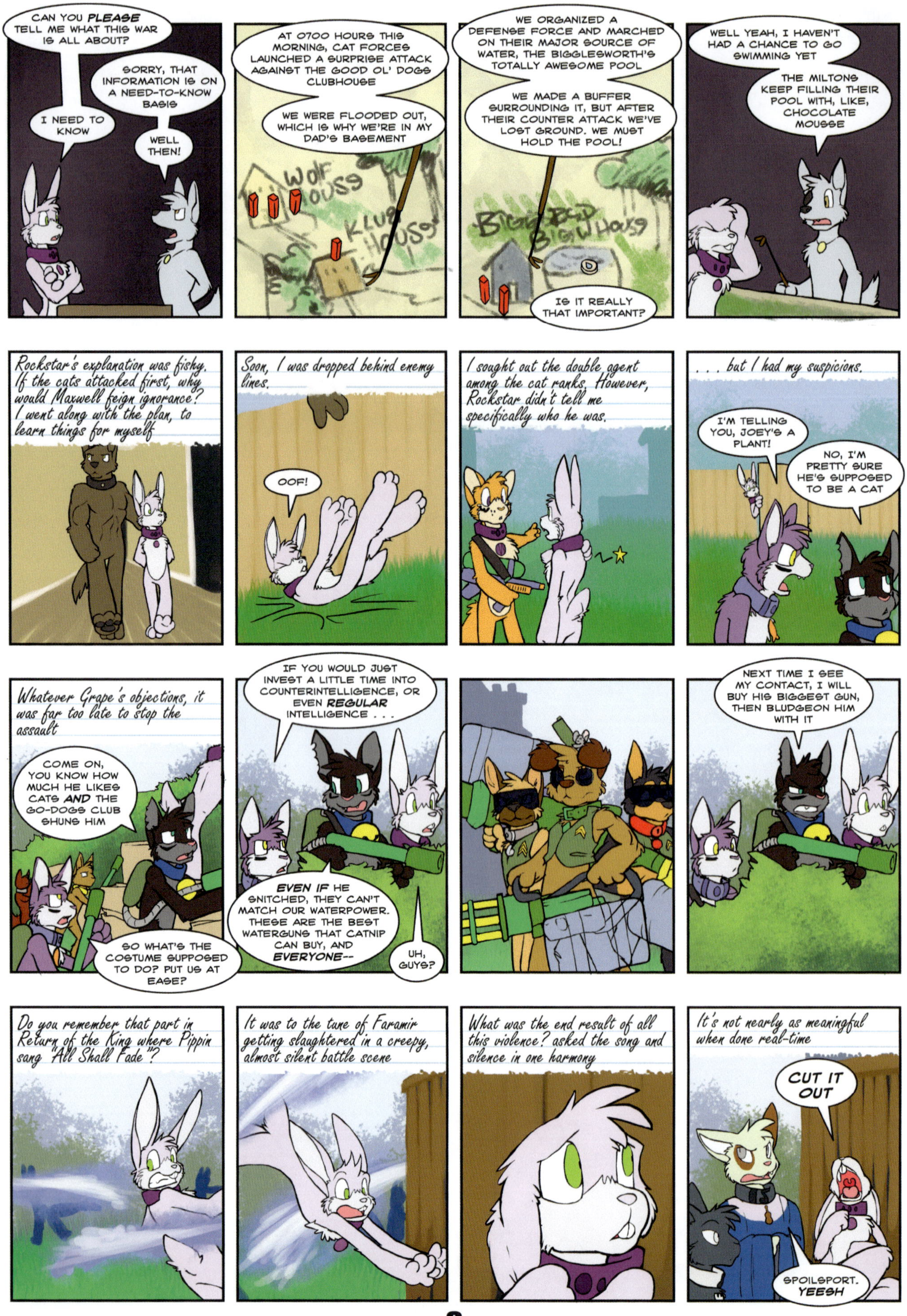
CAN YOU PLEASE TELL ME WHAT THIS WAR IS ALL ABOUT?
SORRY, THAT INFORMATION IS ON A NEED-TO-KNOW BASIS
I NEED TO KNOW
WELL THEN!
AT 0700 HOURS THIS MORNING, CAT FORCES LAUNCHED A SURPRISE ATTACK AGAINST THE GOOD OL' DOGS CLUBHOUSE
WE WERE FLOODED OUT, WHICH IS WHY WE'RE IN MY DAD'S BASEMENT
WOLF HOUSE
KLUB HOUSE
WE ORGANIZED A DEFENSE FORCE AND MARCHED ON THEIR MAJOR SOURCE OF WATER, THE BIGGLESWORTH'S TOTALLY AWESOME POOL
WE MADE A BUFFER SURROUNDING IT, BUT AFTER THEIR COUNTER ATTACK WE'VE LOST GROUND. WE MUST HOLD THE POOL!
IS IT REALLY THAT IMPORTANT?
WELL YEAH, I HAVEN'T HAD A CHANCE TO GO SWIMMING YET
THE MILTONS KEEP FILLING THEIR POOL WITH, LIKE, CHOCOLATE MOUSSE
Rockstar's explanation was fishy. If the cats attacked first, why would Maxwell feign ignorance? I went along with the plan, to learn things for myself
Soon, I was dropped behind enemy lines.
OOF!
I sought out the double agent among the cat ranks. However, Rockstar didn't tell me specifically who he was.
. . . but I had my suspicions.
I'M TELLING YOU, JOEY'S A PLANT!
NO, I'M PRETTY SURE HE'S SUPPOSED TO BE A CAT
Whatever Grape's objections, it was far too late to stop the assault
COME ON, YOU KNOW HOW MUCH HE LIKES CATS AND THE GO-DOGS CLUB SHUNS HIM
SO WHAT'S THE COSTUME SUPPOSED TO DO? PUT US AT EASE?
IF YOU WOULD JUST INVEST A LITTLE TIME INTO COUNTERINTELLIGENCE, OR EVEN REGULAR INTELLIGENCE . . .
EVEN IF HE SNITCHED, THEY CAN'T MATCH OUR WATERPOWER. THESE ARE THE BEST WATERGUNS THAT CATNIP CAN BUY, AND EVERYONE--
UH, GUYS?
NEXT TIME I SEE MY CONTACT, I WILL BUY HIS BIGGEST GUN, THEN BLUDGEON HIM WITH IT
Do you remember that part in Return of the King where Pippin sang "All Shall Fade"?
It was to the tune of Faramir getting slaughtered in a creepy, almost silent battle scene
What was the end result of all this violence? asked the song and silence in one harmony
It's not nearly as meaningful when done real-time
CUT IT OUT
SPOILSPORT. YEESH

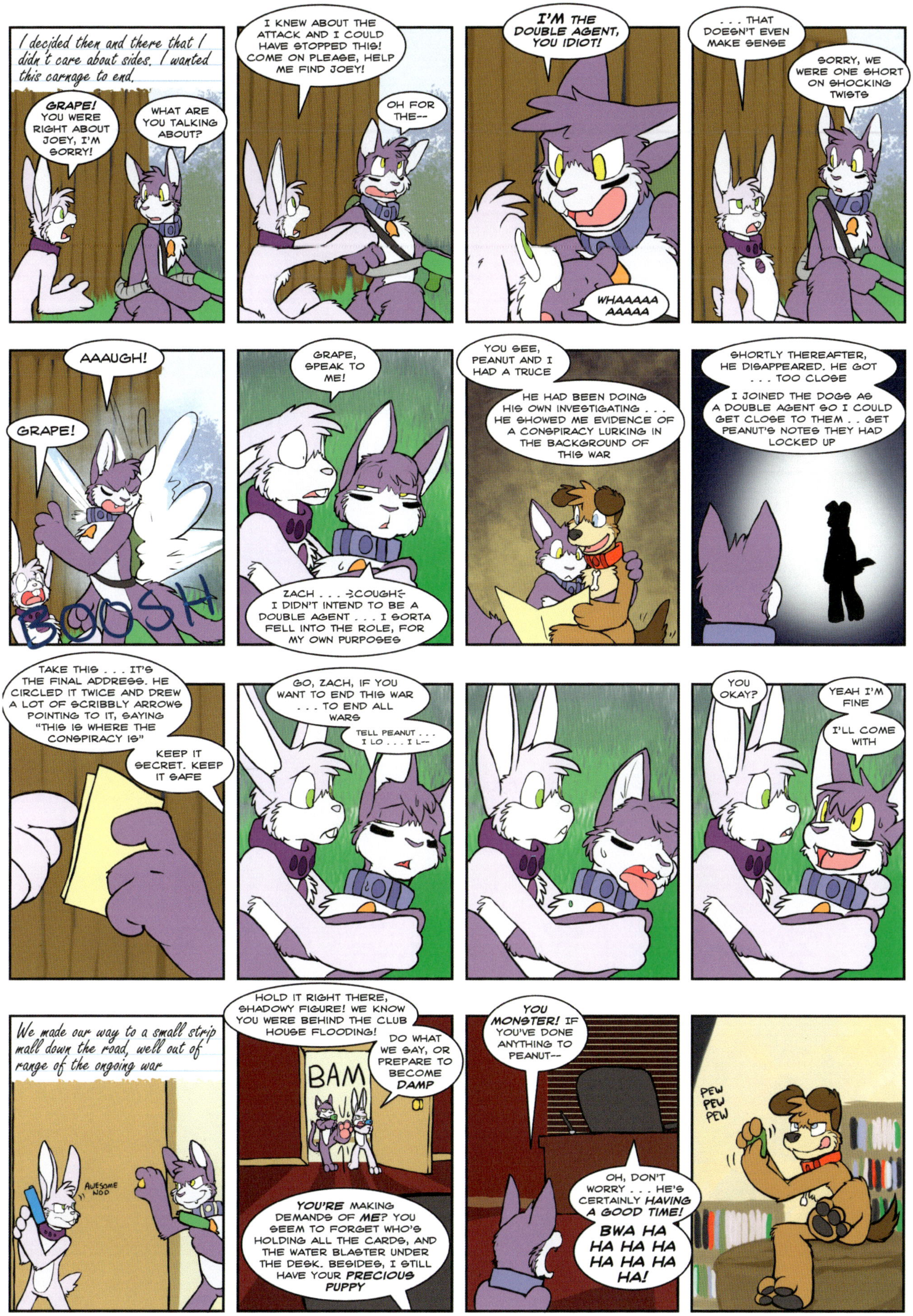

I decided then and there that I didn't care about sides. I wanted this carnage to end.
GRAPE! YOU WERE RIGHT ABOUT JOEY, I'M SORRY!
WHAT ARE YOU TALKING ABOUT?
I KNEW ABOUT THE ATTACK AND I COULD HAVE STOPPED THIS! COME ON PLEASE, HELP ME FIND JOEY!
OH FOR THE--
I'M THE DOUBLE AGENT, YOU IDIOT!
WHAAAAA AAAAA
. . . THAT DOESN'T EVEN MAKE SENSE
SORRY, WE WERE ONE SHORT ON SHOCKING TWISTS
AAAUGH!
GRAPE!
BOOSH
GRAPE, SPEAK TO ME!
ZACH . . . ≯COUGH≮ I DIDN'T INTEND TO BE A DOUBLE AGENT . . . I SORTA FELL INTO THE ROLE, FOR MY OWN PURPOSES
YOU SEE, PEANUT AND I HAD A TRUCE
HE HAD BEEN DOING HIS OWN INVESTIGATING . . . HE SHOWED ME EVIDENCE OF A CONSPIRACY LURKING IN THE BACKGROUND OF THIS WAR
SHORTLY THEREAFTER, HE DISAPPEARED. HE GOT . . . TOO CLOSE
I JOINED THE DOGS AS A DOUBLE AGENT SO I COULD GET CLOSE TO THEM . . GET PEANUT'S NOTES THEY HAD LOCKED UP
TAKE THIS . . . IT'S THE FINAL ADDRESS. HE CIRCLED IT TWICE AND DREW A LOT OF SCRIBBLY ARROWS POINTING TO IT, SAYING "THIS IS WHERE THE CONSPIRACY IS"
KEEP IT SECRET. KEEP IT SAFE
GO, ZACH, IF YOU WANT TO END THIS WAR . . . TO END ALL WARS
TELL PEANUT . . . I LO . . . I L--
YOU OKAY?
YEAH I'M FINE
I'LL COME WITH
We made our way to a small strip mall down the road, well out of range of the ongoing war
AWESOME NOD
HOLD IT RIGHT THERE, SHADOWY FIGURE! WE KNOW YOU WERE BEHIND THE CLUB HOUSE FLOODING!
DO WHAT WE SAY, OR PREPARE TO BECOME DAMP
BAM
YOU'RE MAKING DEMANDS OF ME? YOU SEEM TO FORGET WHO'S HOLDING ALL THE CARDS, AND THE WATER BLASTER UNDER THE DESK. BESIDES, I STILL HAVE YOUR PRECIOUS PUPPY
YOU MONSTER! IF YOU'VE DONE ANYTHING TO PEANUT--
OH, DON'T WORRY . . . HE'S CERTAINLY HAVING A GOOD TIME!
BWA HA HA HA HA HA HA HA HA!
PEW PEW PEW

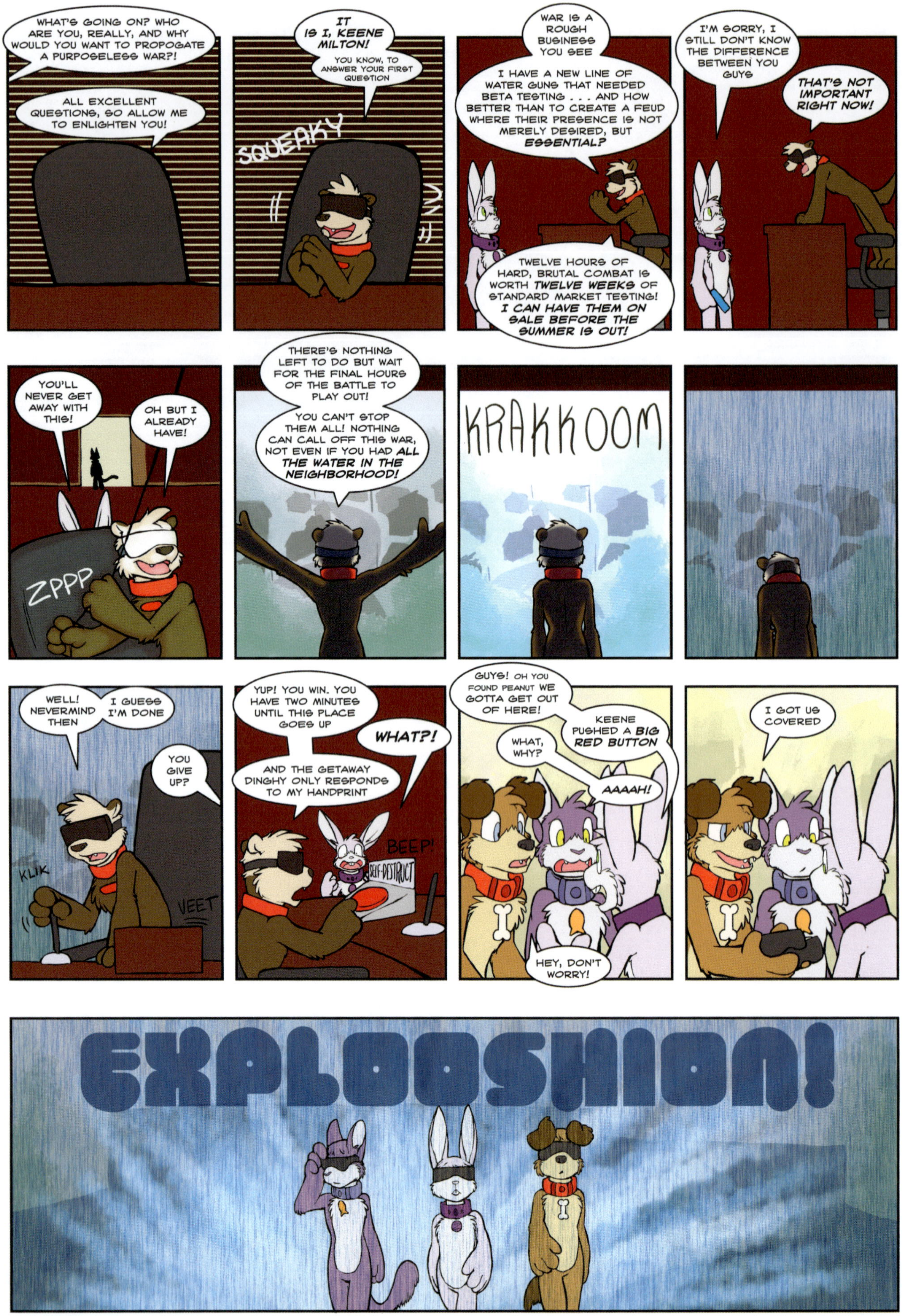

WHAT'S GOING ON? WHO ARE YOU, REALLY, AND WHY WOULD YOU WANT TO PROPOGATE A PURPOSELESS WAR?!
ALL EXCELLENT QUESTIONS, SO ALLOW ME TO ENLIGHTEN YOU!
SQUEAKY
IT IS I, KEENE MILTON!
YOU KNOW, TO ANSWER YOUR FIRST QUESTION
WAR IS A ROUGH BUSINESS YOU SEE
I HAVE A NEW LINE OF WATER GUNS THAT NEEDED BETA TESTING . . . AND HOW BETTER THAN TO CREATE A FEUD WHERE THEIR PRESENCE IS NOT MERELY DESIRED, BUT ESSENTIAL?
TWELVE HOURS OF HARD, BRUTAL COMBAT IS WORTH TWELVE WEEKS OF STANDARD MARKET TESTING! I CAN HAVE THEM ON SALE BEFORE THE SUMMER IS OUT!
I'M SORRY, I STILL DON'T KNOW THE DIFFERENCE BETWEEN YOU GUYS
THAT'S NOT IMPORTANT RIGHT NOW!
YOU'LL NEVER GET AWAY WITH THIS!
OH BUT I ALREADY HAVE!
ZPPP
THERE'S NOTHING LEFT TO DO BUT WAIT FOR THE FINAL HOURS OF THE BATTLE TO PLAY OUT!
YOU CAN'T STOP THEM ALL! NOTHING CAN CALL OFF THIS WAR, NOT EVEN IF YOU HAD ALL THE WATER IN THE NEIGHBORHOOD!
KRAKKOOM
WELL! NEVERMIND THEN
I GUESS I'M DONE
YOU GIVE UP?
KLIK
VEET
YUP! YOU WIN. YOU HAVE TWO MINUTES UNTIL THIS PLACE GOES UP
WHAT?!
AND THE GETAWAY DINGHY ONLY RESPONDS TO MY HANDPRINT
BEEP!
SELF-DESTRUCT
GUYS! OH YOU FOUND PEANUT WE GOTTA GET OUT OF HERE!
WHAT, WHY?
KEENE PUSHED A BIG RED BUTTON
AAAAH!
HEY, DON'T WORRY!
I GOT US COVERED
EXPLOOSHION!

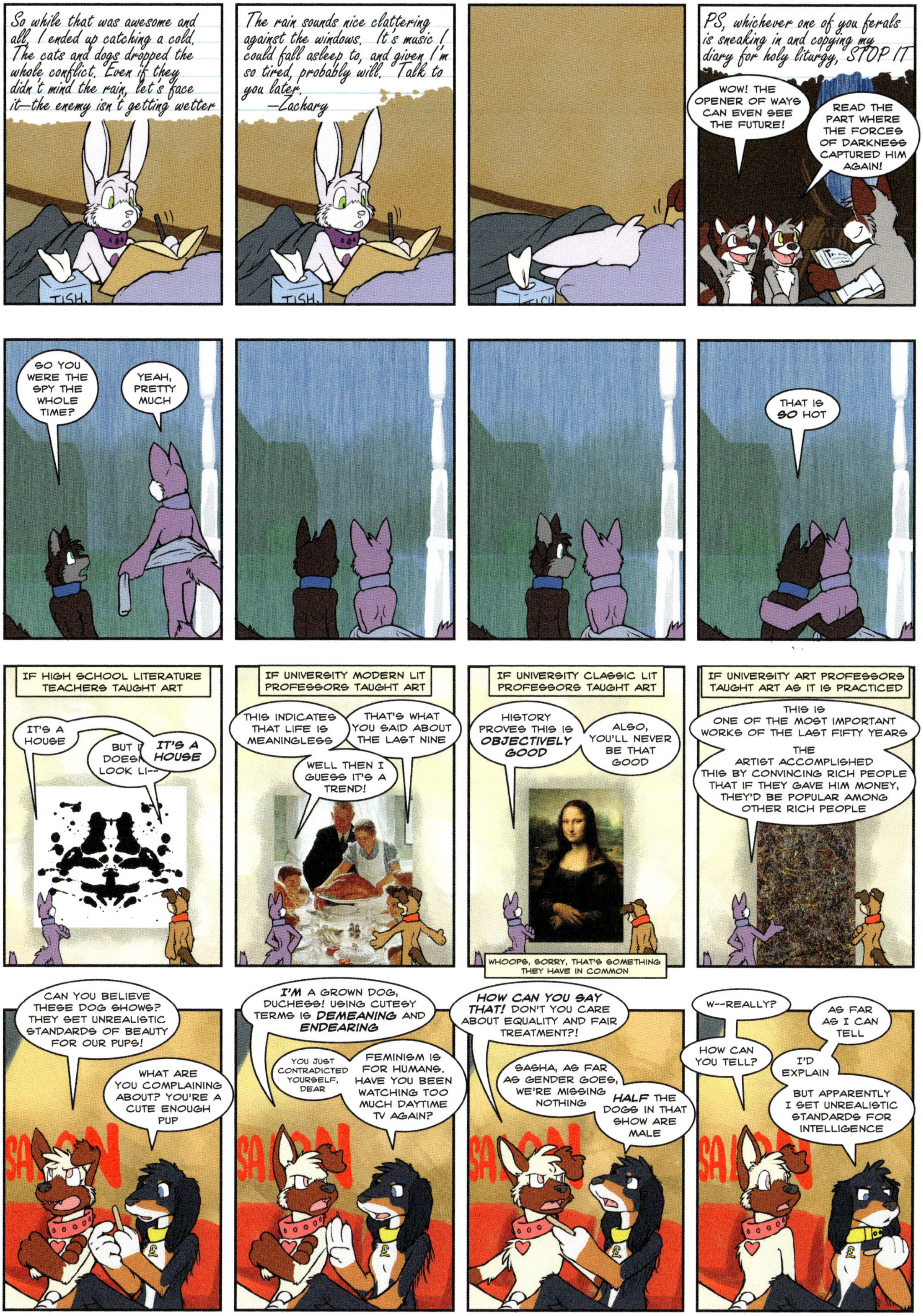
So while that was awesome and all, I ended up catching a cold. The cats and dogs dropped the whole conflict. Even if they didn't mind the rain, let's face it—the enemy isn't getting wetter
TISH.
The rain sounds nice clattering against the windows. It's music I could fall asleep to, and given I'm so tired, probably will. Talk to you later.
—Zachary
TISH.
PS, whichever one of you ferals is sneaking in and copying my diary for holy liturgy, STOP IT
WOW! THE OPENER OF WAYS CAN EVEN SEE THE FUTURE!
READ THE PART WHERE THE FORCES OF DARKNESS CAPTURED HIM AGAIN!
SO YOU WERE THE SPY THE WHOLE TIME?
YEAH, PRETTY MUCH
THAT IS SO HOT
IF HIGH SCHOOL LITERATURE TEACHERS TAUGHT ART
IT'S A HOUSE
BUT IT DOESN'T LOOK LI--
IT'S A HOUSE
IF UNIVERSITY MODERN LIT PROFESSORS TAUGHT ART
THIS INDICATES THAT LIFE IS MEANINGLESS
THAT'S WHAT YOU SAID ABOUT THE LAST NINE
WELL THEN I GUESS IT'S A TREND!
IF UNIVERSITY CLASSIC LIT PROFESSORS TAUGHT ART
HISTORY PROVES THIS IS OBJECTIVELY GOOD
ALSO, YOU'LL NEVER BE THAT GOOD
WHOOPS, SORRY, THAT'S SOMETHING THEY HAVE IN COMMON
IF UNIVERSITY ART PROFESSORS TAUGHT ART AS IT IS PRACTICED
THIS IS ONE OF THE MOST IMPORTANT WORKS OF THE LAST FIFTY YEARS
THE ARTIST ACCOMPLISHED THIS BY CONVINCING RICH PEOPLE THAT IF THEY GAVE HIM MONEY, THEY'D BE POPULAR AMONG OTHER RICH PEOPLE
CAN YOU BELIEVE THESE DOG SHOWS? THEY SET UNREALISTIC STANDARDS OF BEAUTY FOR OUR PUPS!
WHAT ARE YOU COMPLAINING ABOUT? YOU'RE A CUTE ENOUGH PUP
I'M A GROWN DOG, DUCHESS! USING CUTESY TERMS IS DEMEANING AND ENDEARING
YOU JUST CONTRADICTED YOURSELF, DEAR
FEMINISM IS FOR HUMANS. HAVE YOU BEEN WATCHING TOO MUCH DAYTIME TV AGAIN?
HOW CAN YOU SAY THAT! DON'T YOU CARE ABOUT EQUALITY AND FAIR TREATMENT?!
SASHA, AS FAR AS GENDER GOES, WE'RE MISSING NOTHING
HALF THE DOGS IN THAT SHOW ARE MALE
W--REALLY?
HOW CAN YOU TELL?
AS FAR AS I CAN TELL
I'D EXPLAIN
BUT APPARENTLY I SET UNREALISTIC STANDARDS FOR INTELLIGENCE

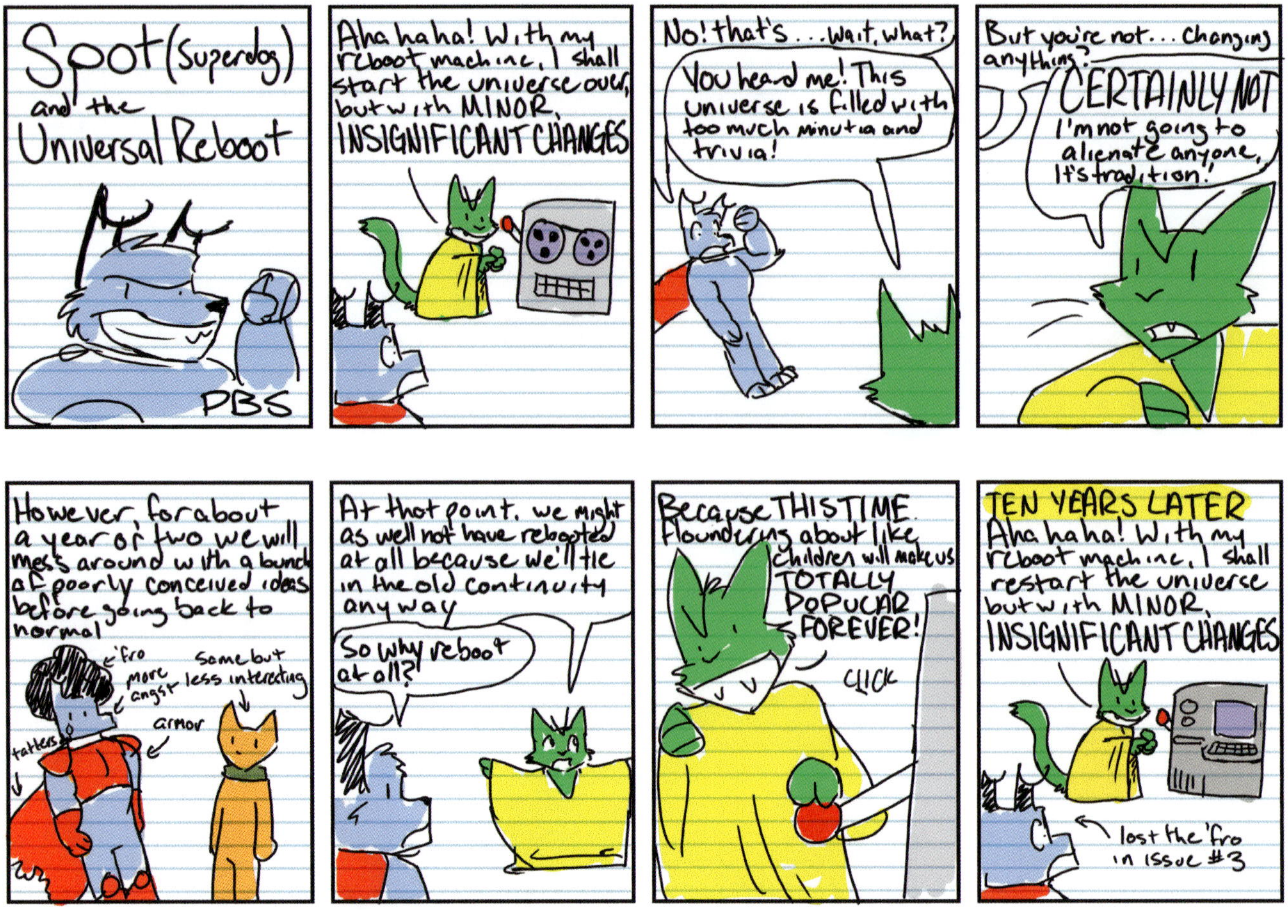
Spot (Superdog) and the Universal Reboot
PBS
Ahahaha! With my reboot machine, I shall start the universe over, but with MINOR, INSIGNIFICANT CHANGES
No! that's . . . wait, what?
You heard me! This universe is filled with too much minutia and trivia!
But you're not... changing anything?
CERTAINLY NOT I'm not going to alienate anyone, It's tradition!
However, for about a year or two we will mess around with a bunch of poorly conceived ideas before going back to normal
'fro
more angst
same but less interesting
armor
tatters
At that point, we might as well not have rebooted at all because we'll tie in the old continuity anyway
So why reboot at all?
Because THIS TIME floundering about like children will make us TOTALLY POPULAR FOREVER!
CLICK
TEN YEARS LATER
Ahahaha! With my reboot machine, I shall restart the universe but with MINOR, INSIGNIFICANT CHANGES
lost the 'fro in issue #3

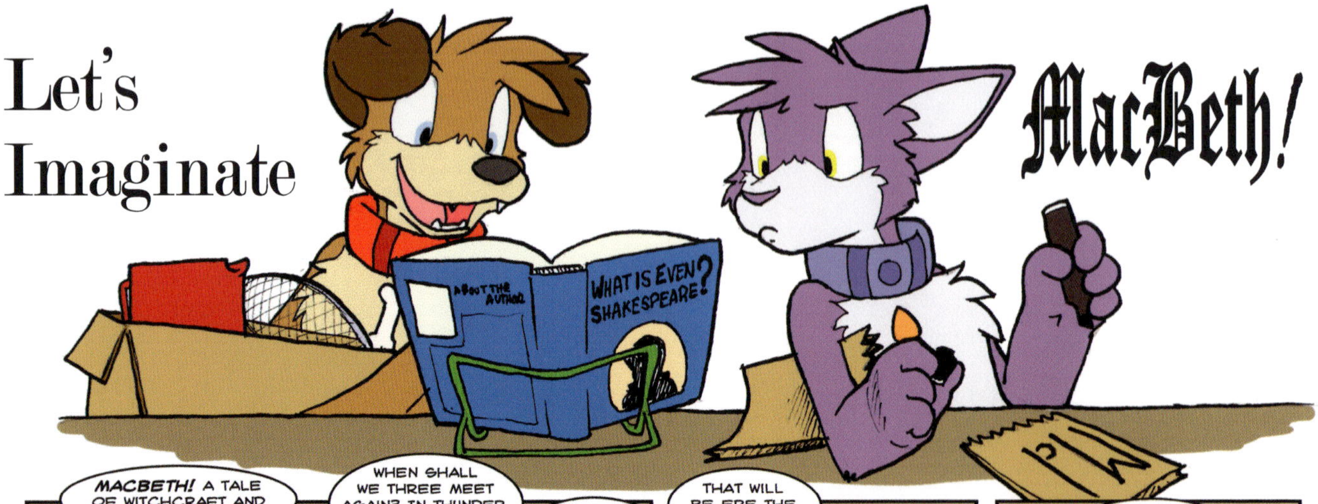
Let's Imagine
MacBeth!
ABOUT THE AUTHOR
WHAT IS EVEN SHAKESPEARE?

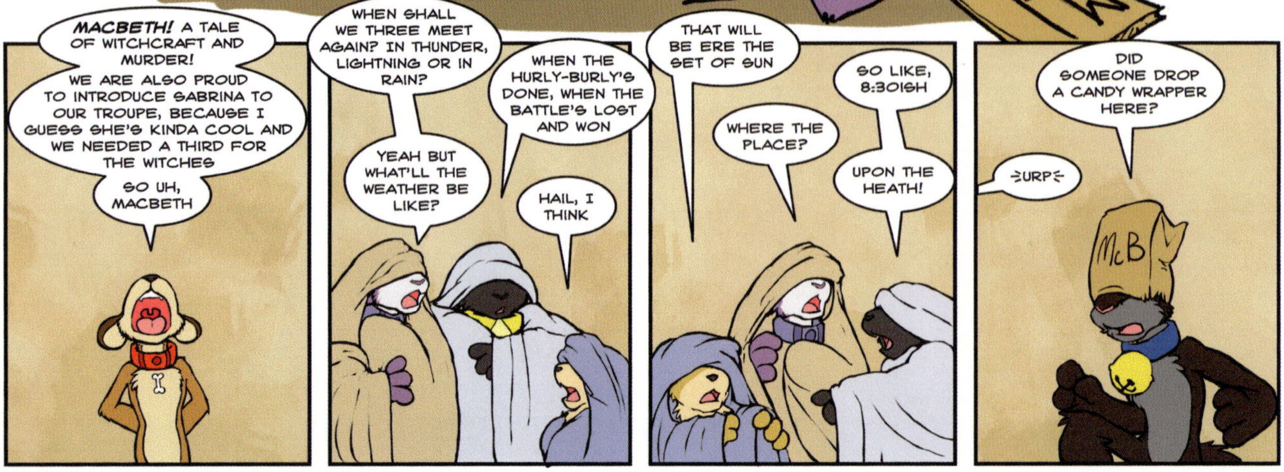
MACBETH! A TALE OF WITCHCRAFT AND MURDER!
WE ARE ALSO PROUD TO INTRODUCE SABRINA TO OUR TROUPE, BECAUSE I GUESS SHE'S KINDA COOL AND WE NEEDED A THIRD FOR THE WITCHES
SO UH, MACBETH
WHEN SHALL WE THREE MEET AGAIN? IN THUNDER, LIGHTNING OR IN RAIN?
YEAH BUT WHAT'LL THE WEATHER BE LIKE?
WHEN THE HURLY-BURLY'S DONE, WHEN THE BATTLE'S LOST AND WON
HAIL, I THINK
THAT WILL BE ERE THE SET OF SUN
SO LIKE, 8:30ISH
WHERE THE PLACE?
UPON THE HEATH!
DID SOMEONE DROP A CANDY WRAPPER HERE?
URP
McB

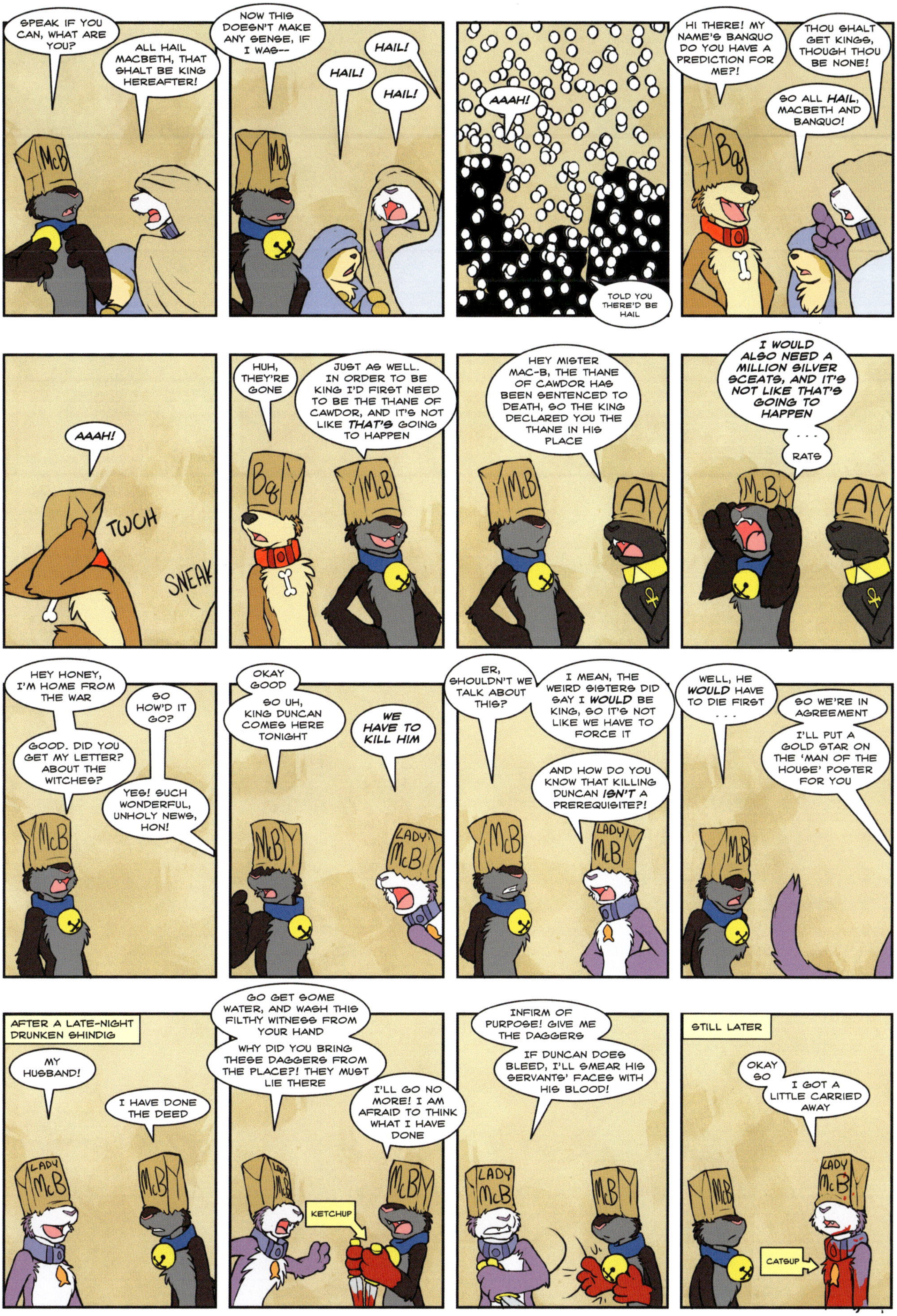
SPEAK IF YOU CAN, WHAT ARE YOU?
ALL HAIL MACBETH, THAT SHALT BE KING HEREAFTER!
NOW THIS DOESN'T MAKE ANY SENSE, IF I WAS--
HAIL!
HAIL!
HAIL!
AAAH!
TOLD YOU THERE'D BE HAIL
HI THERE! MY NAME'S BANQUO DO YOU HAVE A PREDICTION FOR ME?!
THOU SHALT GET KINGS, THOUGH THOU BE NONE!
SO ALL HAIL, MACBETH AND BANQUO!
AAAH!
TWCH
SNEAK
HUH, THEY'RE GONE
JUST AS WELL. IN ORDER TO BE KING I'D FIRST NEED TO BE THE THANE OF CAWDOR, AND IT'S NOT LIKE THAT'S GOING TO HAPPEN
HEY MISTER MAC-B, THE THANE OF CAWDOR HAS BEEN SENTENCED TO DEATH, SO THE KING DECLARED YOU THE THANE IN HIS PLACE
I WOULD ALSO NEED A MILLION SILVER SCEATS, AND IT'S NOT LIKE THAT'S GOING TO HAPPEN
. . .
RATS
HEY HONEY, I'M HOME FROM THE WAR
SO HOW'D IT GO?
GOOD. DID YOU GET MY LETTER? ABOUT THE WITCHES?
YES! SUCH WONDERFUL, UNHOLY NEWS, HON!
OKAY GOOD
SO UH, KING DUNCAN COMES HERE TONIGHT
WE HAVE TO KILL HIM
ER, SHOULDN'T WE TALK ABOUT THIS?
I MEAN, THE WEIRD SISTERS DID SAY I WOULD BE KING, SO IT'S NOT LIKE WE HAVE TO FORCE IT
AND HOW DO YOU KNOW THAT KILLING DUNCAN ISN'T A PREREQUISITE?!
WELL, HE WOULD HAVE TO DIE FIRST . . .
SO WE'RE IN AGREEMENT
I'LL PUT A GOLD STAR ON THE 'MAN OF THE HOUSE' POSTER FOR YOU
AFTER A LATE-NIGHT DRUNKEN SHINDIG
MY HUSBAND!
I HAVE DONE THE DEED
GO GET SOME WATER, AND WASH THIS FILTHY WITNESS FROM YOUR HAND
WHY DID YOU BRING THESE DAGGERS FROM THE PLACE?! THEY MUST LIE THERE
I'LL GO NO MORE! I AM AFRAID TO THINK WHAT I HAVE DONE
KETCHUP
INFIRM OF PURPOSE! GIVE ME THE DAGGERS
IF DUNCAN DOES BLEED, I'LL SMEAR HIS SERVANTS' FACES WITH HIS BLOOD!
STILL LATER
OKAY SO
I GOT A LITTLE CARRIED AWAY
CATSUP

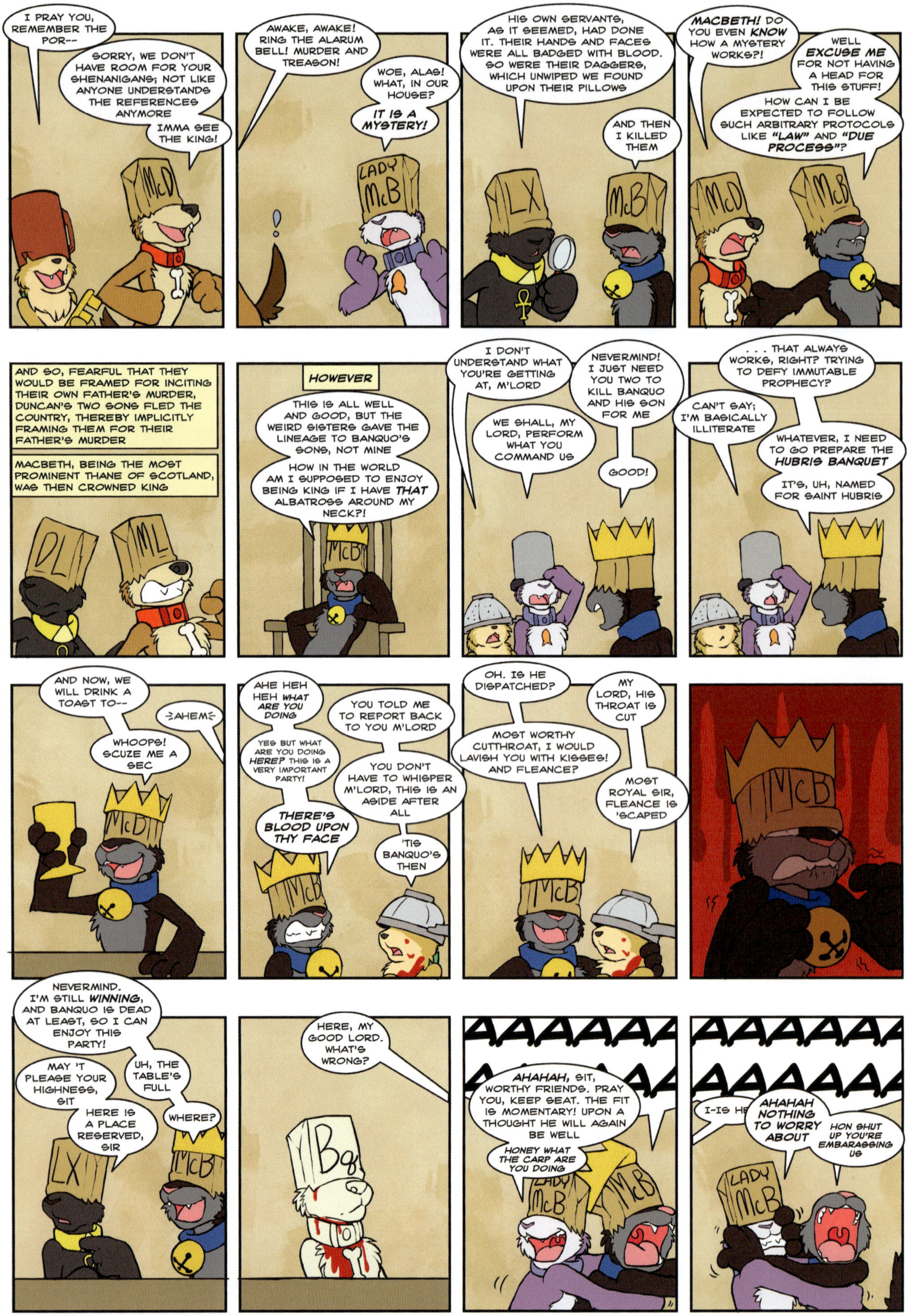

I PRAY YOU, REMEMBER THE POR--
SORRY, WE DON'T HAVE ROOM FOR YOUR SHENANIGANS; NOT LIKE ANYONE UNDERSTANDS THE REFERENCES ANYMORE
IMMA SEE THE KING!
McD
AWAKE, AWAKE! RING THE ALARUM BELL! MURDER AND TREASON!
WOE, ALAS! WHAT, IN OUR HOUSE?
IT IS A MYSTERY!
LADY McB
HIS OWN SERVANTS, AS IT SEEMED, HAD DONE IT. THEIR HANDS AND FACES WERE ALL BADGED WITH BLOOD. SO WERE THEIR DAGGERS, WHICH UNWIPED WE FOUND UPON THEIR PILLOWS
AND THEN I KILLED THEM
LX
McB
MACBETH! DO YOU EVEN KNOW HOW A MYSTERY WORKS?!
WELL EXCUSE ME FOR NOT HAVING A HEAD FOR THIS STUFF!
HOW CAN I BE EXPECTED TO FOLLOW SUCH ARBITRARY PROTOCOLS LIKE "LAW" AND "DUE PROCESS"?
McD
McB
AND SO, FEARFUL THAT THEY WOULD BE FRAMED FOR INCITING THEIR OWN FATHER'S MURDER, DUNCAN'S TWO SONS FLED THE COUNTRY, THEREBY IMPLICITLY FRAMING THEM FOR THEIR FATHER'S MURDER
MACBETH, BEING THE MOST PROMINENT THANE OF SCOTLAND, WAS THEN CROWNED KING
DL
ML
HOWEVER
THIS IS ALL WELL AND GOOD, BUT THE WEIRD SISTERS GAVE THE LINEAGE TO BANQUO'S SONS, NOT MINE
HOW IN THE WORLD AM I SUPPOSED TO ENJOY BEING KING IF I HAVE THAT ALBATROSS AROUND MY NECK?!
McB
I DON'T UNDERSTAND WHAT YOU'RE GETTING AT, M'LORD
NEVERMIND! I JUST NEED YOU TWO TO KILL BANQUO AND HIS SON FOR ME
WE SHALL, MY LORD, PERFORM WHAT YOU COMMAND US
GOOD!
. . . THAT ALWAYS WORKS, RIGHT? TRYING TO DEFY IMMUTABLE PROPHECY?
CAN'T SAY; I'M BASICALLY ILLITERATE
WHATEVER, I NEED TO GO PREPARE THE HUBRIS BANQUET
IT'S, UH, NAMED FOR SAINT HUBRIS
AND NOW, WE WILL DRINK A TOAST TO--
AHEM
WHOOPS! SCUZE ME A SEC
McB
AHE HEH HEH WHAT ARE YOU DOING
YOU TOLD ME TO REPORT BACK TO YOU M'LORD
YES BUT WHAT ARE YOU DOING HERE? THIS IS A VERY IMPORTANT PARTY!
YOU DON'T HAVE TO WHISPER M'LORD, THIS IS AN ASIDE AFTER ALL
THERE'S BLOOD UPON THY FACE
'TIS BANQUO'S THEN
McB
OH. IS HE DISPATCHED?
MY LORD, HIS THROAT IS CUT
MOST WORTHY CUTTHROAT, I WOULD LAVISH YOU WITH KISSES! AND FLEANCE?
MOST ROYAL SIR, FLEANCE IS 'SCAPED
McB
McB
NEVERMIND. I'M STILL WINNING, AND BANQUO IS DEAD AT LEAST, SO I CAN ENJOY THIS PARTY!
MAY 'T PLEASE YOUR HIGHNESS, SIT
UH, THE TABLE'S FULL
HERE IS A PLACE RESERVED, SIR
WHERE?
LX
McB
HERE, MY GOOD LORD. WHAT'S WRONG?
Bq
AAAAAAAAAAAAA
AHAHAH, SIT, WORTHY FRIENDS. PRAY YOU, KEEP SEAT. THE FIT IS MOMENTARY! UPON A THOUGHT HE WILL AGAIN BE WELL
HONEY WHAT THE CARP ARE YOU DOING
LADY McB
McB
AAAAAAAAAAA
I-IS HE
AHAHAH NOTHING TO WORRY ABOUT
HON SHUT UP YOU'RE EMBARASSING US
LADY McB

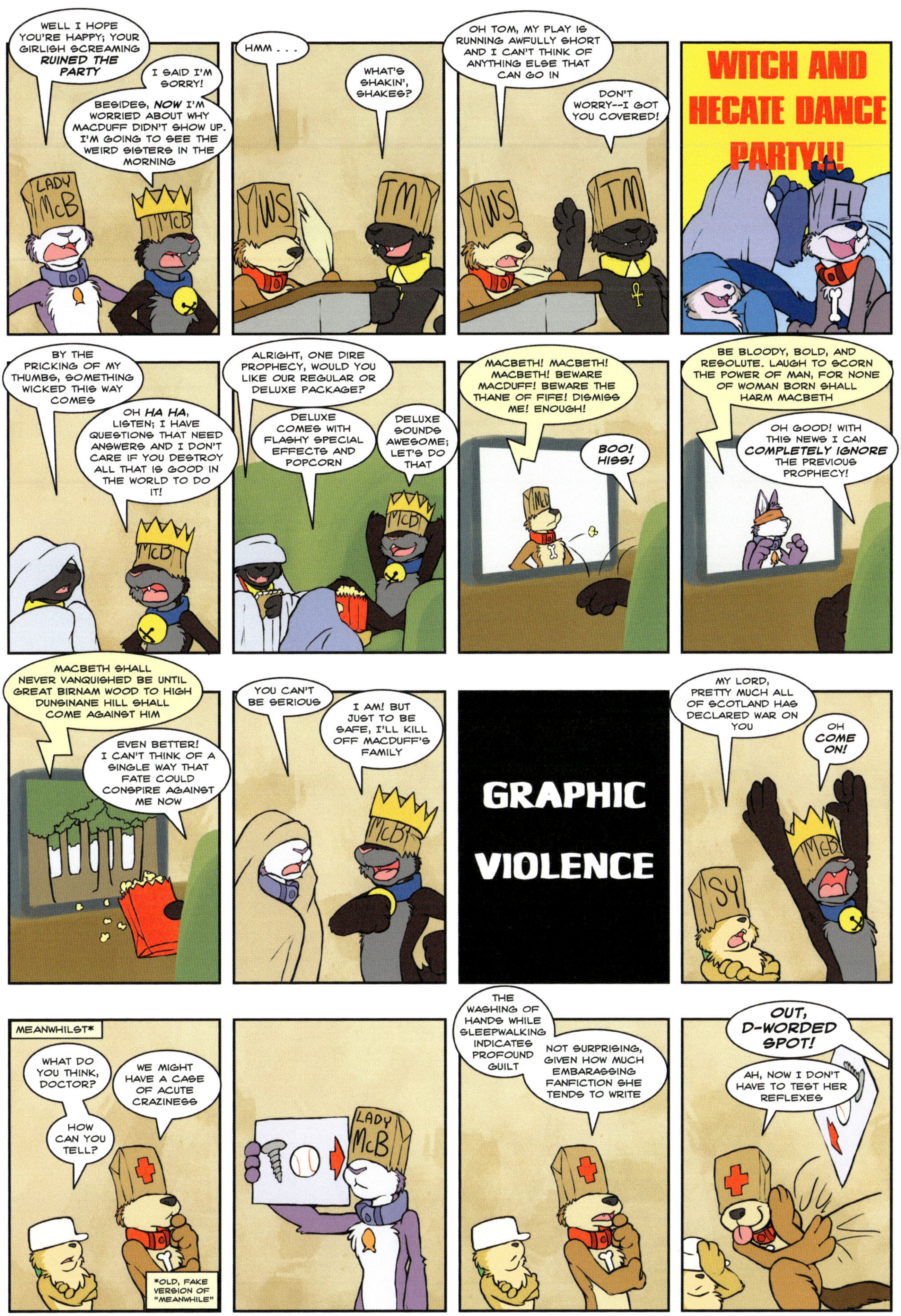
WELL I HOPE YOU'RE HAPPY; YOUR GIRLISH SCREAMING RUINED THE PARTY
I SAID I'M SORRY!
BESIDES, NOW I'M WORRIED ABOUT WHY MACDUFF DIDN'T SHOW UP. I'M GOING TO SEE THE WEIRD SISTERS IN THE MORNING
LADY McB
McB
HMM . . .
WHAT'S SHAKIN', SHAKES?
WS
TM
OH TOM, MY PLAY IS RUNNING AWFULLY SHORT AND I CAN'T THINK OF ANYTHING ELSE THAT CAN GO IN
DON'T WORRY--I GOT YOU COVERED!
WITCH AND HECATE DANCE PARTY!!!
H
BY THE PRICKING OF MY THUMBS, SOMETHING WICKED THIS WAY COMES
OH HA HA, LISTEN; I HAVE QUESTIONS THAT NEED ANSWERS AND I DON'T CARE IF YOU DESTROY ALL THAT IS GOOD IN THE WORLD TO DO IT!
ALRIGHT, ONE DIRE PROPHECY, WOULD YOU LIKE OUR REGULAR OR DELUXE PACKAGE?
DELUXE COMES WITH FLASHY SPECIAL EFFECTS AND POPCORN
DELUXE SOUNDS AWESOME; LET'S DO THAT
MACBETH! MACBETH! MACBETH! BEWARE MACDUFF! BEWARE THE THANE OF FIFE! DISMISS ME! ENOUGH!
BOO! HISS!
BE BLOODY, BOLD, AND RESOLUTE. LAUGH TO SCORN THE POWER OF MAN, FOR NONE OF WOMAN BORN SHALL HARM MACBETH
OH GOOD! WITH THIS NEWS I CAN COMPLETELY IGNORE THE PREVIOUS PROPHECY!
MACBETH SHALL NEVER VANQUISHED BE UNTIL GREAT BIRNAM WOOD TO HIGH DUNSINANE HILL SHALL COME AGAINST HIM
EVEN BETTER! I CAN'T THINK OF A SINGLE WAY THAT FATE COULD CONSPIRE AGAINST ME NOW
YOU CAN'T BE SERIOUS
I AM! BUT JUST TO BE SAFE, I'LL KILL OFF MACDUFF'S FAMILY
GRAPHIC VIOLENCE
MY LORD, PRETTY MUCH ALL OF SCOTLAND HAS DECLARED WAR ON YOU
OH COME ON!
SY
MEANWHILST*
WHAT DO YOU THINK, DOCTOR?
WE MIGHT HAVE A CASE OF ACUTE CRAZINESS
HOW CAN YOU TELL?
*OLD, FAKE VERSION OF "MEANWHILE"
THE WASHING OF HANDS WHILE SLEEPWALKING INDICATES PROFOUND GUILT
NOT SURPRISING, GIVEN HOW MUCH EMBARASSING FANFICTION SHE TENDS TO WRITE
OUT, D-WORDED SPOT!
AH, NOW I DON'T HAVE TO TEST HER REFLEXES

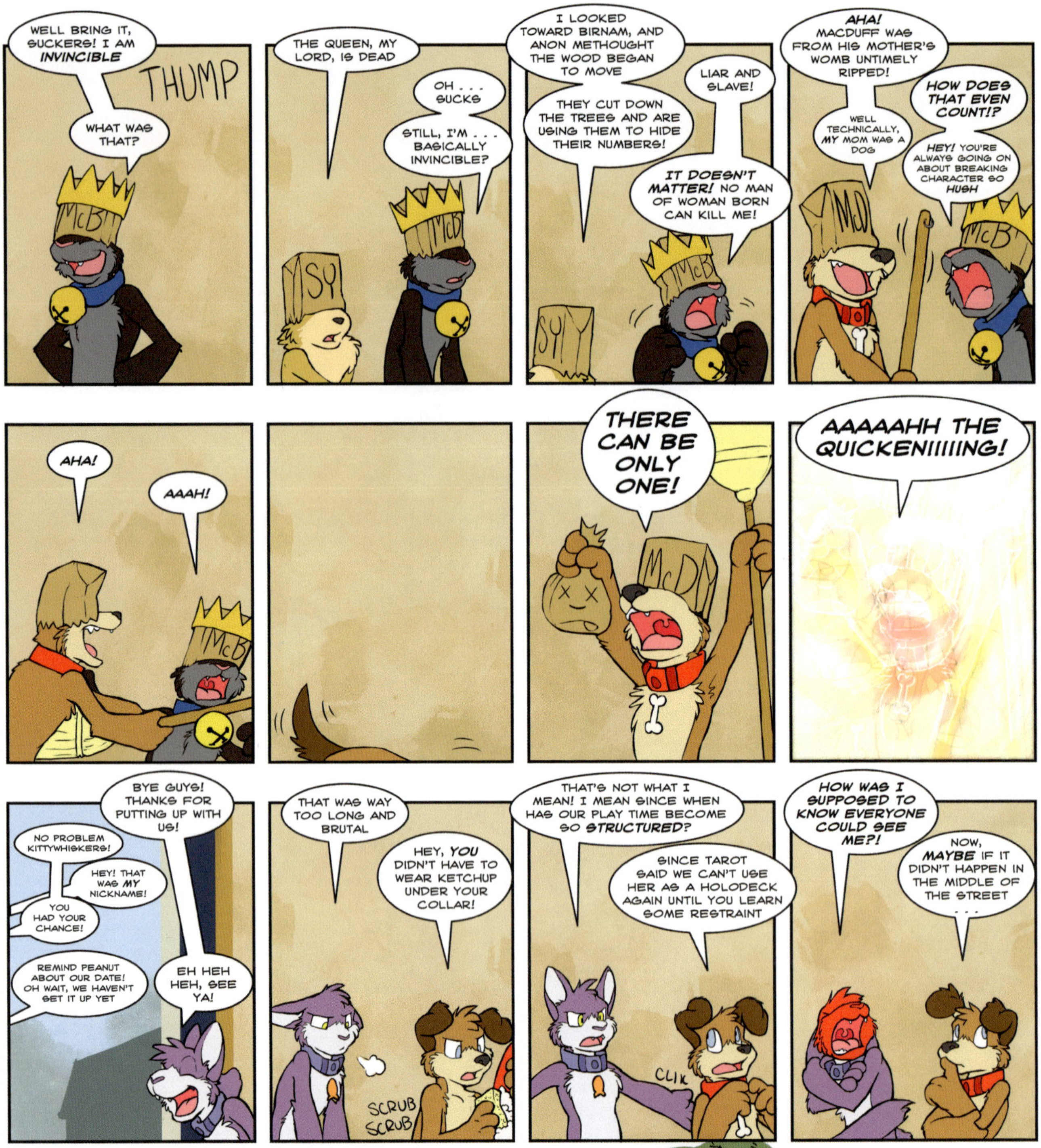
WELL BRING IT, SUCKERS! I AM INVINCIBLE
THUMP
WHAT WAS THAT?
THE QUEEN, MY LORD, IS DEAD
OH . . . SUCKS
STILL, I'M . . . BASICALLY INVINCIBLE?
I LOOKED TOWARD BIRNAM, AND ANON METHOUGHT THE WOOD BEGAN TO MOVE
THEY CUT DOWN THE TREES AND ARE USING THEM TO HIDE THEIR NUMBERS!
LIAR AND SLAVE!
IT DOESN'T MATTER! NO MAN OF WOMAN BORN CAN KILL ME!
AHA! MACDUFF WAS FROM HIS MOTHER'S WOMB UNTIMELY RIPPED!
WELL TECHNICALLY, MY MOM WAS A DOG
HOW DOES THAT EVEN COUNT!?
HEY! YOU'RE ALWAYS GOING ON ABOUT BREAKING CHARACTER SO HUSH
AHA!
AAAH!
THERE CAN BE ONLY ONE!
AAAAAHH THE QUICKENIIIIING!
BYE GUYS! THANKS FOR PUTTING UP WITH US!
NO PROBLEM KITTYWHISKERS!
HEY! THAT WAS MY NICKNAME!
YOU HAD YOUR CHANCE!
REMIND PEANUT ABOUT OUR DATE! OH WAIT, WE HAVEN'T SET IT UP YET
EH HEH HEH, SEE YA!
THAT WAS WAY TOO LONG AND BRUTAL
HEY, YOU DIDN'T HAVE TO WEAR KETCHUP UNDER YOUR COLLAR!
SCRUB SCRUB
THAT'S NOT WHAT I MEAN! I MEAN SINCE WHEN HAS OUR PLAY TIME BECOME SO STRUCTURED?
SINCE TAROT SAID WE CAN'T USE HER AS A HOLODECK AGAIN UNTIL YOU LEARN SOME RESTRAINT
CLIK
HOW WAS I SUPPOSED TO KNOW EVERYONE COULD SEE ME?!
NOW, MAYBE IF IT DIDN'T HAPPEN IN THE MIDDLE OF THE STREET . . .

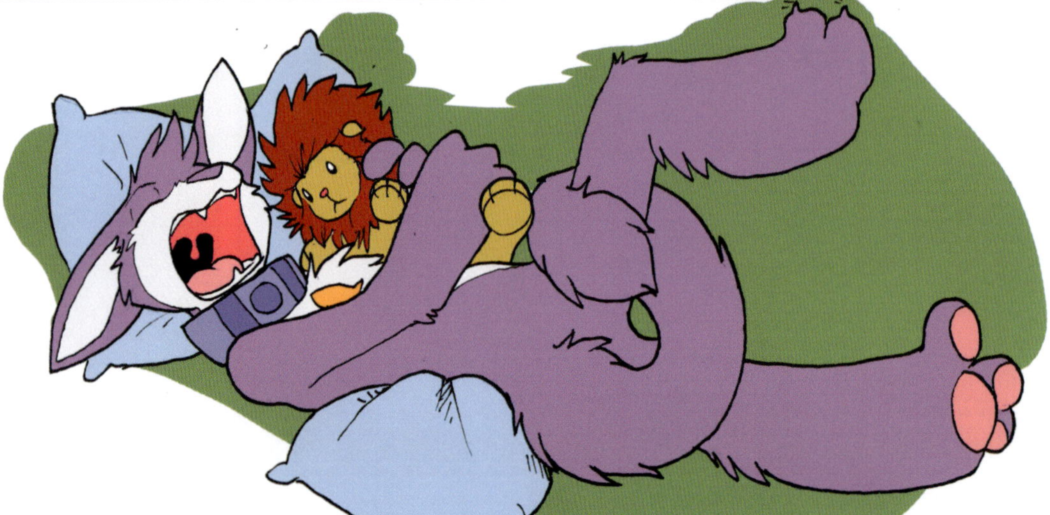

THE INTERVIEW

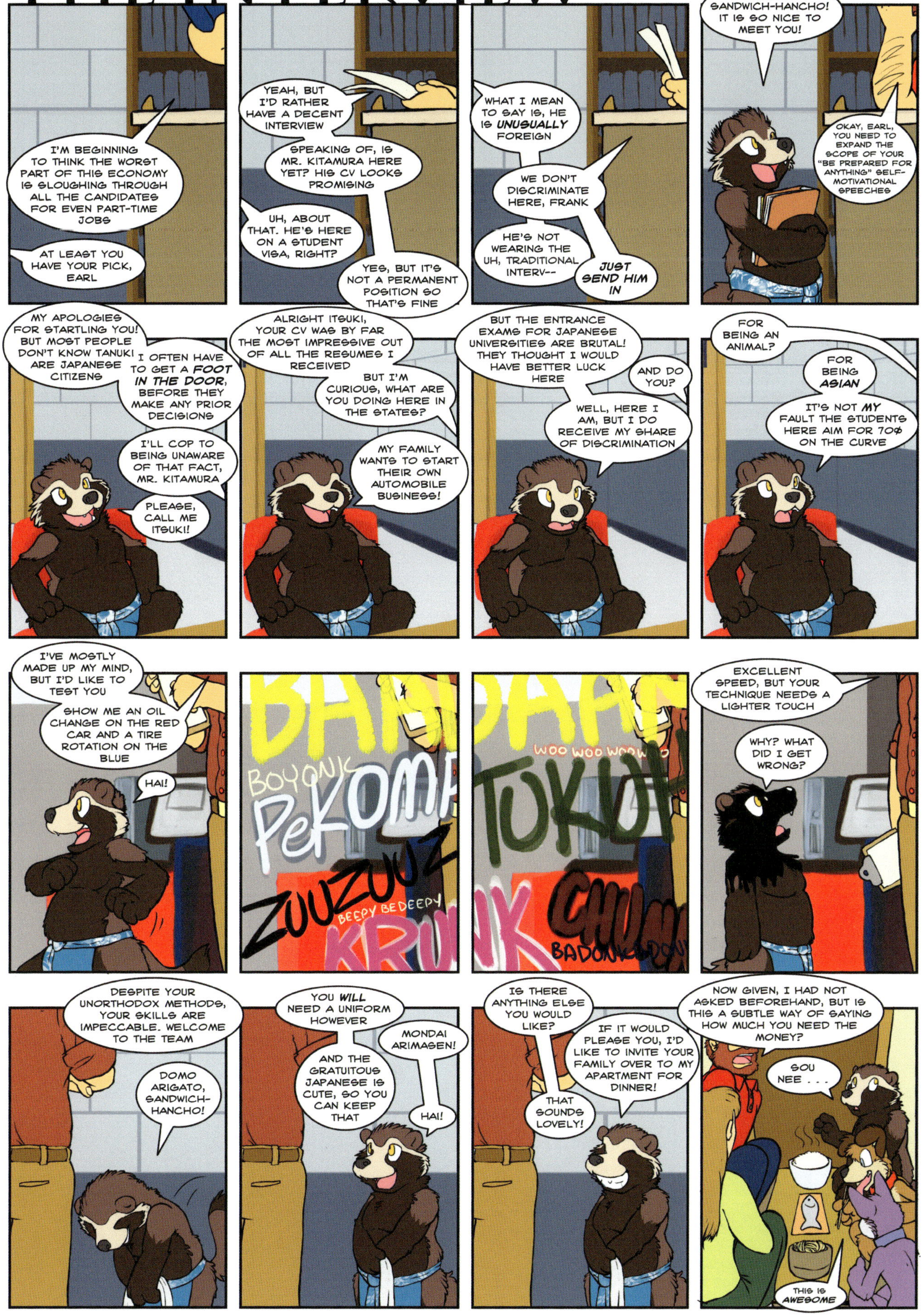
I'M BEGINNING TO THINK THE WORST PART OF THIS ECONOMY IS SLOUGHING THROUGH ALL THE CANDIDATES FOR EVEN PART-TIME JOBS
AT LEAST YOU HAVE YOUR PICK, EARL
YEAH, BUT I'D RATHER HAVE A DECENT INTERVIEW
SPEAKING OF, IS MR. KITAMURA HERE YET? HIS CV LOOKS PROMISING
UH, ABOUT THAT. HE'S HERE ON A STUDENT VISA, RIGHT?
YES, BUT IT'S NOT A PERMANENT POSITION SO THAT'S FINE
WHAT I MEAN TO SAY IS, HE IS UNUSUALLY FOREIGN
WE DON'T DISCRIMINATE HERE, FRANK
HE'S NOT WEARING THE UH, TRADITIONAL INTERV--
JUST SEND HIM IN
KONNICHIWA, SANDWICH-HANCHO! IT IS SO NICE TO MEET YOU!
OKAY, EARL, YOU NEED TO EXPAND THE SCOPE OF YOUR "BE PREPARED FOR ANYTHING" SELF-MOTIVATIONAL SPEECHES
MY APOLOGIES FOR STARTLING YOU! BUT MOST PEOPLE DON'T KNOW TANUKI ARE JAPANESE CITIZENS
I OFTEN HAVE TO GET A FOOT IN THE DOOR, BEFORE THEY MAKE ANY PRIOR DECISIONS
I'LL COP TO BEING UNAWARE OF THAT FACT, MR. KITAMURA
PLEASE, CALL ME ITSUKI!
ALRIGHT ITSUKI, YOUR CV WAS BY FAR THE MOST IMPRESSIVE OUT OF ALL THE RESUMES I RECEIVED
BUT I'M CURIOUS, WHAT ARE YOU DOING HERE IN THE STATES?
MY FAMILY WANTS TO START THEIR OWN AUTOMOBILE BUSINESS!
BUT THE ENTRANCE EXAMS FOR JAPANESE UNIVERSITIES ARE BRUTAL! THEY THOUGHT I WOULD HAVE BETTER LUCK HERE
AND DO YOU?
WELL, HERE I AM, BUT I DO RECEIVE MY SHARE OF DISCRIMINATION
FOR BEING AN ANIMAL?
FOR BEING ASIAN
IT'S NOT MY FAULT THE STUDENTS HERE AIM FOR 70% ON THE CURVE
I'VE MOSTLY MADE UP MY MIND, BUT I'D LIKE TO TEST YOU
SHOW ME AN OIL CHANGE ON THE RED CAR AND A TIRE ROTATION ON THE BLUE
HAI!
BAHDAAH
BOYONK
PeKOMA
ZUUZUUZ
BEEPY BEDEEPY
KRUNK
WOO WOO WOOWOO
TUKUH
CHUN
BADONKADON
EXCELLENT SPEED, BUT YOUR TECHNIQUE NEEDS A LIGHTER TOUCH
WHY? WHAT DID I GET WRONG?
DESPITE YOUR UNORTHODOX METHODS, YOUR SKILLS ARE IMPECCABLE. WELCOME TO THE TEAM
DOMO ARIGATO, SANDWICH-HANCHO!
YOU WILL NEED A UNIFORM HOWEVER
MONDAI ARIMASEN!
AND THE GRATUITOUS JAPANESE IS CUTE, SO YOU CAN KEEP THAT
HAI!
IS THERE ANYTHING ELSE YOU WOULD LIKE?
IF IT WOULD PLEASE YOU, I'D LIKE TO INVITE YOUR FAMILY OVER TO MY APARTMENT FOR DINNER!
THAT SOUNDS LOVELY!
NOW GIVEN, I HAD NOT ASKED BEFOREHAND, BUT IS THIS A SUBTLE WAY OF SAYING HOW MUCH YOU NEED THE MONEY?
SOU NEE . . .
THIS IS AWESOME

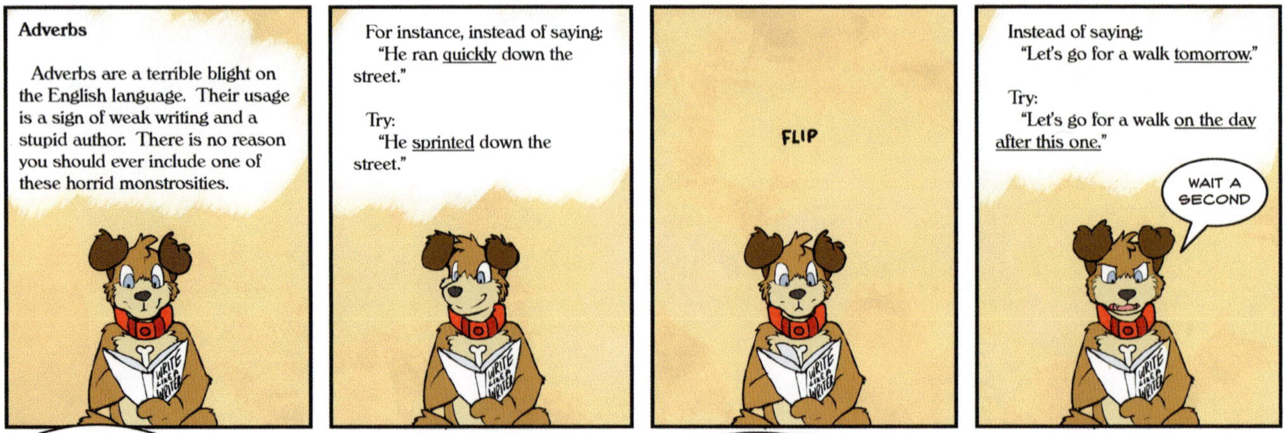
Adverbs
Adverbs are a terrible blight on the English language. Their usage is a sign of weak writing and a stupid author. There is no reason you should ever include one of these horrid monstrosities.
For instance, instead of saying: "He ran quickly down the street."
Try: "He sprinted down the street."
FLIP
Instead of saying: "Let's go for a walk tomorrow."
Try: "Let's go for a walk on the day after this one."
WAIT A SECOND

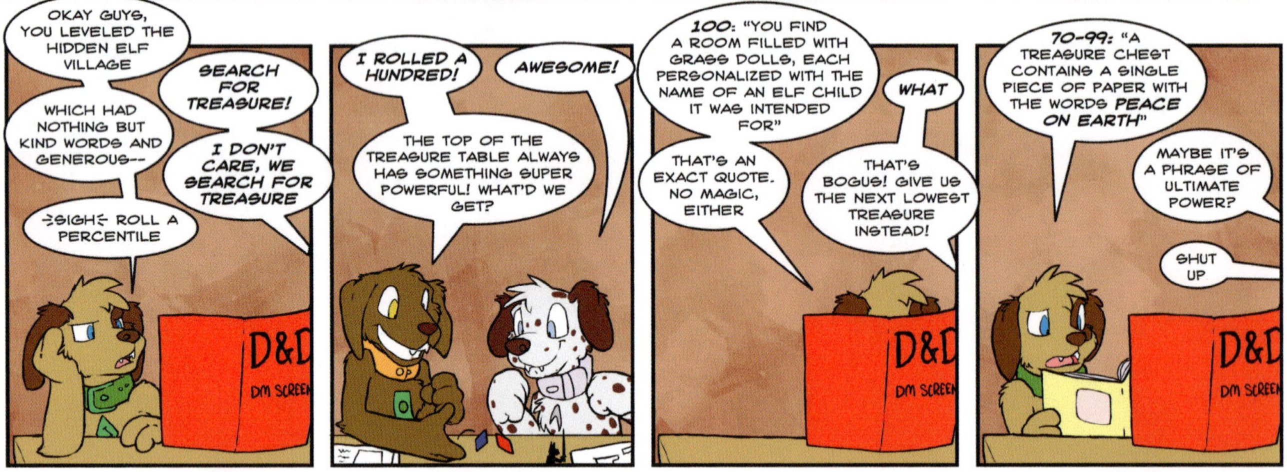
OKAY GUYS, YOU LEVELED THE HIDDEN ELF VILLAGE
SEARCH FOR TREASURE!
WHICH HAD NOTHING BUT KIND WORDS AND GENEROUS--
I DON'T CARE, WE SEARCH FOR TREASURE
SIGH ROLL A PERCENTILE
D&D DM SCREEN
I ROLLED A HUNDRED!
AWESOME!
THE TOP OF THE TREASURE TABLE ALWAYS HAS SOMETHING SUPER POWERFUL! WHAT'D WE GET?
100: "YOU FIND A ROOM FILLED WITH GRASS DOLLS, EACH PERSONALIZED WITH THE NAME OF AN ELF CHILD IT WAS INTENDED FOR"
WHAT
THAT'S AN EXACT QUOTE. NO MAGIC, EITHER
THAT'S BOGUS! GIVE US THE NEXT LOWEST TREASURE INSTEAD!
70-99: "A TREASURE CHEST CONTAINS A SINGLE PIECE OF PAPER WITH THE WORDS PEACE ON EARTH"
MAYBE IT'S A PHRASE OF ULTIMATE POWER?
SHUT UP
D&D DM SCREEN

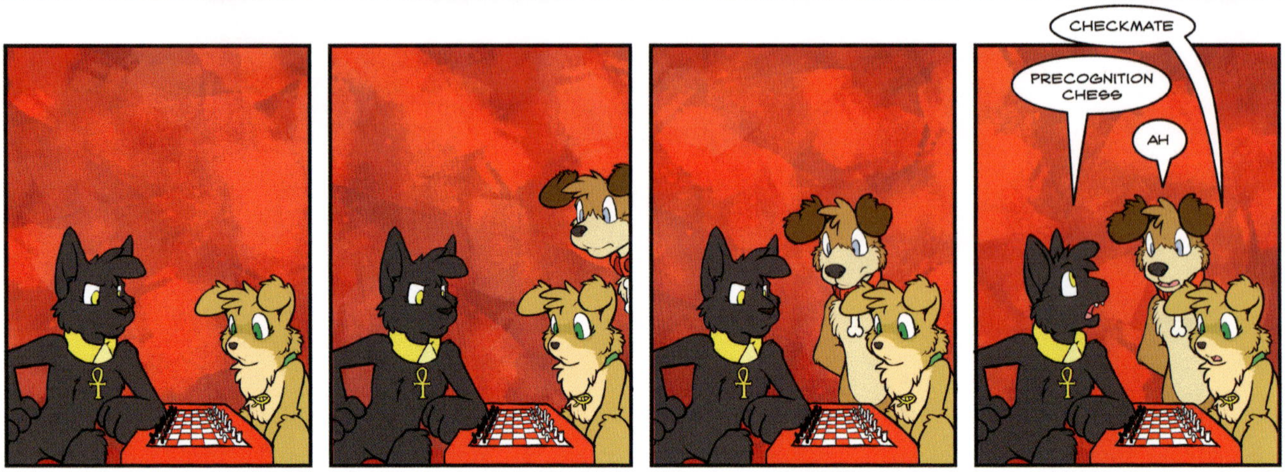
CHECKMATE
PRECOGNITION CHESS
AH

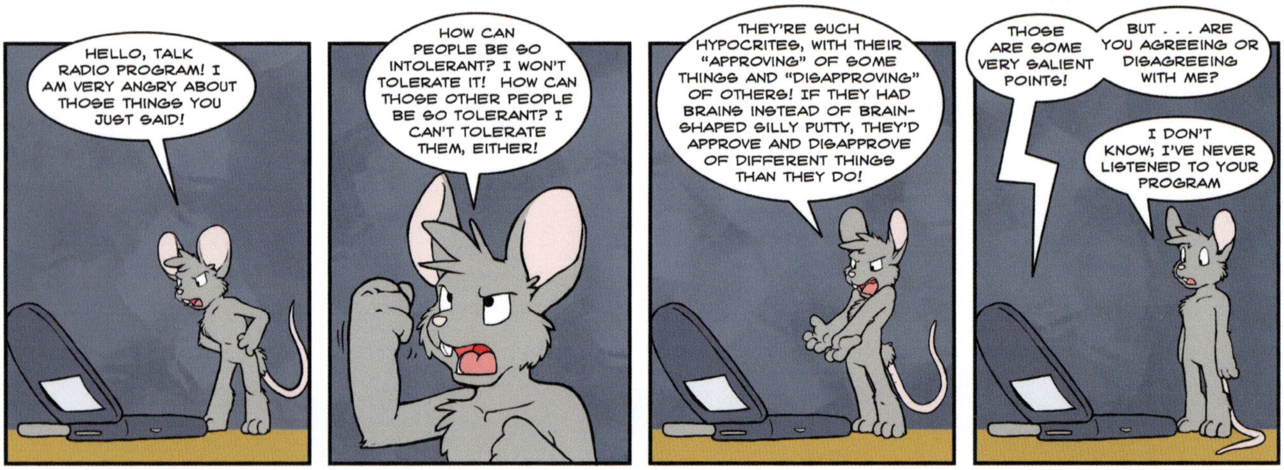
HELLO, TALK RADIO PROGRAM! I AM VERY ANGRY ABOUT THOSE THINGS YOU JUST SAID!
HOW CAN PEOPLE BE SO INTOLERANT? I WON'T TOLERATE IT! HOW CAN THOSE OTHER PEOPLE BE SO TOLERANT? I CAN'T TOLERATE THEM, EITHER!
THEY'RE SUCH HYPOCRITES, WITH THEIR "APPROVING" OF SOME THINGS AND "DISAPPROVING" OF OTHERS! IF THEY HAD BRAINS INSTEAD OF BRAIN-SHAPED SILLY PUTTY, THEY'D APPROVE AND DISAPPROVE OF DIFFERENT THINGS THAN THEY DO!
THOSE ARE SOME VERY SALIENT POINTS!
BUT . . . ARE YOU AGREEING OR DISAGREEING WITH ME?
I DON'T KNOW; I'VE NEVER LISTENED TO YOUR PROGRAM

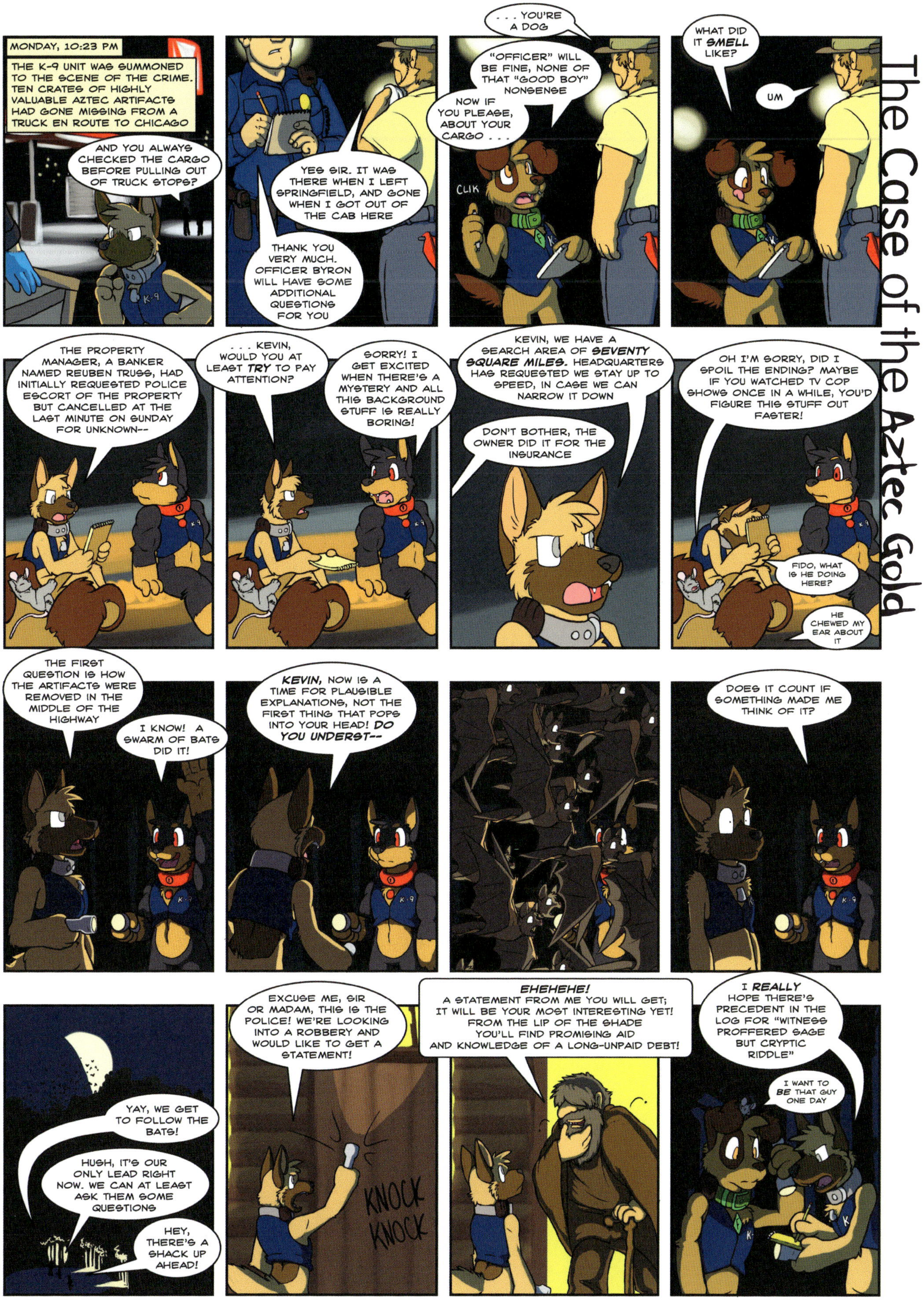

The Case of the Aztec Gold
MONDAY, 10:23 PM
THE K-9 UNIT WAS SUMMONED TO THE SCENE OF THE CRIME. TEN CRATES OF HIGHLY VALUABLE AZTEC ARTIFACTS HAD GONE MISSING FROM A TRUCK EN ROUTE TO CHICAGO
AND YOU ALWAYS CHECKED THE CARGO BEFORE PULLING OUT OF TRUCK STOPS?
YES SIR. IT WAS THERE WHEN I LEFT SPRINGFIELD, AND GONE WHEN I GOT OUT OF THE CAB HERE
THANK YOU VERY MUCH. OFFICER BYRON WILL HAVE SOME ADDITIONAL QUESTIONS FOR YOU
. . . YOU'RE A DOG
"OFFICER" WILL BE FINE, NONE OF THAT "GOOD BOY" NONSENSE
NOW IF YOU PLEASE, ABOUT YOUR CARGO . . .
CLIK
WHAT DID IT SMELL LIKE?
UM
THE PROPERTY MANAGER, A BANKER NAMED REUBEN TRUSS, HAD INITIALLY REQUESTED POLICE ESCORT OF THE PROPERTY BUT CANCELLED AT THE LAST MINUTE ON SUNDAY FOR UNKNOWN--
. . . KEVIN, WOULD YOU AT LEAST TRY TO PAY ATTENTION?
SORRY! I GET EXCITED WHEN THERE'S A MYSTERY AND ALL THIS BACKGROUND STUFF IS REALLY BORING!
KEVIN, WE HAVE A SEARCH AREA OF SEVENTY SQUARE MILES. HEADQUARTERS HAS REQUESTED WE STAY UP TO SPEED, IN CASE WE CAN NARROW IT DOWN
DON'T BOTHER, THE OWNER DID IT FOR THE INSURANCE
OH I'M SORRY, DID I SPOIL THE ENDING? MAYBE IF YOU WATCHED TV COP SHOWS ONCE IN A WHILE, YOU'D FIGURE THIS STUFF OUT FASTER!
FIDO, WHAT IS HE DOING HERE?
HE CHEWED MY EAR ABOUT IT
THE FIRST QUESTION IS HOW THE ARTIFACTS WERE REMOVED IN THE MIDDLE OF THE HIGHWAY
I KNOW! A SWARM OF BATS DID IT!
KEVIN, NOW IS A TIME FOR PLAUSIBLE EXPLANATIONS, NOT THE FIRST THING THAT POPS INTO YOUR HEAD! DO YOU UNDERST--
DOES IT COUNT IF SOMETHING MADE ME THINK OF IT?
YAY, WE GET TO FOLLOW THE BATS!
HUSH, IT'S OUR ONLY LEAD RIGHT NOW. WE CAN AT LEAST ASK THEM SOME QUESTIONS
HEY, THERE'S A SHACK UP AHEAD!
EXCUSE ME, SIR OR MADAM, THIS IS THE POLICE! WE'RE LOOKING INTO A ROBBERY AND WOULD LIKE TO GET A STATEMENT!
KNOCK KNOCK
EHEHEHE!
A STATEMENT FROM ME YOU WILL GET;
IT WILL BE YOUR MOST INTERESTING YET!
FROM THE LIP OF THE SHADE
YOU'LL FIND PROMISING AID
AND KNOWLEDGE OF A LONG-UNPAID DEBT!
I REALLY HOPE THERE'S PRECEDENT IN THE LOG FOR "WITNESS PROFFERED SAGE BUT CRYPTIC RIDDLE"
I WANT TO BE THAT GUY ONE DAY

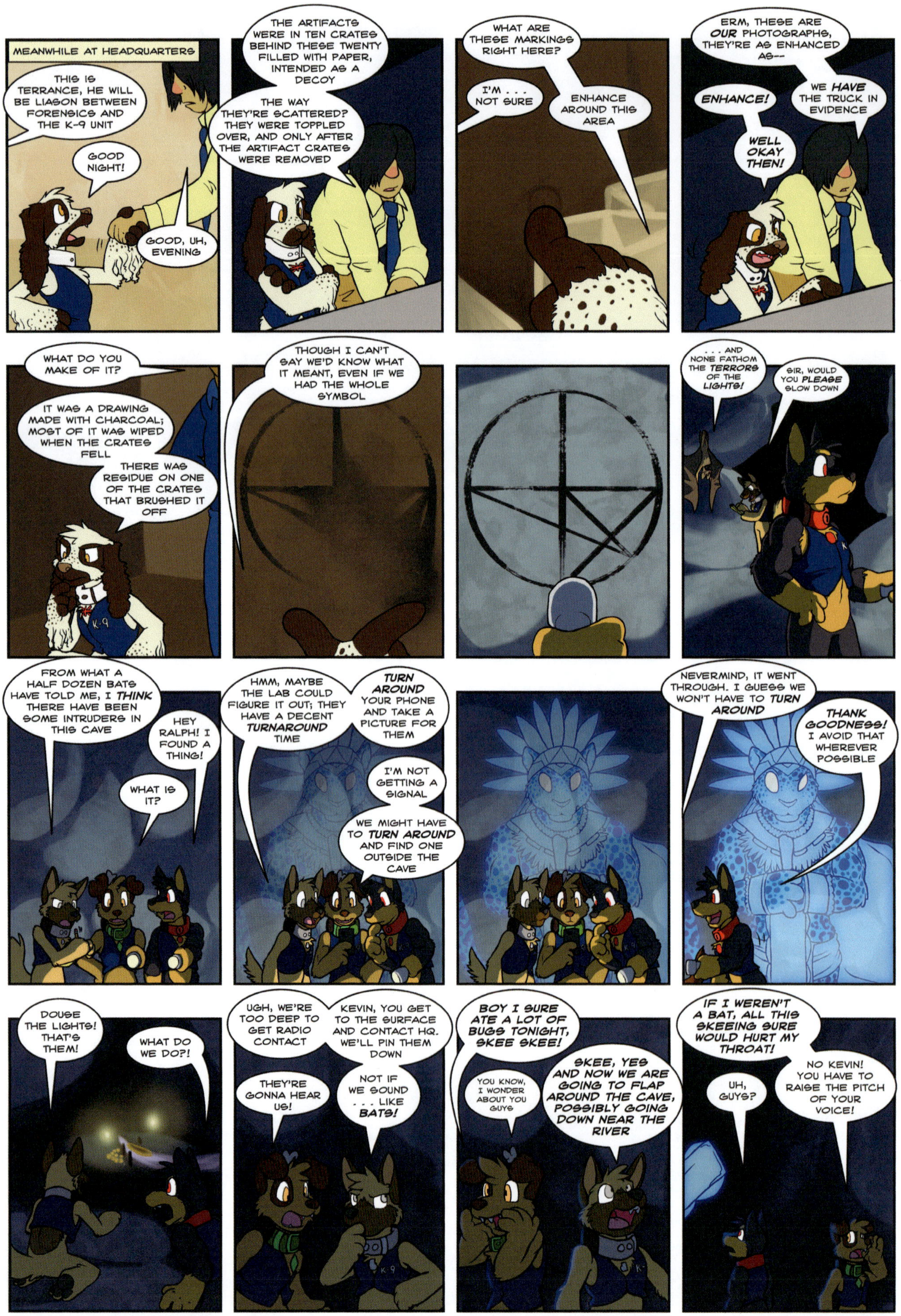
MEANWHILE AT HEADQUARTERS
THIS IS TERRANCE, HE WILL BE LIASON BETWEEN FORENSICS AND THE K-9 UNIT
GOOD NIGHT!
GOOD, UH, EVENING
THE ARTIFACTS WERE IN TEN CRATES BEHIND THESE TWENTY FILLED WITH PAPER, INTENDED AS A DECOY
THE WAY THEY'RE SCATTERED? THEY WERE TOPPLED OVER, AND ONLY AFTER THE ARTIFACT CRATES WERE REMOVED
WHAT ARE THESE MARKINGS RIGHT HERE?
I'M . . . NOT SURE
ENHANCE AROUND THIS AREA
ERM, THESE ARE OUR PHOTOGRAPHS, THEY'RE AS ENHANCED AS--
ENHANCE!
WE HAVE THE TRUCK IN EVIDENCE
WELL OKAY THEN!
WHAT DO YOU MAKE OF IT?
IT WAS A DRAWING MADE WITH CHARCOAL; MOST OF IT WAS WIPED WHEN THE CRATES FELL
THERE WAS RESIDUE ON ONE OF THE CRATES THAT BRUSHED IT OFF
THOUGH I CAN'T SAY WE'D KNOW WHAT IT MEANT, EVEN IF WE HAD THE WHOLE SYMBOL
. . . AND NONE FATHOM THE TERRORS OF THE LIGHTS!
SIR, WOULD YOU PLEASE SLOW DOWN
FROM WHAT A HALF DOZEN BATS HAVE TOLD ME, I THINK THERE HAVE BEEN SOME INTRUDERS IN THIS CAVE
HEY RALPH! I FOUND A THING!
WHAT IS IT?
HMM, MAYBE THE LAB COULD FIGURE IT OUT; THEY HAVE A DECENT TURNAROUND TIME
TURN AROUND YOUR PHONE AND TAKE A PICTURE FOR THEM
I'M NOT GETTING A SIGNAL
WE MIGHT HAVE TO TURN AROUND AND FIND ONE OUTSIDE THE CAVE
NEVERMIND, IT WENT THROUGH. I GUESS WE WON'T HAVE TO TURN AROUND
THANK GOODNESS! I AVOID THAT WHEREVER POSSIBLE
DOUSE THE LIGHTS! THAT'S THEM!
WHAT DO WE DO?!
UGH, WE'RE TOO DEEP TO GET RADIO CONTACT
KEVIN, YOU GET TO THE SURFACE AND CONTACT HQ. WE'LL PIN THEM DOWN
THEY'RE GONNA HEAR US!
NOT IF WE SOUND . . . LIKE BATS!
BOY I SURE ATE A LOT OF BUGS TONIGHT, SKEE SKEE!
YOU KNOW, I WONDER ABOUT YOU GUYS
SKEE, YES AND NOW WE ARE GOING TO FLAP AROUND THE CAVE, POSSIBLY GOING DOWN NEAR THE RIVER
IF I WEREN'T A BAT, ALL THIS SKEEING SURE WOULD HURT MY THROAT!
UH, GUYS?
NO KEVIN! YOU HAVE TO RAISE THE PITCH OF YOUR VOICE!

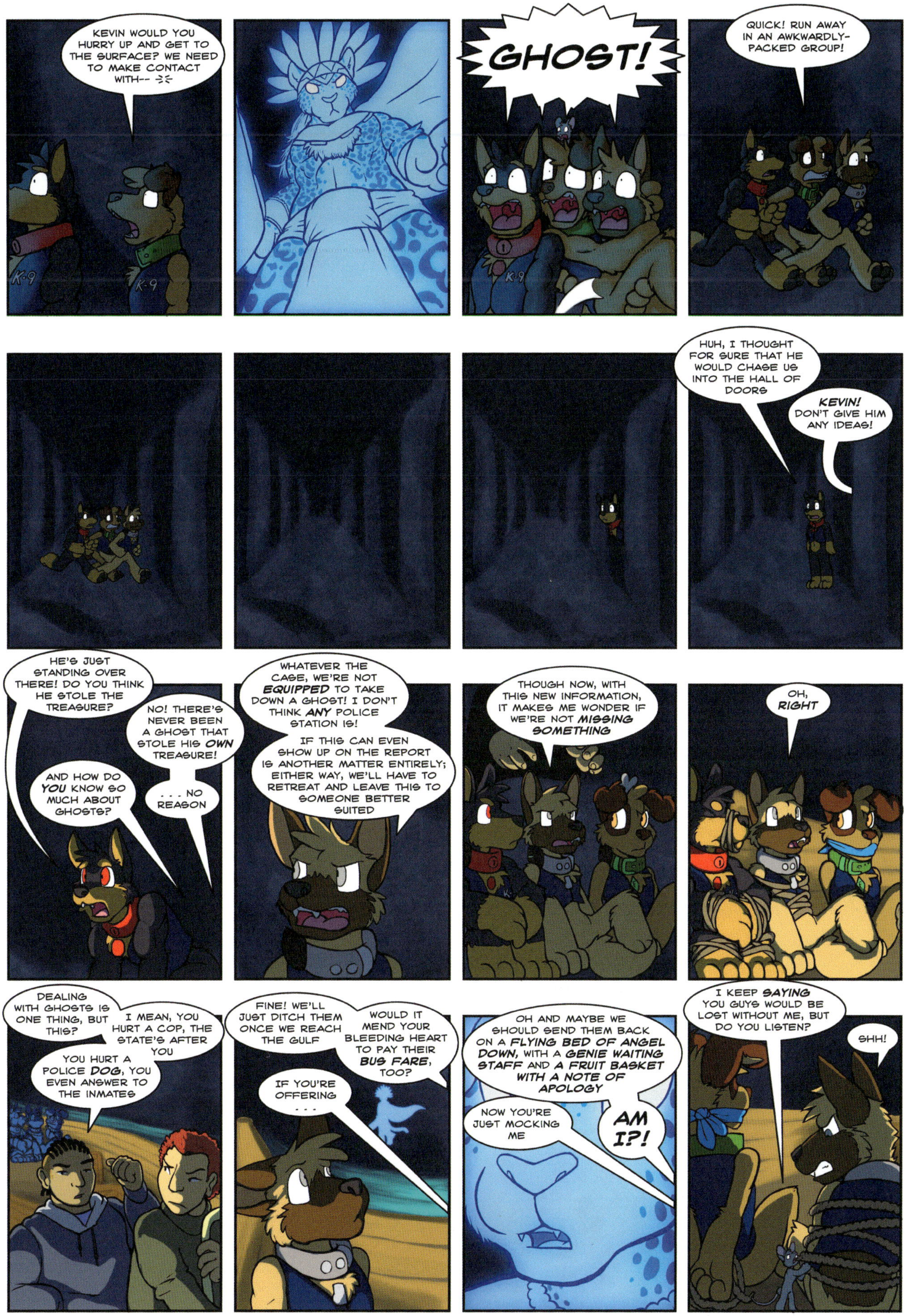
KEVIN WOULD YOU HURRY UP AND GET TO THE SURFACE? WE NEED TO MAKE CONTACT WITH--
K-9
K-9
GHOST!
K-9
QUICK! RUN AWAY IN AN AWKWARDLY-PACKED GROUP!
HUH, I THOUGHT FOR SURE THAT HE WOULD CHASE US INTO THE HALL OF DOORS
KEVIN! DON'T GIVE HIM ANY IDEAS!
HE'S JUST STANDING OVER THERE! DO YOU THINK HE STOLE THE TREASURE?
NO! THERE'S NEVER BEEN A GHOST THAT STOLE HIS OWN TREASURE!
AND HOW DO YOU KNOW SO MUCH ABOUT GHOSTS?
. . . NO REASON
WHATEVER THE CASE, WE'RE NOT EQUIPPED TO TAKE DOWN A GHOST! I DON'T THINK ANY POLICE STATION IS!
IF THIS CAN EVEN SHOW UP ON THE REPORT IS ANOTHER MATTER ENTIRELY; EITHER WAY, WE'LL HAVE TO RETREAT AND LEAVE THIS TO SOMEONE BETTER SUITED
THOUGH NOW, WITH THIS NEW INFORMATION, IT MAKES ME WONDER IF WE'RE NOT MISSING SOMETHING
OH, RIGHT
DEALING WITH GHOSTS IS ONE THING, BUT THIS?
I MEAN, YOU HURT A COP, THE STATE'S AFTER YOU
YOU HURT A POLICE DOG, YOU EVEN ANSWER TO THE INMATES
FINE! WE'LL JUST DITCH THEM ONCE WE REACH THE GULF
WOULD IT MEND YOUR BLEEDING HEART TO PAY THEIR BUS FARE, TOO?
IF YOU'RE OFFERING . . .
OH AND MAYBE WE SHOULD SEND THEM BACK ON A FLYING BED OF ANGEL DOWN, WITH A GENIE WAITING STAFF AND A FRUIT BASKET WITH A NOTE OF APOLOGY
NOW YOU'RE JUST MOCKING ME
AM I?!
I KEEP SAYING YOU GUYS WOULD BE LOST WITHOUT ME, BUT DO YOU LISTEN?
SHH!

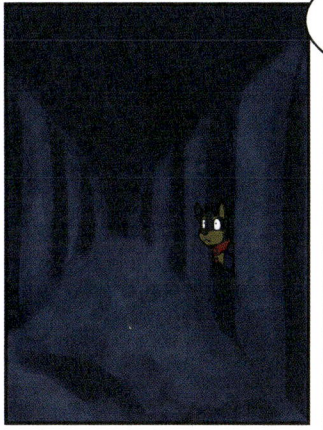

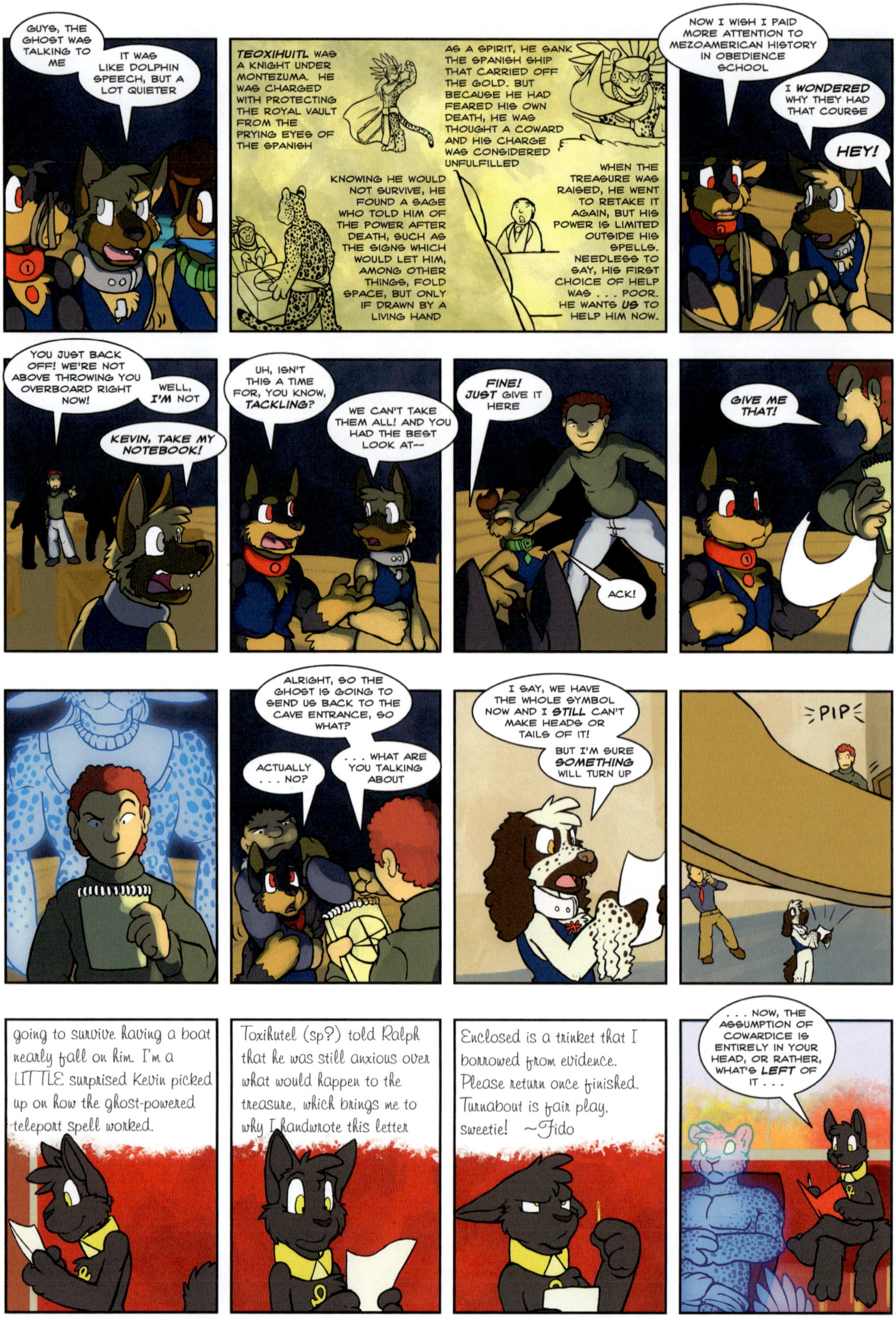

GUYS, THE GHOST WAS TALKING TO ME
IT WAS LIKE DOLPHIN SPEECH, BUT A LOT QUIETER
TEOXIHUITL WAS A KNIGHT UNDER MONTEZUMA. HE WAS CHARGED WITH PROTECTING THE ROYAL VAULT FROM THE PRYING EYES OF THE SPANISH
AS A SPIRIT, HE SANK THE SPANISH SHIP THAT CARRIED OFF THE GOLD. BUT BECAUSE HE HAD FEARED HIS OWN DEATH, HE WAS THOUGHT A COWARD AND HIS CHARGE WAS CONSIDERED UNFULFILLED
KNOWING HE WOULD NOT SURVIVE, HE FOUND A SAGE WHO TOLD HIM OF THE POWER AFTER DEATH, SUCH AS THE SIGNS WHICH WOULD LET HIM, AMONG OTHER THINGS, FOLD SPACE, BUT ONLY IF DRAWN BY A LIVING HAND
WHEN THE TREASURE WAS RAISED, HE WENT TO RETAKE IT AGAIN, BUT HIS POWER IS LIMITED OUTSIDE HIS SPELLS. NEEDLESS TO SAY, HIS FIRST CHOICE OF HELP WAS . . . POOR. HE WANTS US TO HELP HIM NOW.
NOW I WISH I PAID MORE ATTENTION TO MEZOAMERICAN HISTORY IN OBEDIENCE SCHOOL
I WONDERED WHY THEY HAD THAT COURSE
HEY!
YOU JUST BACK OFF! WE'RE NOT ABOVE THROWING YOU OVERBOARD RIGHT NOW!
WELL, I'M NOT
KEVIN, TAKE MY NOTEBOOK!
UH, ISN'T THIS A TIME FOR, YOU KNOW, TACKLING?
WE CAN'T TAKE THEM ALL! AND YOU HAD THE BEST LOOK AT--
FINE! JUST GIVE IT HERE
ACK!
GIVE ME THAT!
ALRIGHT, SO THE GHOST IS GOING TO SEND US BACK TO THE CAVE ENTRANCE, SO WHAT?
ACTUALLY . . . NO?
. . . WHAT ARE YOU TALKING ABOUT
I SAY, WE HAVE THE WHOLE SYMBOL NOW AND I STILL CAN'T MAKE HEADS OR TAILS OF IT!
BUT I'M SURE SOMETHING WILL TURN UP
PIP
going to survive having a boat nearly fall on him. I'm a LITTLE surprised Kevin picked up on how the ghost-powered teleport spell worked.
Toxihutel (sp?) told Ralph that he was still anxious over what would happen to the treasure, which brings me to why I handwrote this letter
Enclosed is a trinket that I borrowed from evidence. Please return once finished. Turnabout is fair play, sweetie! ~Fido
. . . NOW, THE ASSUMPTION OF COWARDICE IS ENTIRELY IN YOUR HEAD, OR RATHER, WHAT'S LEFT OF IT . . .

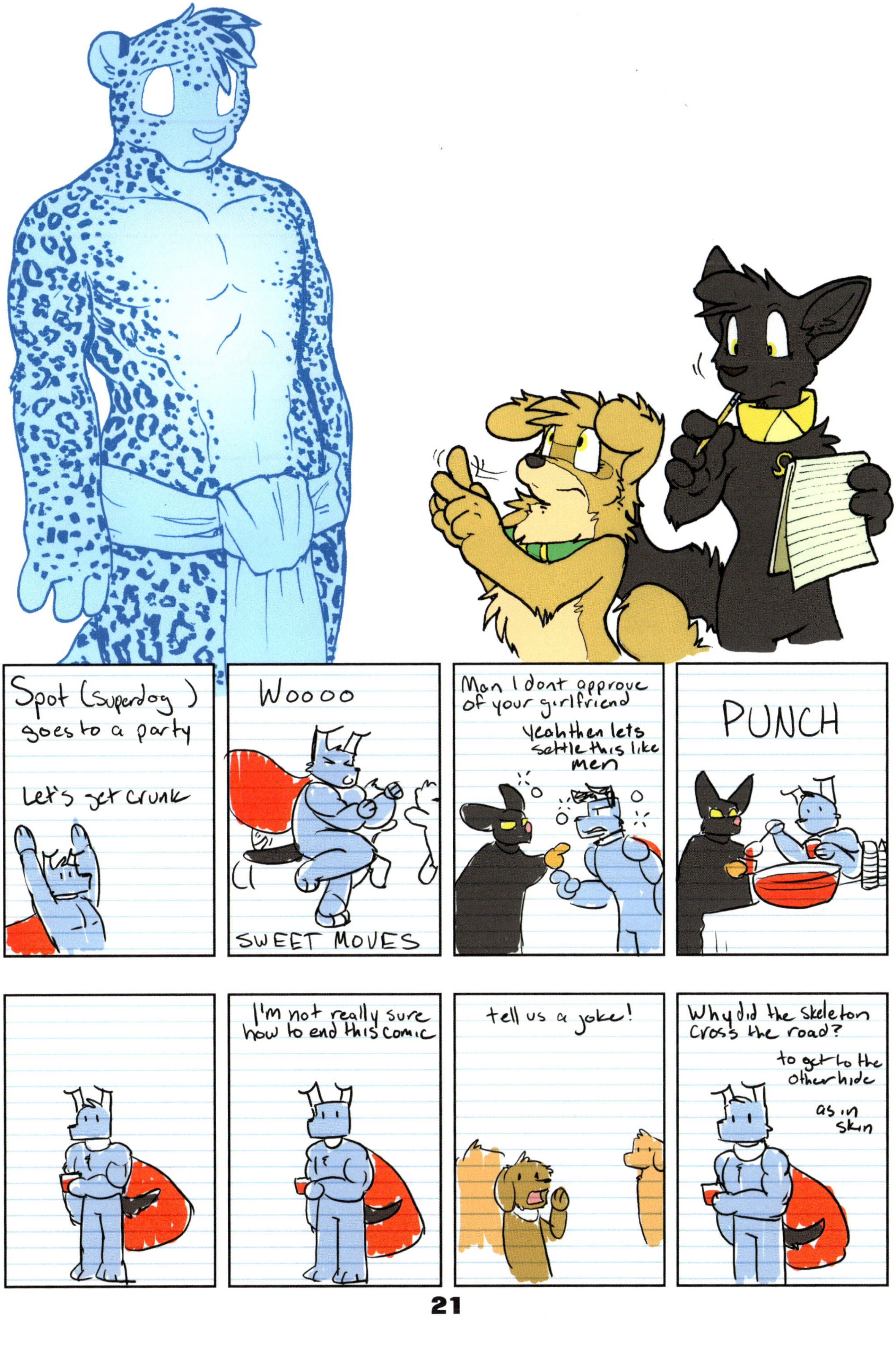
Spot (superdog) goes to a party
Let's get crunk
Woooo
SWEET MOVES
Man I dont approve of your girlfriend
Yeah then lets settle this like men
PUNCH
I'm not really sure how to end this comic
tell us a joke!
Why did the skeleton cross the road?
to get to the other hide
as in skin

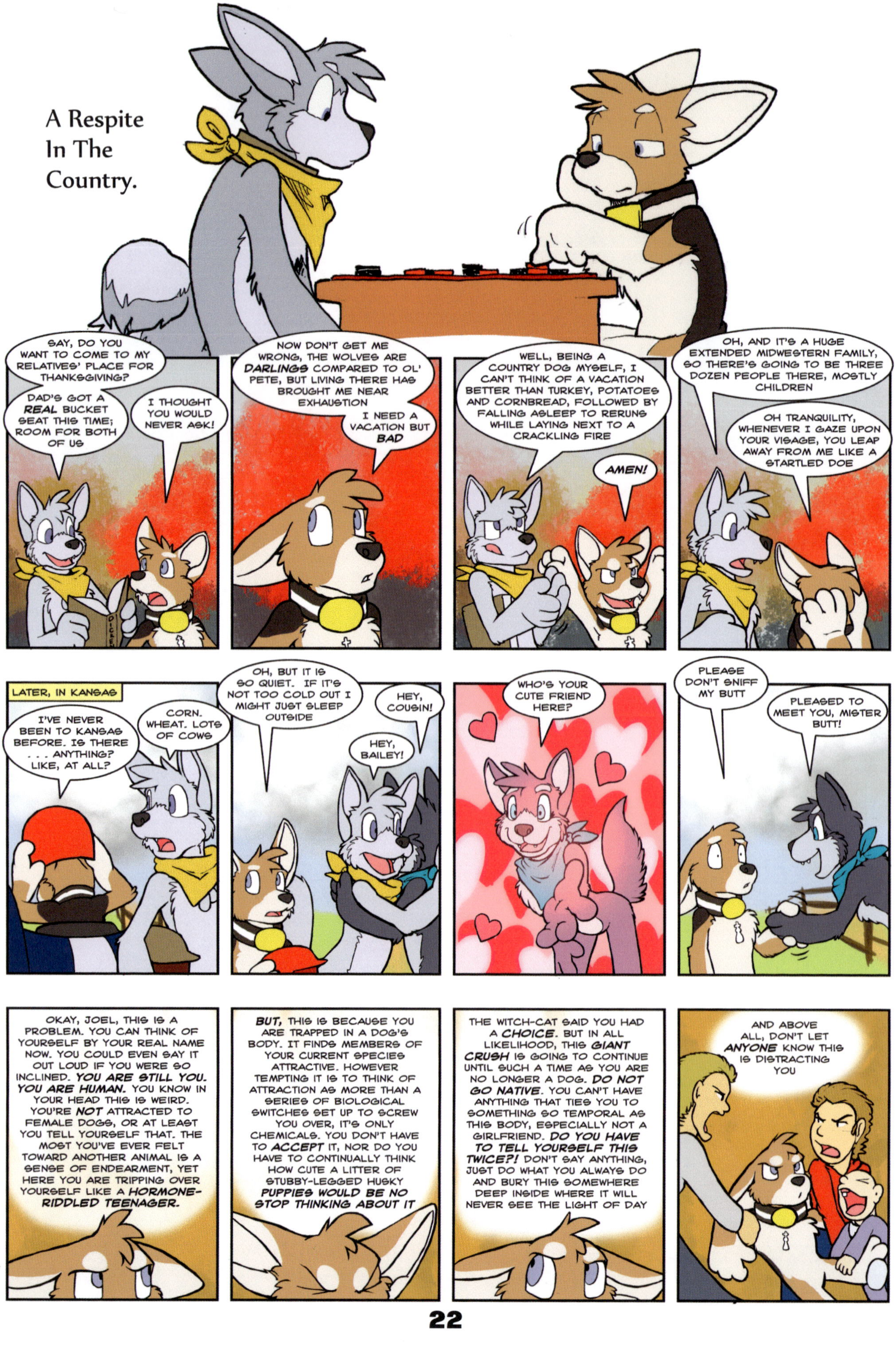
A Respite In The Country.
SAY, DO YOU WANT TO COME TO MY RELATIVES' PLACE FOR THANKSGIVING?
DAD'S GOT A REAL BUCKET SEAT THIS TIME; ROOM FOR BOTH OF US
I THOUGHT YOU WOULD NEVER ASK!
NOW DON'T GET ME WRONG, THE WOLVES ARE DARLINGS COMPARED TO OL' PETE, BUT LIVING THERE HAS BROUGHT ME NEAR EXHAUSTION
I NEED A VACATION BUT BAD
WELL, BEING A COUNTRY DOG MYSELF, I CAN'T THINK OF A VACATION BETTER THAN TURKEY, POTATOES AND CORNBREAD, FOLLOWED BY FALLING ASLEEP TO RERUNS WHILE LAYING NEXT TO A CRACKLING FIRE
AMEN!
OH, AND IT'S A HUGE EXTENDED MIDWESTERN FAMILY, SO THERE'S GOING TO BE THREE DOZEN PEOPLE THERE, MOSTLY CHILDREN
OH TRANQUILITY, WHENEVER I GAZE UPON YOUR VISAGE, YOU LEAP AWAY FROM ME LIKE A STARTLED DOE
LATER, IN KANSAS
I'VE NEVER BEEN TO KANSAS BEFORE. IS THERE . . . ANYTHING? LIKE, AT ALL?
CORN. WHEAT. LOTS OF COWS
OH, BUT IT IS SO QUIET. IF IT'S NOT TOO COLD OUT I MIGHT JUST SLEEP OUTSIDE
HEY, COUSIN!
HEY, BAILEY!
WHO'S YOUR CUTE FRIEND HERE?
PLEASE DON'T SNIFF MY BUTT
PLEASED TO MEET YOU, MISTER BUTT!
OKAY, JOEL, THIS IS A PROBLEM. YOU CAN THINK OF YOURSELF BY YOUR REAL NAME NOW. YOU COULD EVEN SAY IT OUT LOUD IF YOU WERE SO INCLINED. YOU ARE STILL YOU. YOU ARE HUMAN. YOU KNOW IN YOUR HEAD THIS IS WEIRD. YOU'RE NOT ATTRACTED TO FEMALE DOGS, OR AT LEAST YOU TELL YOURSELF THAT. THE MOST YOU'VE EVER FELT TOWARD ANOTHER ANIMAL IS A SENSE OF ENDEARMENT, YET HERE YOU ARE TRIPPING OVER YOURSELF LIKE A HORMONE-RIDDLED TEENAGER.
BUT, THIS IS BECAUSE YOU ARE TRAPPED IN A DOG'S BODY. IT FINDS MEMBERS OF YOUR CURRENT SPECIES ATTRACTIVE. HOWEVER TEMPTING IT IS TO THINK OF ATTRACTION AS MORE THAN A SERIES OF BIOLOGICAL SWITCHES SET UP TO SCREW YOU OVER, IT'S ONLY CHEMICALS. YOU DON'T HAVE TO ACCEPT IT, NOR DO YOU HAVE TO CONTINUALLY THINK HOW CUTE A LITTER OF STUBBY-LEGGED HUSKY PUPPIES WOULD BE NO STOP THINKING ABOUT IT
THE WITCH-CAT SAID YOU HAD A CHOICE. BUT IN ALL LIKELIHOOD, THIS GIANT CRUSH IS GOING TO CONTINUE UNTIL SUCH A TIME AS YOU ARE NO LONGER A DOG. DO NOT GO NATIVE. YOU CAN'T HAVE ANYTHING THAT TIES YOU TO SOMETHING SO TEMPORAL AS THIS BODY, ESPECIALLY NOT A GIRLFRIEND. DO YOU HAVE TO TELL YOURSELF THIS TWICE?! DON'T SAY ANYTHING, JUST DO WHAT YOU ALWAYS DO AND BURY THIS SOMEWHERE DEEP INSIDE WHERE IT WILL NEVER SEE THE LIGHT OF DAY
AND ABOVE ALL, DON'T LET ANYONE KNOW THIS IS DISTRACTING YOU

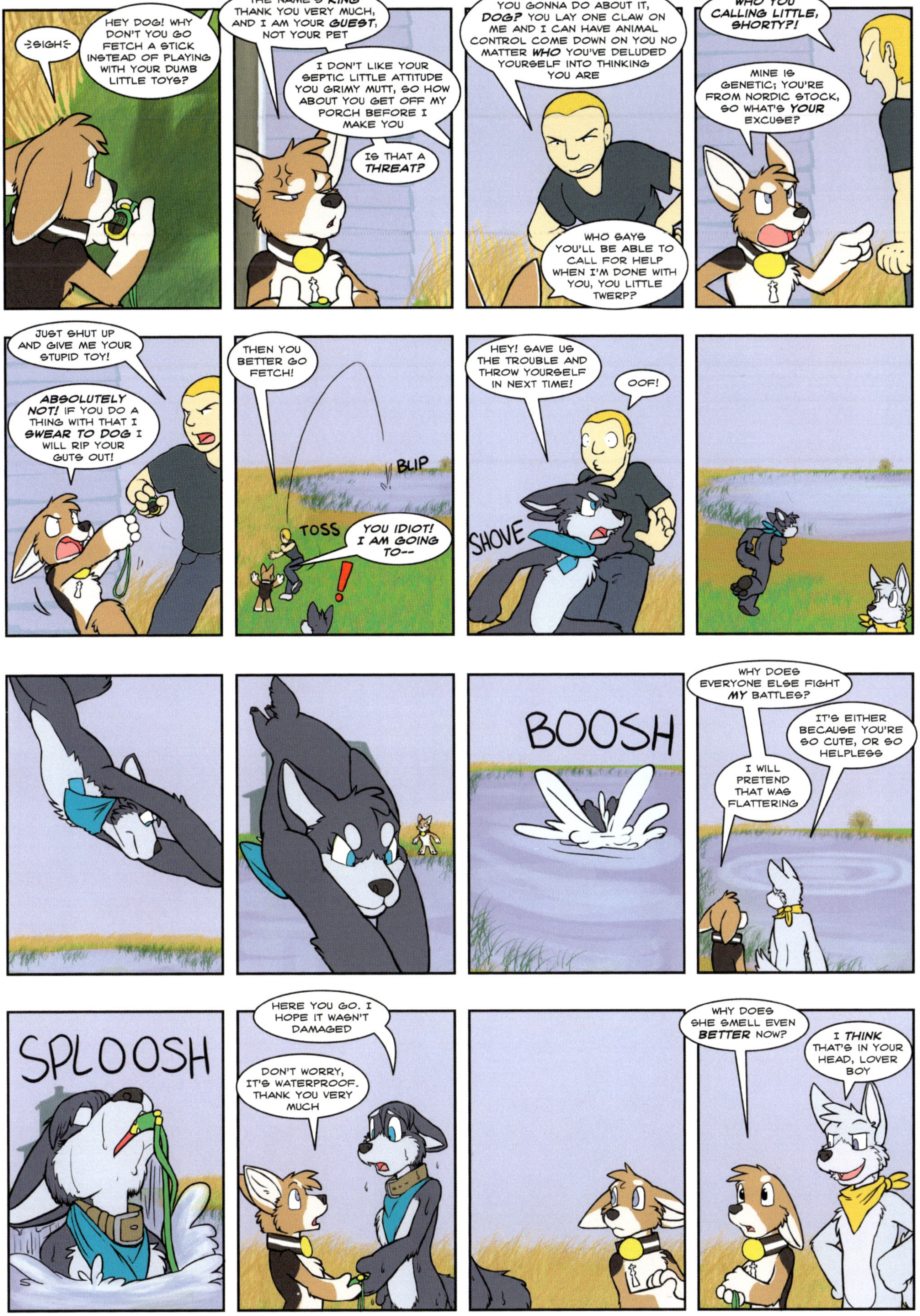

HEY DOG! WHY DON'T YOU GO FETCH A STICK INSTEAD OF PLAYING WITH YOUR DUMB LITTLE TOYS?
SIGH
THE NAME'S KING THANK YOU VERY MUCH, AND I AM YOUR GUEST, NOT YOUR PET
I DON'T LIKE YOUR SEPTIC LITTLE ATTITUDE YOU GRIMY MUTT, SO HOW ABOUT YOU GET OFF MY PORCH BEFORE I MAKE YOU
IS THAT A THREAT?
YEAH, AND WHAT ARE YOU GONNA DO ABOUT IT, DOG? YOU LAY ONE CLAW ON ME AND I CAN HAVE ANIMAL CONTROL COME DOWN ON YOU NO MATTER WHO YOU'VE DELUDED YOURSELF INTO THINKING YOU ARE
WHO SAYS YOU'LL BE ABLE TO CALL FOR HELP WHEN I'M DONE WITH YOU, YOU LITTLE TWERP?
WHO YOU CALLING LITTLE, SHORTY?!
MINE IS GENETIC; YOU'RE FROM NORDIC STOCK, SO WHAT'S YOUR EXCUSE?
JUST SHUT UP AND GIVE ME YOUR STUPID TOY!
ABSOLUTELY NOT! IF YOU DO A THING WITH THAT I SWEAR TO DOG I WILL RIP YOUR GUTS OUT!
THEN YOU BETTER GO FETCH!
BLIP
TOSS
YOU IDIOT! I AM GOING TO--
!
HEY! SAVE US THE TROUBLE AND THROW YOURSELF IN NEXT TIME!
OOF!
SHOVE
BOOSH
WHY DOES EVERYONE ELSE FIGHT MY BATTLES?
IT'S EITHER BECAUSE YOU'RE SO CUTE, OR SO HELPLESS
I WILL PRETEND THAT WAS FLATTERING
SPLOOSH
HERE YOU GO. I HOPE IT WASN'T DAMAGED
DON'T WORRY, IT'S WATERPROOF. THANK YOU VERY MUCH
WHY DOES SHE SMELL EVEN BETTER NOW?
I THINK THAT'S IN YOUR HEAD, LOVER BOY

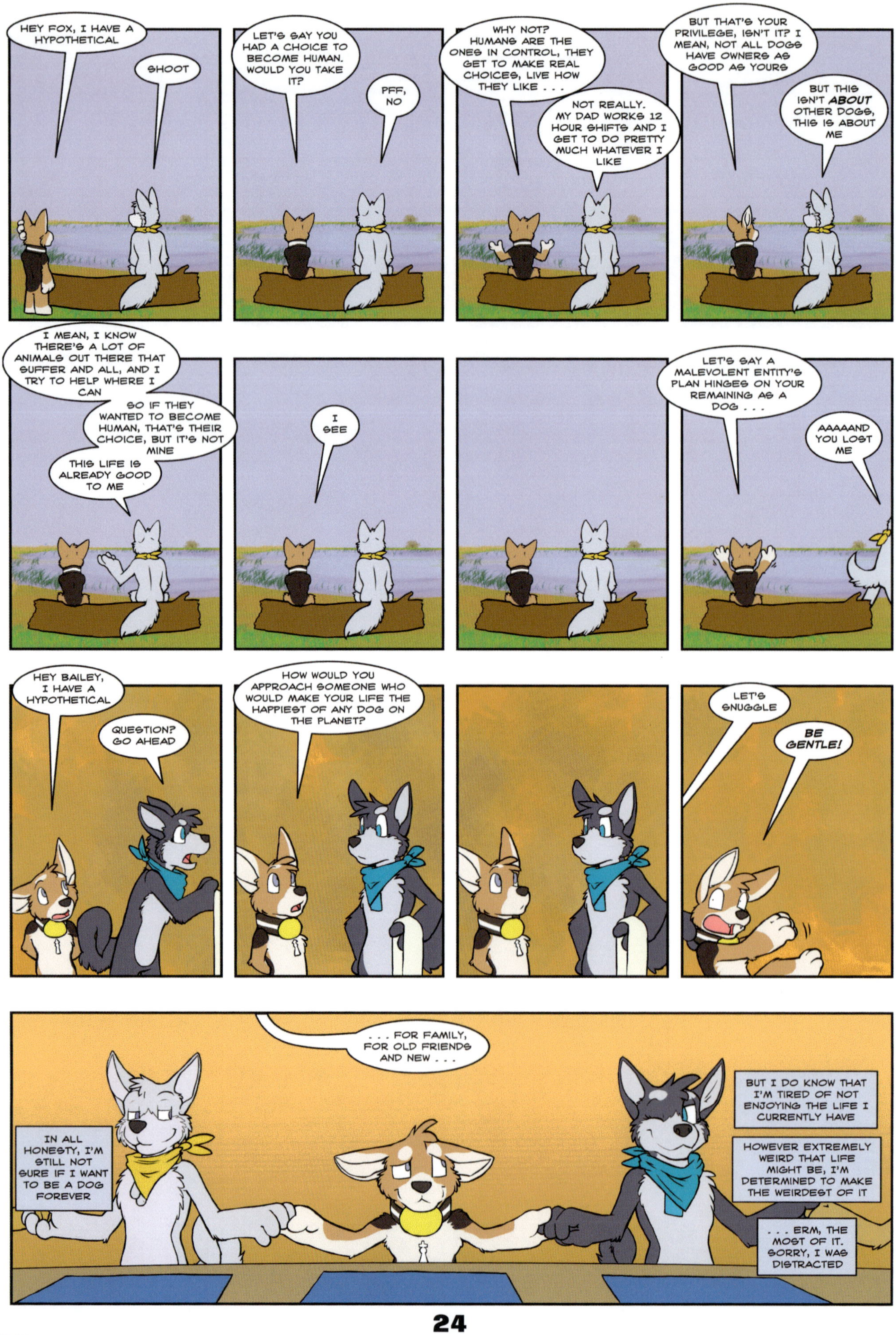
HEY FOX, I HAVE A HYPOTHETICAL
SHOOT
LET'S SAY YOU HAD A CHOICE TO BECOME HUMAN. WOULD YOU TAKE IT?
PFF, NO
WHY NOT? HUMANS ARE THE ONES IN CONTROL, THEY GET TO MAKE REAL CHOICES, LIVE HOW THEY LIKE . . .
NOT REALLY. MY DAD WORKS 12 HOUR SHIFTS AND I GET TO DO PRETTY MUCH WHATEVER I LIKE
BUT THAT'S YOUR PRIVILEGE, ISN'T IT? I MEAN, NOT ALL DOGS HAVE OWNERS AS GOOD AS YOURS
BUT THIS ISN'T ABOUT OTHER DOGS, THIS IS ABOUT ME
I MEAN, I KNOW THERE'S A LOT OF ANIMALS OUT THERE THAT SUFFER AND ALL, AND I TRY TO HELP WHERE I CAN
SO IF THEY WANTED TO BECOME HUMAN, THAT'S THEIR CHOICE, BUT IT'S NOT MINE
THIS LIFE IS ALREADY GOOD TO ME
I SEE
LET'S SAY A MALEVOLENT ENTITY'S PLAN HINGES ON YOUR REMAINING AS A DOG . . .
AAAAAND YOU LOST ME
HEY BAILEY, I HAVE A HYPOTHETICAL
QUESTION? GO AHEAD
HOW WOULD YOU APPROACH SOMEONE WHO WOULD MAKE YOUR LIFE THE HAPPIEST OF ANY DOG ON THE PLANET?
LET'S SNUGGLE
BE GENTLE!
. . . FOR FAMILY, FOR OLD FRIENDS AND NEW . . .
IN ALL HONESTY, I'M STILL NOT SURE IF I WANT TO BE A DOG FOREVER
BUT I DO KNOW THAT I'M TIRED OF NOT ENJOYING THE LIFE I CURRENTLY HAVE
HOWEVER EXTREMELY WEIRD THAT LIFE MIGHT BE, I'M DETERMINED TO MAKE THE WEIRDEST OF IT
. . . ERM, THE MOST OF IT. SORRY, I WAS DISTRACTED

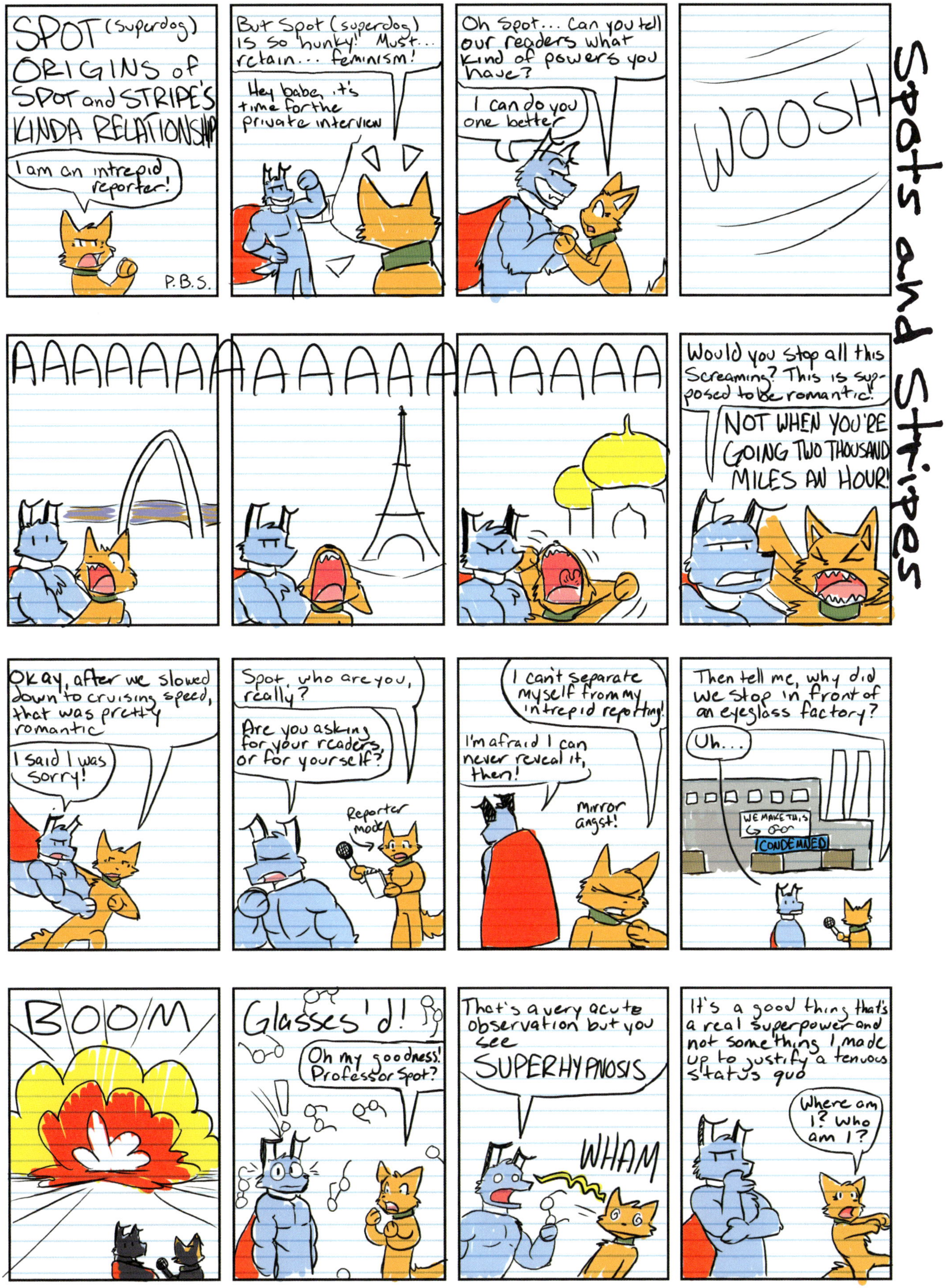
Spots and Stripes
SPOT (superdog) ORIGINS of SPOT and STRIPE'S KINDA RELATIONSHIP
I am an intrepid reporter!
P.B.S.
But Spot (superdog) is so hunky! Must... retain... feminism!
Hey babe, it's time for the private interview
Oh Spot... Can you tell our readers what kind of powers you have?
I can do you one better
WOOSH
AAAAAAAAAAAAAAAAA
Would you stop all this Screaming? This is supposed to be romantic!
NOT WHEN YOU'RE GOING TWO THOUSAND MILES AN HOUR!
Okay, after we slowed down to cruising speed, that was pretty romantic
I said I was sorry!
Spot, who are you, really?
Are you asking for your readers, or for yourself?
Reporter mode
I can't separate myself from my intrepid reporting!
I'm afraid I can never reveal it, then!
mirror angst!
Then tell me, why did we stop in front of an eyeglass factory?
Uh...
WE MAKE THIS
CONDEMNED
BOOM
Glasses'd!
Oh my goodness! Professor Spot?
That's a very acute observation but you see
SUPERHYPNOSIS
WHAM
It's a good thing that's a real superpower and not something I made up to justify a tenuous status quo
Where am I? Who am I?

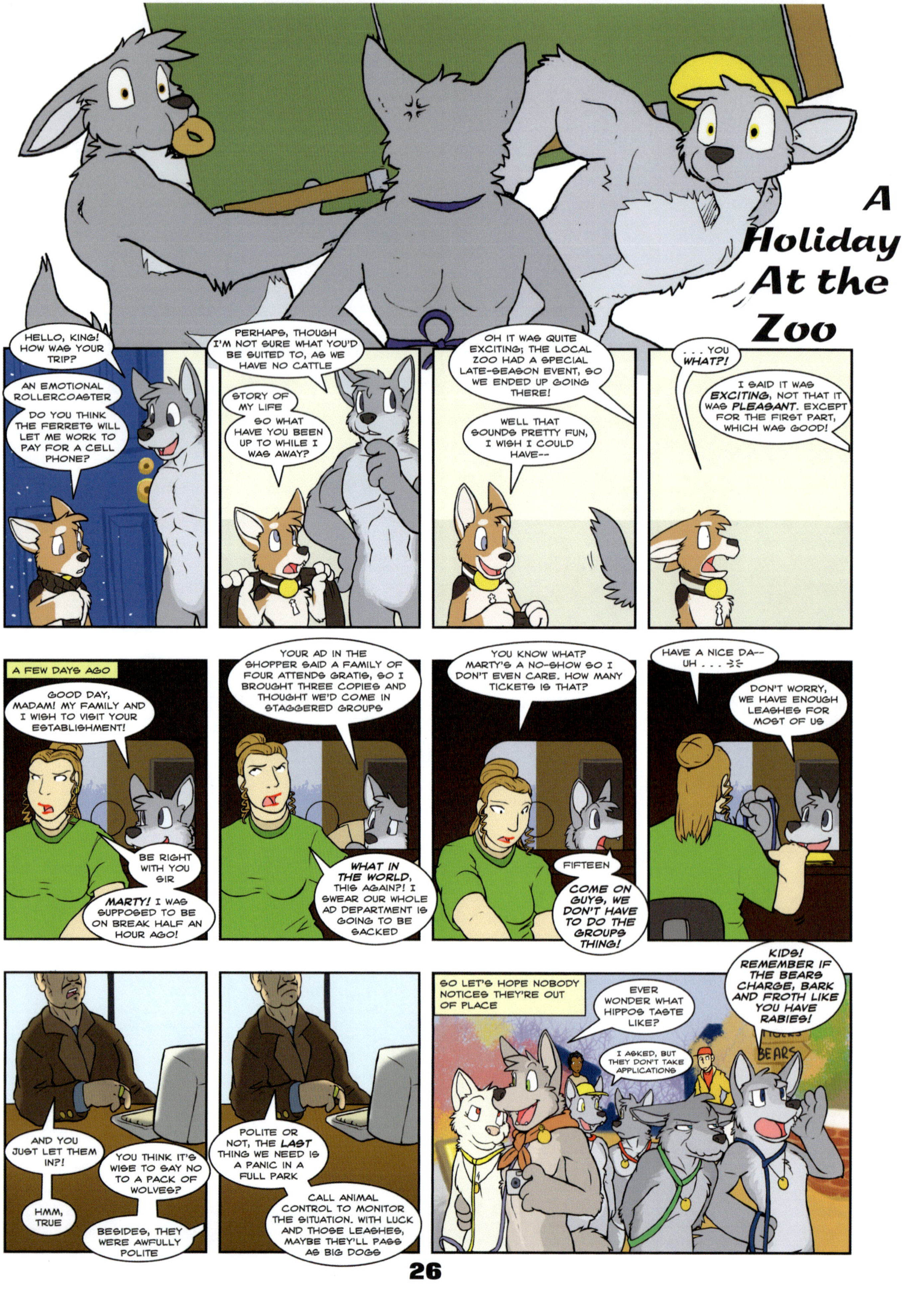
A Holiday At the Zoo
HELLO, KING! HOW WAS YOUR TRIP?
AN EMOTIONAL ROLLERCOASTER
DO YOU THINK THE FERRETS WILL LET ME WORK TO PAY FOR A CELL PHONE?
PERHAPS, THOUGH I'M NOT SURE WHAT YOU'D BE SUITED TO, AS WE HAVE NO CATTLE
STORY OF MY LIFE
SO WHAT HAVE YOU BEEN UP TO WHILE I WAS AWAY?
OH IT WAS QUITE EXCITING; THE LOCAL ZOO HAD A SPECIAL LATE-SEASON EVENT, SO WE ENDED UP GOING THERE!
WELL THAT SOUNDS PRETTY FUN, I WISH I COULD HAVE--
. . . YOU WHAT?!
I SAID IT WAS EXCITING, NOT THAT IT WAS PLEASANT. EXCEPT FOR THE FIRST PART, WHICH WAS GOOD!
A FEW DAYS AGO
GOOD DAY, MADAM! MY FAMILY AND I WISH TO VISIT YOUR ESTABLISHMENT!
BE RIGHT WITH YOU SIR
MARTY! I WAS SUPPOSED TO BE ON BREAK HALF AN HOUR AGO!
YOUR AD IN THE SHOPPER SAID A FAMILY OF FOUR ATTENDS GRATIS, SO I BROUGHT THREE COPIES AND THOUGHT WE'D COME IN STAGGERED GROUPS
WHAT IN THE WORLD, THIS AGAIN?! I SWEAR OUR WHOLE AD DEPARTMENT IS GOING TO BE SACKED
YOU KNOW WHAT? MARTY'S A NO-SHOW SO I DON'T EVEN CARE. HOW MANY TICKETS IS THAT?
FIFTEEN
COME ON GUYS, WE DON'T HAVE TO DO THE GROUPS THING!
HAVE A NICE DA-- UH . . .
DON'T WORRY, WE HAVE ENOUGH LEASHES FOR MOST OF US
AND YOU JUST LET THEM IN?!
YOU THINK IT'S WISE TO SAY NO TO A PACK OF WOLVES?
HMM, TRUE
BESIDES, THEY WERE AWFULLY POLITE
POLITE OR NOT, THE LAST THING WE NEED IS A PANIC IN A FULL PARK
CALL ANIMAL CONTROL TO MONITOR THE SITUATION. WITH LUCK AND THOSE LEASHES, MAYBE THEY'LL PASS AS BIG DOGS
SO LET'S HOPE NOBODY NOTICES THEY'RE OUT OF PLACE
EVER WONDER WHAT HIPPOS TASTE LIKE?
I ASKED, BUT THEY DON'T TAKE APPLICATIONS
KIDS! REMEMBER IF THE BEARS CHARGE, BARK AND FROTH LIKE YOU HAVE RABIES!
BEARS

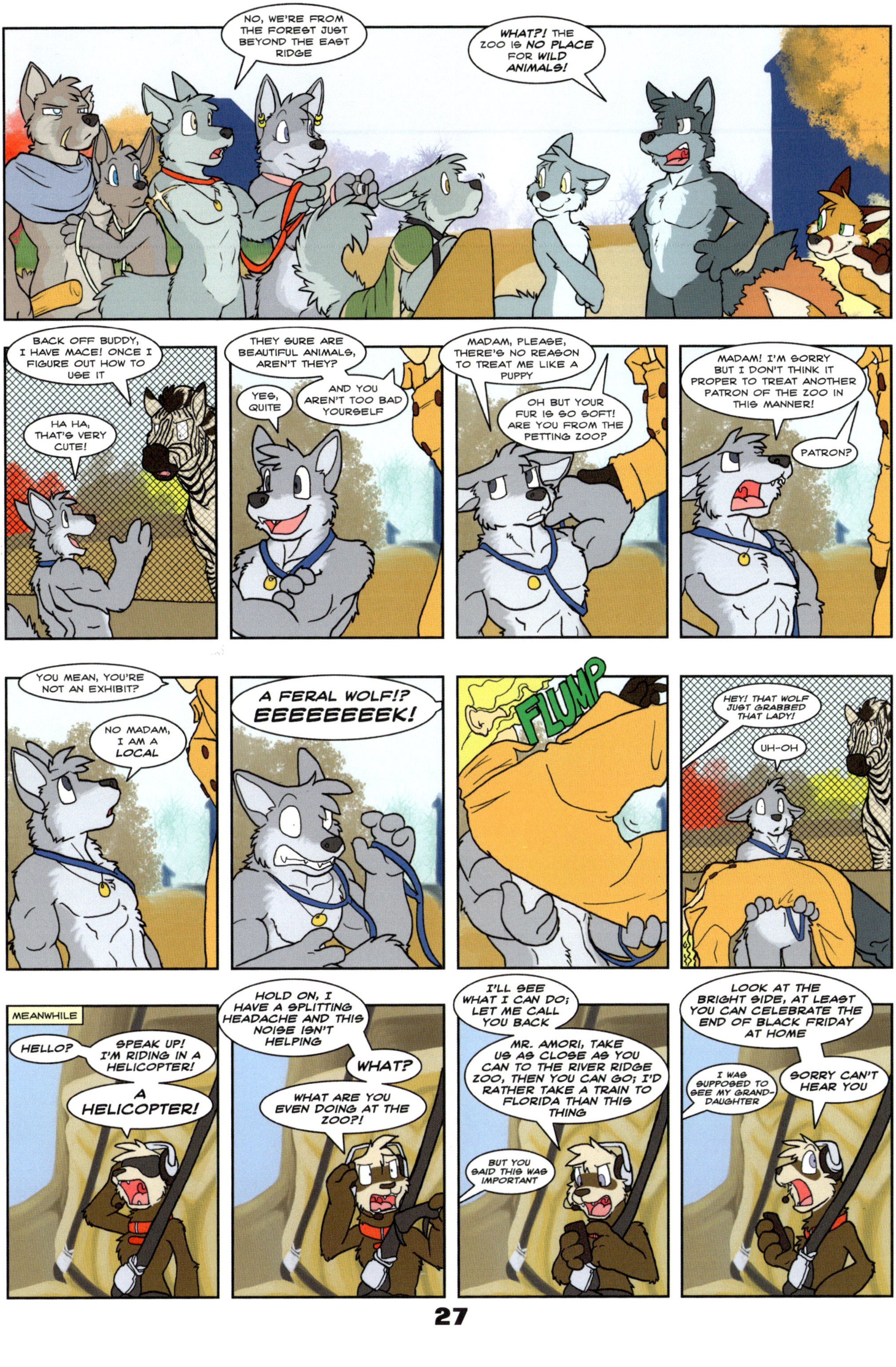
NO, WE'RE FROM THE FOREST JUST BEYOND THE EAST RIDGE
WHAT?! THE ZOO IS NO PLACE FOR WILD ANIMALS!
BACK OFF BUDDY, I HAVE MACE! ONCE I FIGURE OUT HOW TO USE IT
HA HA, THAT'S VERY CUTE!
THEY SURE ARE BEAUTIFUL ANIMALS, AREN'T THEY?
YES, QUITE
AND YOU AREN'T TOO BAD YOURSELF
MADAM, PLEASE, THERE'S NO REASON TO TREAT ME LIKE A PUPPY
OH BUT YOUR FUR IS SO SOFT! ARE YOU FROM THE PETTING ZOO?
MADAM! I'M SORRY BUT I DON'T THINK IT PROPER TO TREAT ANOTHER PATRON OF THE ZOO IN THIS MANNER!
PATRON?
YOU MEAN, YOU'RE NOT AN EXHIBIT?
NO MADAM, I AM A LOCAL
A FERAL WOLF!? EEEEEEEEK!
FLUMP
HEY! THAT WOLF JUST GRABBED THAT LADY!
UH-OH
MEANWHILE
HELLO?
SPEAK UP! I'M RIDING IN A HELICOPTER!
A HELICOPTER!
HOLD ON, I HAVE A SPLITTING HEADACHE AND THIS NOISE ISN'T HELPING
WHAT?
WHAT ARE YOU EVEN DOING AT THE ZOO?!
I'LL SEE WHAT I CAN DO; LET ME CALL YOU BACK
MR. AMORI, TAKE US AS CLOSE AS YOU CAN TO THE RIVER RIDGE ZOO, THEN YOU CAN GO; I'D RATHER TAKE A TRAIN TO FLORIDA THAN THIS THING
BUT YOU SAID THIS WAS IMPORTANT
LOOK AT THE BRIGHT SIDE, AT LEAST YOU CAN CELEBRATE THE END OF BLACK FRIDAY AT HOME
I WAS SUPPOSED TO SEE MY GRAND-DAUGHTER
SORRY CAN'T HEAR YOU

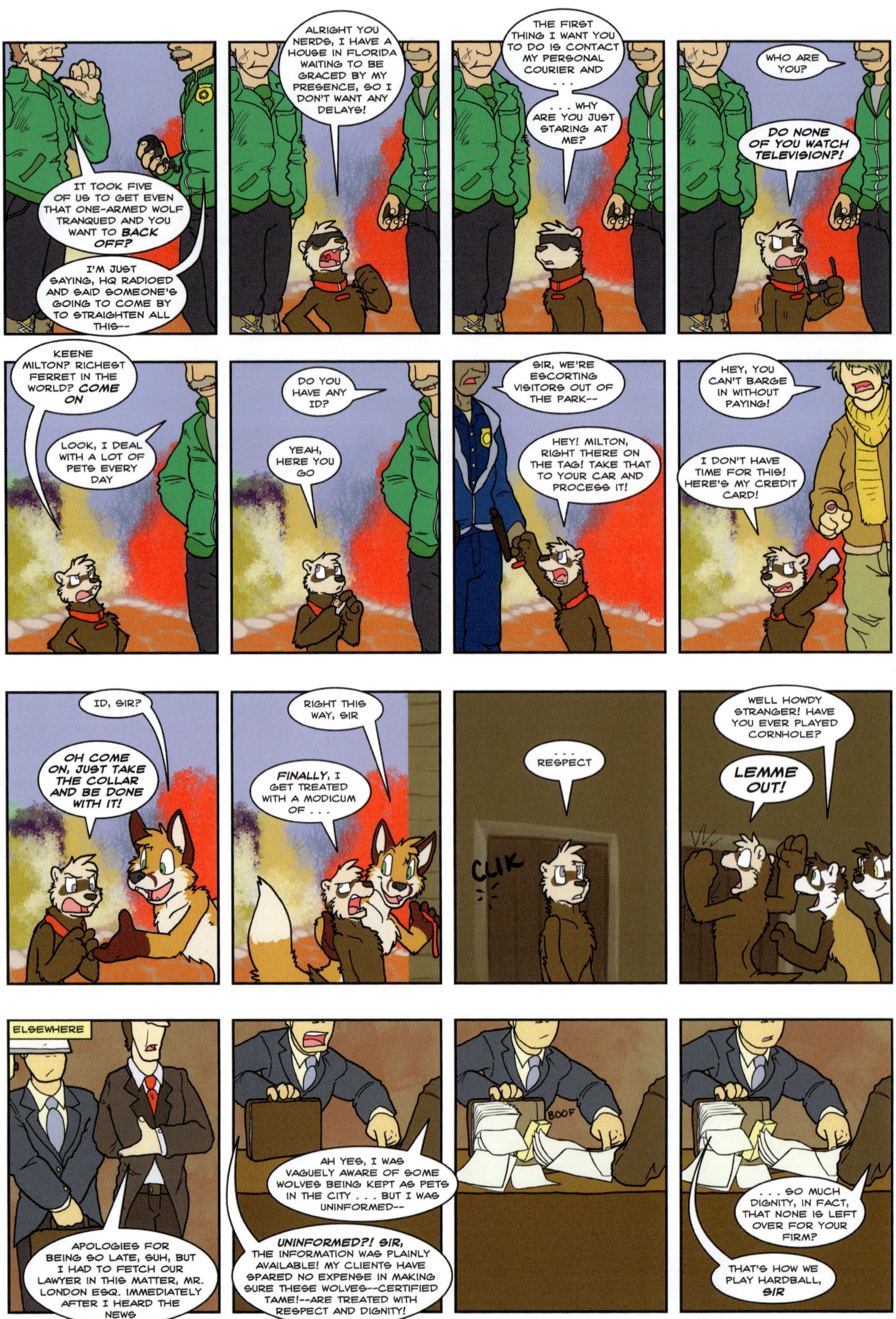
IT TOOK FIVE OF US TO GET EVEN THAT ONE-ARMED WOLF TRANQUED AND YOU WANT TO BACK OFF?
I'M JUST SAYING, HQ RADIOED AND SAID SOMEONE'S GOING TO COME BY TO STRAIGHTEN ALL THIS--
ALRIGHT YOU NERDS, I HAVE A HOUSE IN FLORIDA WAITING TO BE GRACED BY MY PRESENCE, SO I DON'T WANT ANY DELAYS!
THE FIRST THING I WANT YOU TO DO IS CONTACT MY PERSONAL COURIER AND . . .
. . . WHY ARE YOU JUST STARING AT ME?
WHO ARE YOU?
DO NONE OF YOU WATCH TELEVISION?!
KEENE MILTON? RICHEST FERRET IN THE WORLD? COME ON
LOOK, I DEAL WITH A LOT OF PETS EVERY DAY
DO YOU HAVE ANY ID?
YEAH, HERE YOU GO
SIR, WE'RE ESCORTING VISITORS OUT OF THE PARK--
HEY! MILTON, RIGHT THERE ON THE TAG! TAKE THAT TO YOUR CAR AND PROCESS IT!
HEY, YOU CAN'T BARGE IN WITHOUT PAYING!
I DON'T HAVE TIME FOR THIS! HERE'S MY CREDIT CARD!
ID, SIR?
OH COME ON, JUST TAKE THE COLLAR AND BE DONE WITH IT!
RIGHT THIS WAY, SIR
FINALLY, I GET TREATED WITH A MODICUM OF . . .
. . . RESPECT
CLIK
WELL HOWDY STRANGER! HAVE YOU EVER PLAYED CORNHOLE?
LEMME OUT!
ELSEWHERE
APOLOGIES FOR BEING SO LATE, SUH, BUT I HAD TO FETCH OUR LAWYER IN THIS MATTER, MR. LONDON ESQ. IMMEDIATELY AFTER I HEARD THE NEWS
AH YES, I WAS VAGUELY AWARE OF SOME WOLVES BEING KEPT AS PETS IN THE CITY . . . BUT I WAS UNINFORMED--
UNINFORMED?! SIR, THE INFORMATION WAS PLAINLY AVAILABLE! MY CLIENTS HAVE SPARED NO EXPENSE IN MAKING SURE THESE WOLVES--CERTIFIED TAME!--ARE TREATED WITH RESPECT AND DIGNITY!
BOOF
. . . SO MUCH DIGNITY, IN FACT, THAT NONE IS LEFT OVER FOR YOUR FIRM?
THAT'S HOW WE PLAY HARDBALL, SIR

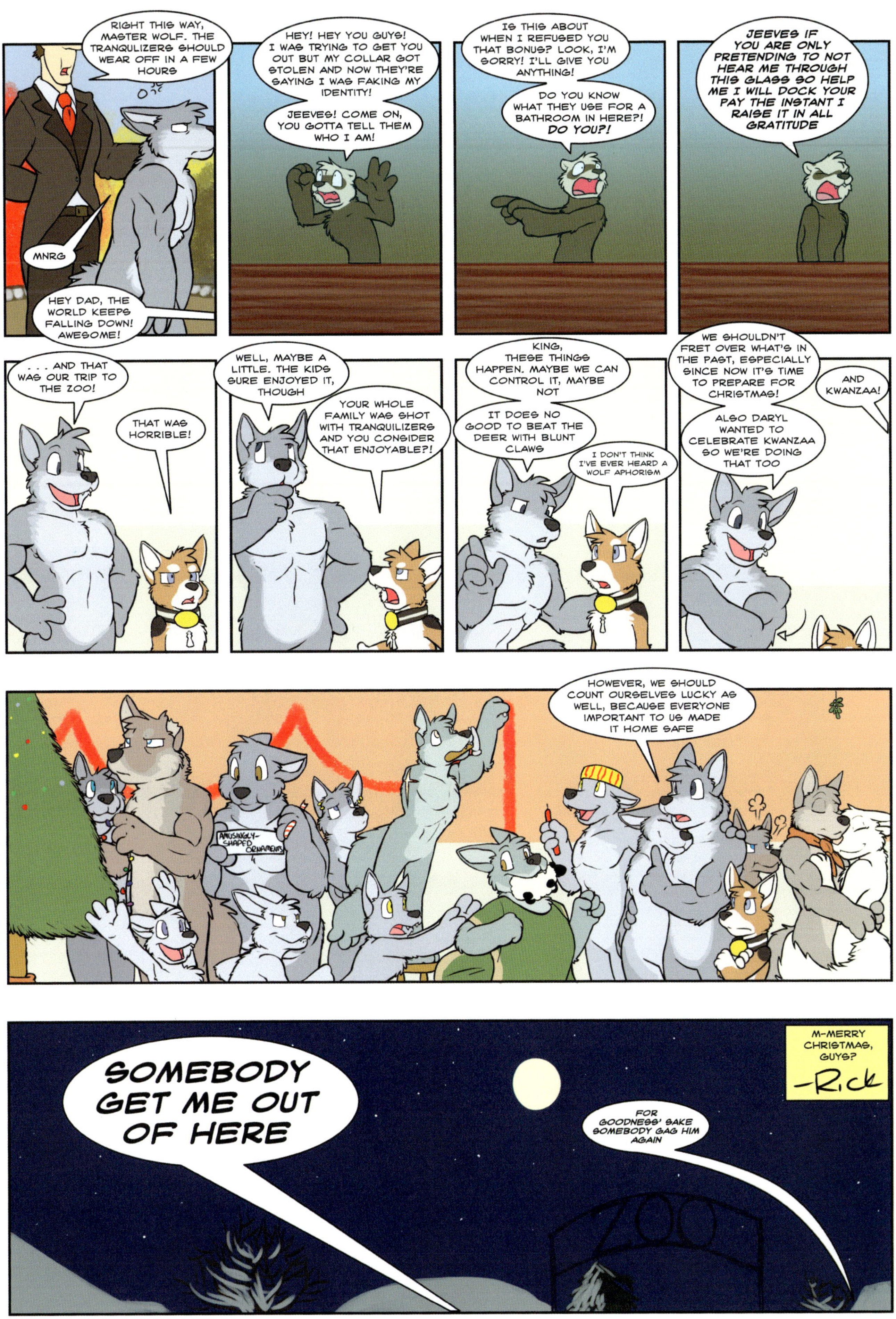
RIGHT THIS WAY, MASTER WOLF. THE TRANQULIZERS SHOULD WEAR OFF IN A FEW HOURS
MNRG
HEY DAD, THE WORLD KEEPS FALLING DOWN! AWESOME!
HEY! HEY YOU GUYS! I WAS TRYING TO GET YOU OUT BUT MY COLLAR GOT STOLEN AND NOW THEY'RE SAYING I WAS FAKING MY IDENTITY!
JEEVES! COME ON, YOU GOTTA TELL THEM WHO I AM!
IS THIS ABOUT WHEN I REFUSED YOU THAT BONUS? LOOK, I'M SORRY! I'LL GIVE YOU ANYTHING!
DO YOU KNOW WHAT THEY USE FOR A BATHROOM IN HERE?! DO YOU?!
JEEVES IF YOU ARE ONLY PRETENDING TO NOT HEAR ME THROUGH THIS GLASS SO HELP ME I WILL DOCK YOUR PAY THE INSTANT I RAISE IT IN ALL GRATITUDE
. . . AND THAT WAS OUR TRIP TO THE ZOO!
THAT WAS HORRIBLE!
WELL, MAYBE A LITTLE. THE KIDS SURE ENJOYED IT, THOUGH
YOUR WHOLE FAMILY WAS SHOT WITH TRANQUILIZERS AND YOU CONSIDER THAT ENJOYABLE?!
KING, THESE THINGS HAPPEN. MAYBE WE CAN CONTROL IT, MAYBE NOT
IT DOES NO GOOD TO BEAT THE DEER WITH BLUNT CLAWS
I DON'T THINK I'VE EVER HEARD A WOLF APHORISM
WE SHOULDN'T FRET OVER WHAT'S IN THE PAST, ESPECIALLY SINCE NOW IT'S TIME TO PREPARE FOR CHRISTMAS!
AND KWANZAA!
ALSO DARYL WANTED TO CELEBRATE KWANZAA SO WE'RE DOING THAT TOO
AMUSINGLY-SHAPED ORNAMENTS
HOWEVER, WE SHOULD COUNT OURSELVES LUCKY AS WELL, BECAUSE EVERYONE IMPORTANT TO US MADE IT HOME SAFE
SOMEBODY GET ME OUT OF HERE
FOR GOODNESS' SAKE SOMEBODY GAG HIM AGAIN
ZOO
M-MERRY CHRISTMAS, GUYS?
-Rick

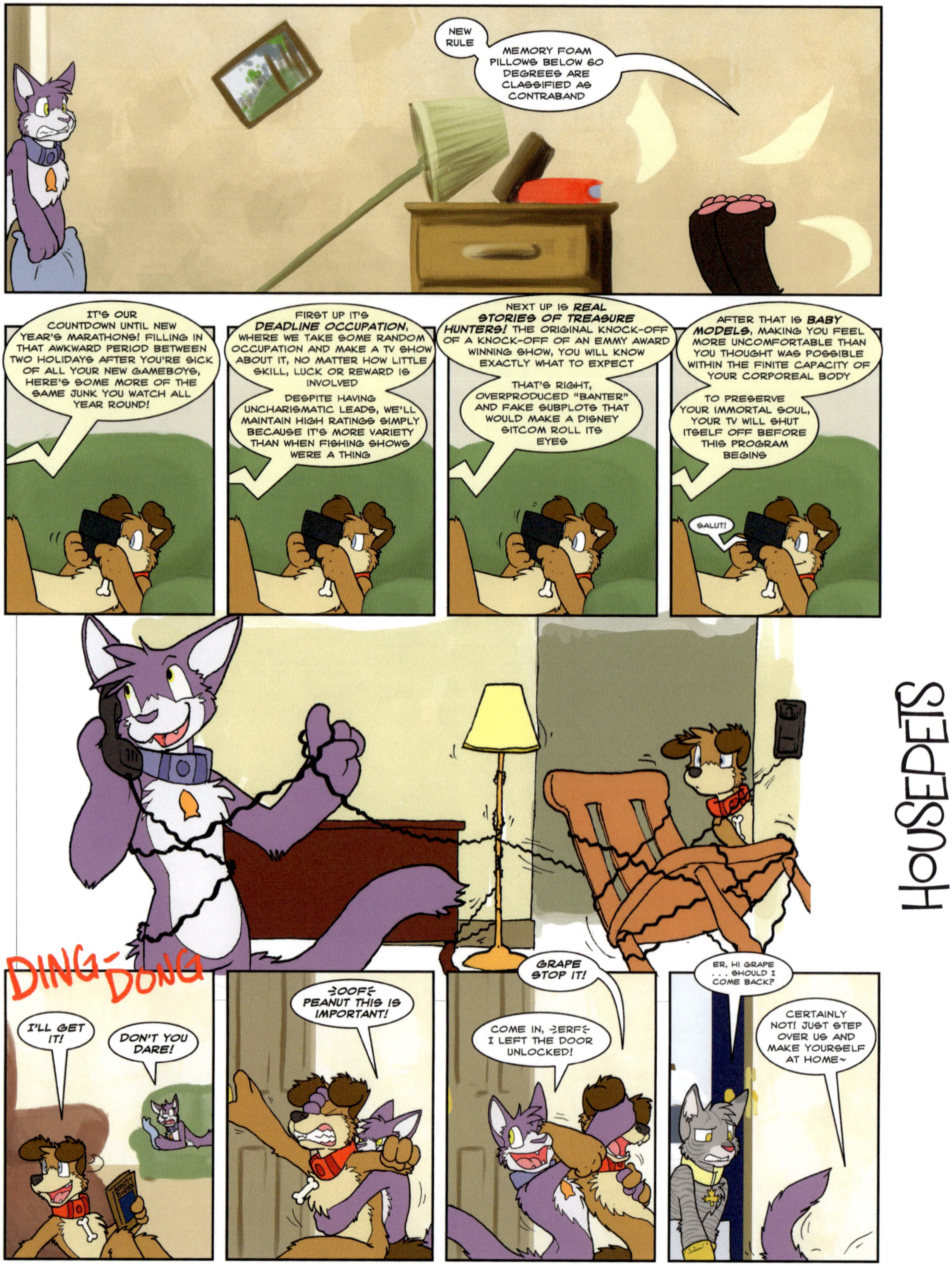
NEW RULE
MEMORY FOAM PILLOWS BELOW 60 DEGREES ARE CLASSIFIED AS CONTRABAND
IT'S OUR COUNTDOWN UNTIL NEW YEAR'S MARATHONS! FILLING IN THAT AWKWARD PERIOD BETWEEN TWO HOLIDAYS AFTER YOU'RE SICK OF ALL YOUR NEW GAMEBOYS, HERE'S SOME MORE OF THE SAME JUNK YOU WATCH ALL YEAR ROUND!
FIRST UP IT'S *DEADLINE OCCUPATION*, WHERE WE TAKE SOME RANDOM OCCUPATION AND MAKE A TV SHOW ABOUT IT, NO MATTER HOW LITTLE SKILL, LUCK OR REWARD IS INVOLVED
DESPITE HAVING UNCHARISMATIC LEADS, WE'LL MAINTAIN HIGH RATINGS SIMPLY BECAUSE IT'S MORE VARIETY THAN WHEN FISHING SHOWS WERE A THING
NEXT UP IS ***REAL STORIES OF TREASURE HUNTERS!*** THE ORIGINAL KNOCK-OFF OF A KNOCK-OFF OF AN EMMY AWARD WINNING SHOW, YOU WILL KNOW EXACTLY WHAT TO EXPECT
THAT'S RIGHT, OVERPRODUCED "BANTER" AND FAKE SUBPLOTS THAT WOULD MAKE A DISNEY SITCOM ROLL ITS EYES
AFTER THAT IS **BABY MODELS**, MAKING YOU FEEL MORE UNCOMFORTABLE THAN YOU THOUGHT WAS POSSIBLE WITHIN THE FINITE CAPACITY OF YOUR CORPOREAL BODY
TO PRESERVE YOUR IMMORTAL SOUL, YOUR TV WILL SHUT ITSELF OFF BEFORE THIS PROGRAM BEGINS
SALUT!
HOUSEPETS
DING-DONG
I'LL GET IT!
DON'T YOU DARE!
-OOF- PEANUT THIS IS IMPORTANT!
GRAPE STOP IT!
COME IN, -ERF- I LEFT THE DOOR UNLOCKED!
ER, HI GRAPE . . . SHOULD I COME BACK?
CERTAINLY NOT! JUST STEP OVER US AND MAKE YOURSELF AT HOME~

BABIES!

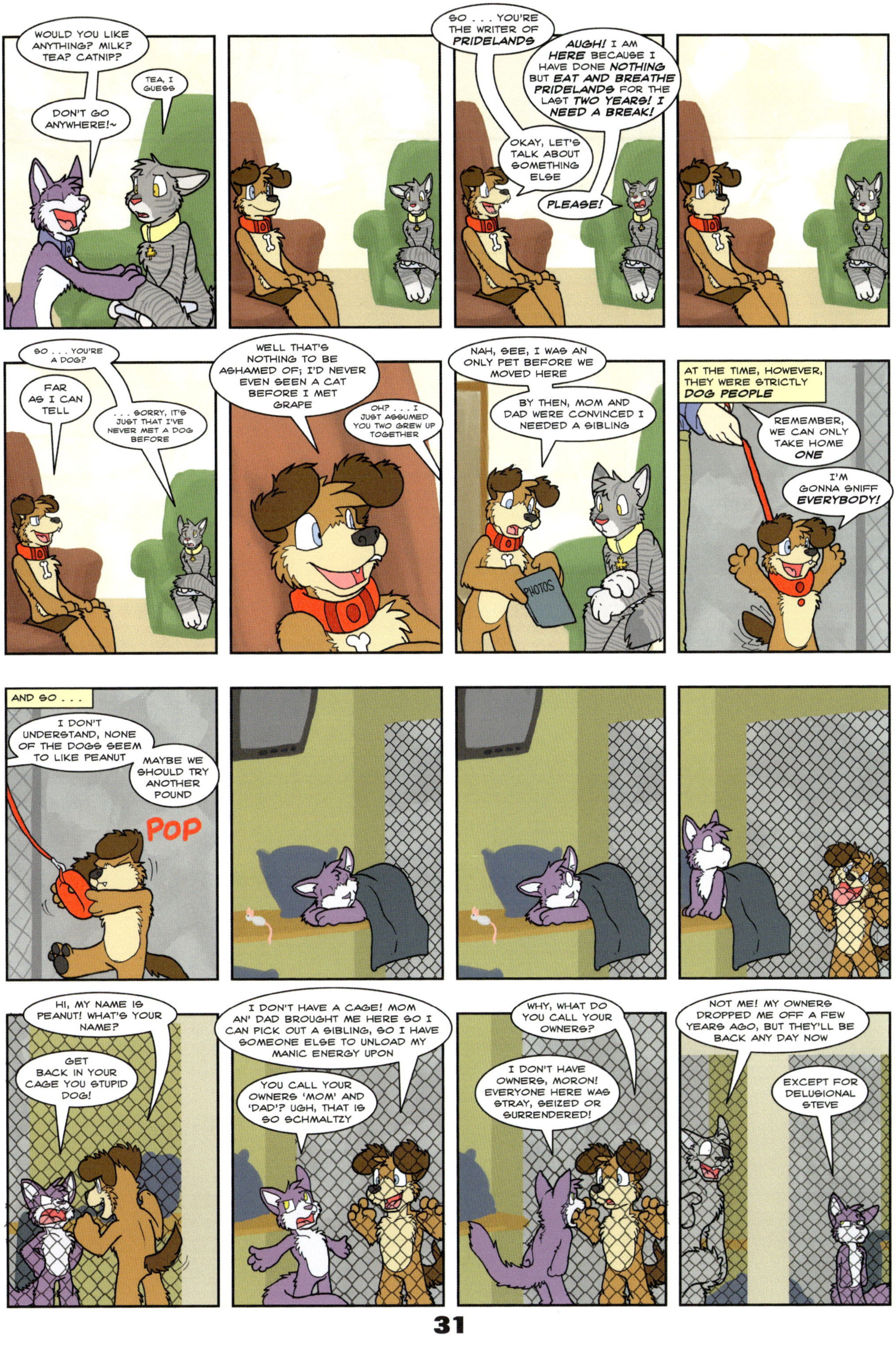

WOULD YOU LIKE ANYTHING? MILK? TEA? CATNIP?
TEA, I GUESS
DON'T GO ANYWHERE!~
SO . . . YOU'RE THE WRITER OF PRIDELANDS
AUGH! I AM HERE BECAUSE I HAVE DONE NOTHING BUT EAT AND BREATHE PRIDELANDS FOR THE LAST TWO YEARS! I NEED A BREAK!
OKAY, LET'S TALK ABOUT SOMETHING ELSE
PLEASE!
SO . . . YOU'RE A DOG?
FAR AS I CAN TELL
. . . SORRY, IT'S JUST THAT I'VE NEVER MET A DOG BEFORE
WELL THAT'S NOTHING TO BE ASHAMED OF; I'D NEVER EVEN SEEN A CAT BEFORE I MET GRAPE
OH? . . . I JUST ASSUMED YOU TWO GREW UP TOGETHER
NAH, SEE, I WAS AN ONLY PET BEFORE WE MOVED HERE
BY THEN, MOM AND DAD WERE CONVINCED I NEEDED A SIBLING
PHOTOS
AT THE TIME, HOWEVER, THEY WERE STRICTLY DOG PEOPLE
REMEMBER, WE CAN ONLY TAKE HOME ONE
I'M GONNA SNIFF EVERYBODY!
AND SO . . .
I DON'T UNDERSTAND, NONE OF THE DOGS SEEM TO LIKE PEANUT
MAYBE WE SHOULD TRY ANOTHER POUND
POP
HI, MY NAME IS PEANUT! WHAT'S YOUR NAME?
GET BACK IN YOUR CAGE YOU STUPID DOG!
I DON'T HAVE A CAGE! MOM AN' DAD BROUGHT ME HERE SO I CAN PICK OUT A SIBLING, SO I HAVE SOMEONE ELSE TO UNLOAD MY MANIC ENERGY UPON
YOU CALL YOUR OWNERS 'MOM' AND 'DAD'? UGH, THAT IS SO SCHMALTZY
WHY, WHAT DO YOU CALL YOUR OWNERS?
I DON'T HAVE OWNERS, MORON! EVERYONE HERE WAS STRAY, SEIZED OR SURRENDERED!
NOT ME! MY OWNERS DROPPED ME OFF A FEW YEARS AGO, BUT THEY'LL BE BACK ANY DAY NOW
EXCEPT FOR DELUSIONAL STEVE

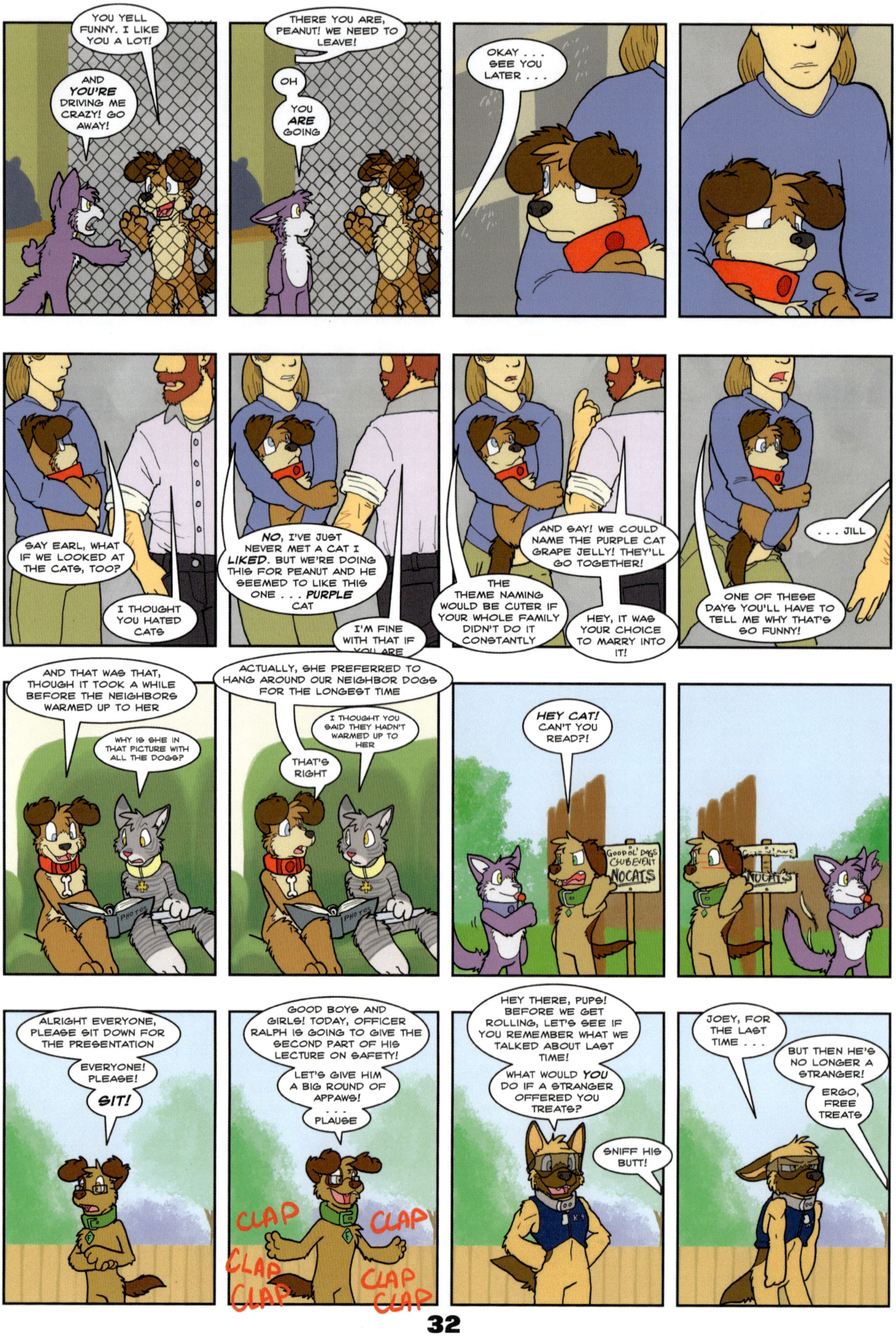
YOU YELL FUNNY. I LIKE YOU A LOT!
AND YOU'RE DRIVING ME CRAZY! GO AWAY!
THERE YOU ARE, PEANUT! WE NEED TO LEAVE!
OH
YOU ARE GOING
OKAY . . . SEE YOU LATER . . .
SAY EARL, WHAT IF WE LOOKED AT THE CATS, TOO?
I THOUGHT YOU HATED CATS
NO, I'VE JUST NEVER MET A CAT I LIKED. BUT WE'RE DOING THIS FOR PEANUT AND HE SEEMED TO LIKE THIS ONE . . . PURPLE CAT
I'M FINE WITH THAT IF YOU ARE
AND SAY! WE COULD NAME THE PURPLE CAT GRAPE JELLY! THEY'LL GO TOGETHER!
THE THEME NAMING WOULD BE CUTER IF YOUR WHOLE FAMILY DIDN'T DO IT CONSTANTLY
HEY, IT WAS YOUR CHOICE TO MARRY INTO IT!
. . . JILL
ONE OF THESE DAYS YOU'LL HAVE TO TELL ME WHY THAT'S SO FUNNY!
AND THAT WAS THAT, THOUGH IT TOOK A WHILE BEFORE THE NEIGHBORS WARMED UP TO HER
WHY IS SHE IN THAT PICTURE WITH ALL THE DOGS?
PHOTOS
ACTUALLY, SHE PREFERRED TO HANG AROUND OUR NEIGHBOR DOGS FOR THE LONGEST TIME
I THOUGHT YOU SAID THEY HADN'T WARMED UP TO HER
THAT'S RIGHT
HEY CAT! CAN'T YOU READ?!
GOOD OL' DOGS CLUB EVENT NO CATS
ALRIGHT EVERYONE, PLEASE SIT DOWN FOR THE PRESENTATION
EVERYONE! PLEASE!
SIT!
GOOD BOYS AND GIRLS! TODAY, OFFICER RALPH IS GOING TO GIVE THE SECOND PART OF HIS LECTURE ON SAFETY!
LET'S GIVE HIM A BIG ROUND OF APPAWS!
. . . PLAUSE
CLAP CLAP CLAP CLAP CLAP CLAP
HEY THERE, PUPS! BEFORE WE GET ROLLING, LET'S SEE IF YOU REMEMBER WHAT WE TALKED ABOUT LAST TIME!
WHAT WOULD YOU DO IF A STRANGER OFFERED YOU TREATS?
SNIFF HIS BUTT!
JOEY, FOR THE LAST TIME . . .
BUT THEN HE'S NO LONGER A STRANGER!
ERGO, FREE TREATS

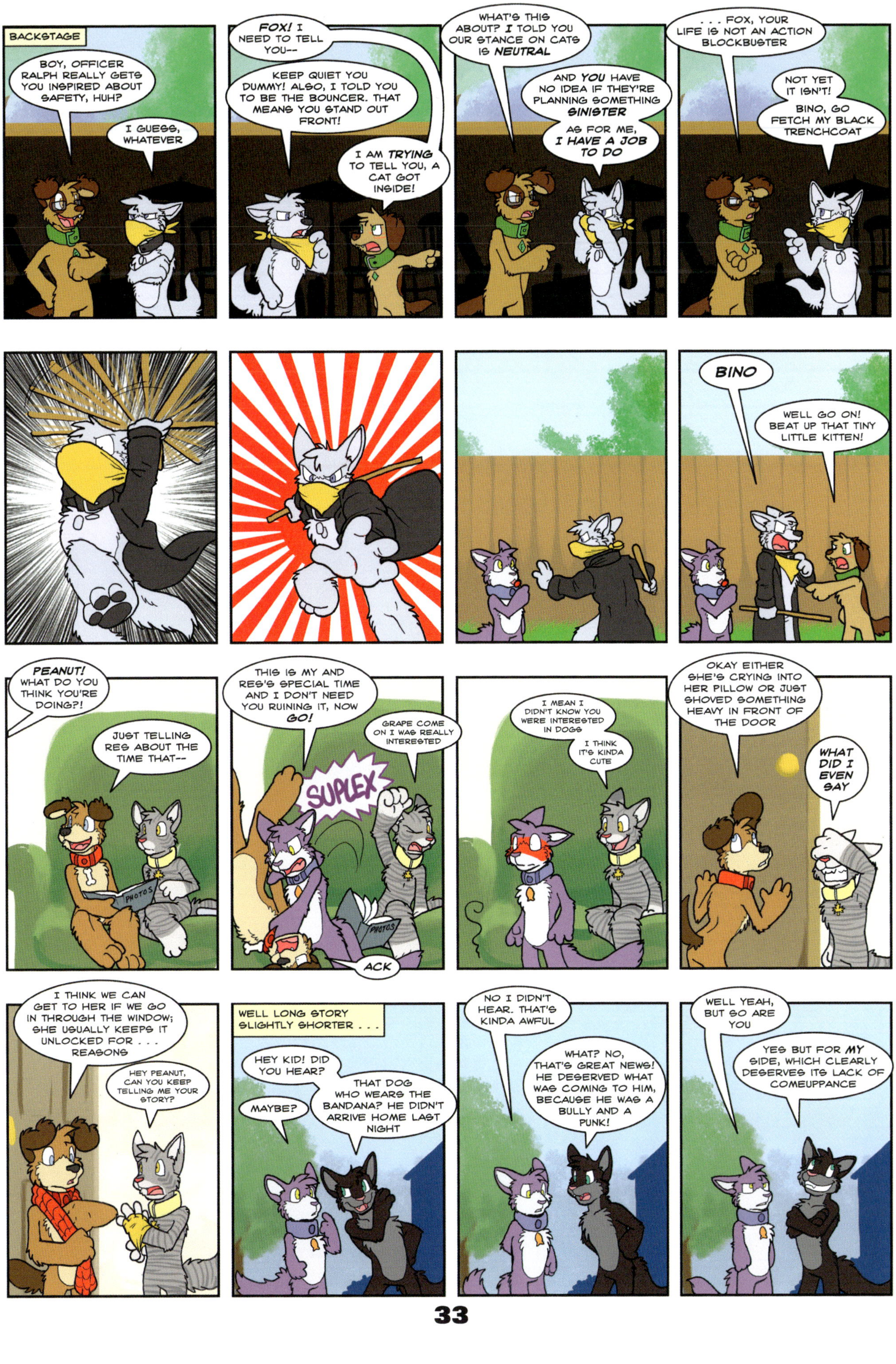
BACKSTAGE
BOY, OFFICER RALPH REALLY GETS YOU INSPIRED ABOUT SAFETY, HUH?
I GUESS, WHATEVER
FOX! I NEED TO TELL YOU--
KEEP QUIET YOU DUMMY! ALSO, I TOLD YOU TO BE THE BOUNCER. THAT MEANS YOU STAND OUT FRONT!
I AM TRYING TO TELL YOU, A CAT GOT INSIDE!
WHAT'S THIS ABOUT? I TOLD YOU OUR STANCE ON CATS IS NEUTRAL
AND YOU HAVE NO IDEA IF THEY'RE PLANNING SOMETHING SINISTER
AS FOR ME, I HAVE A JOB TO DO
. . . FOX, YOUR LIFE IS NOT AN ACTION BLOCKBUSTER
NOT YET IT ISN'T!
BINO, GO FETCH MY BLACK TRENCHCOAT
BINO
WELL GO ON! BEAT UP THAT TINY LITTLE KITTEN!
PEANUT! WHAT DO YOU THINK YOU'RE DOING?!
JUST TELLING RES ABOUT THE TIME THAT--
PHOTOS
THIS IS MY AND RES'S SPECIAL TIME AND I DON'T NEED YOU RUINING IT, NOW GO!
GRAPE COME ON I WAS REALLY INTERESTED
SUPLEX
ACK
I MEAN I DIDN'T KNOW YOU WERE INTERESTED IN DOGS
I THINK IT'S KINDA CUTE
OKAY EITHER SHE'S CRYING INTO HER PILLOW OR JUST SHOVED SOMETHING HEAVY IN FRONT OF THE DOOR
WHAT DID I EVEN SAY
I THINK WE CAN GET TO HER IF WE GO IN THROUGH THE WINDOW; SHE USUALLY KEEPS IT UNLOCKED FOR . . . REASONS
HEY PEANUT, CAN YOU KEEP TELLING ME YOUR STORY?
WELL LONG STORY SLIGHTLY SHORTER . . .
HEY KID! DID YOU HEAR?
MAYBE?
THAT DOG WHO WEARS THE BANDANA? HE DIDN'T ARRIVE HOME LAST NIGHT
NO I DIDN'T HEAR. THAT'S KINDA AWFUL
WHAT? NO, THAT'S GREAT NEWS! HE DESERVED WHAT WAS COMING TO HIM, BECAUSE HE WAS A BULLY AND A PUNK!
WELL YEAH, BUT SO ARE YOU
YES BUT FOR MY SIDE, WHICH CLEARLY DESERVES ITS LACK OF COMEUPPANCE

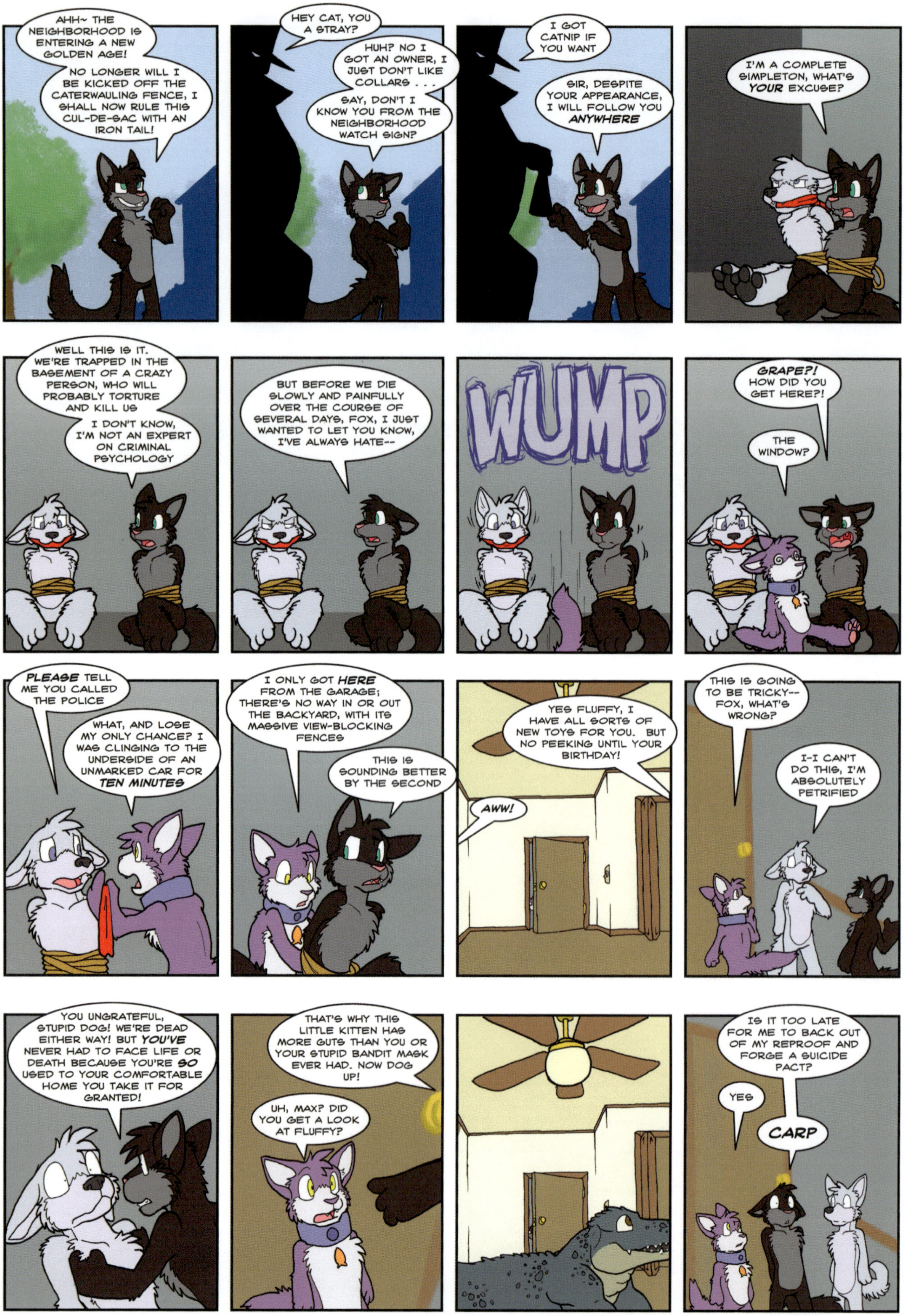
AHH~ THE NEIGHBORHOOD IS ENTERING A NEW GOLDEN AGE!
NO LONGER WILL I BE KICKED OFF THE CATERWAULING FENCE, I SHALL NOW RULE THIS CUL-DE-SAC WITH AN IRON TAIL!
HEY CAT, YOU A STRAY?
HUH? NO I GOT AN OWNER, I JUST DON'T LIKE COLLARS . . .
SAY, DON'T I KNOW YOU FROM THE NEIGHBORHOOD WATCH SIGN?
I GOT CATNIP IF YOU WANT
SIR, DESPITE YOUR APPEARANCE, I WILL FOLLOW YOU ANYWHERE
I'M A COMPLETE SIMPLETON, WHAT'S YOUR EXCUSE?
WELL THIS IS IT. WE'RE TRAPPED IN THE BASEMENT OF A CRAZY PERSON, WHO WILL PROBABLY TORTURE AND KILL US
I DON'T KNOW, I'M NOT AN EXPERT ON CRIMINAL PSYCHOLOGY
BUT BEFORE WE DIE SLOWLY AND PAINFULLY OVER THE COURSE OF SEVERAL DAYS, FOX, I JUST WANTED TO LET YOU KNOW, I'VE ALWAYS HATE--
WUMP
GRAPE?! HOW DID YOU GET HERE?!
THE WINDOW?
PLEASE TELL ME YOU CALLED THE POLICE
WHAT, AND LOSE MY ONLY CHANCE? I WAS CLINGING TO THE UNDERSIDE OF AN UNMARKED CAR FOR TEN MINUTES
I ONLY GOT HERE FROM THE GARAGE; THERE'S NO WAY IN OR OUT THE BACKYARD, WITH ITS MASSIVE VIEW-BLOCKING FENCES
THIS IS SOUNDING BETTER BY THE SECOND
YES FLUFFY, I HAVE ALL SORTS OF NEW TOYS FOR YOU. BUT NO PEEKING UNTIL YOUR BIRTHDAY!
AWW!
THIS IS GOING TO BE TRICKY-- FOX, WHAT'S WRONG?
I-I CAN'T DO THIS, I'M ABSOLUTELY PETRIFIED
YOU UNGRATEFUL, STUPID DOG! WE'RE DEAD EITHER WAY! BUT YOU'VE NEVER HAD TO FACE LIFE OR DEATH BECAUSE YOU'RE SO USED TO YOUR COMFORTABLE HOME YOU TAKE IT FOR GRANTED!
THAT'S WHY THIS LITTLE KITTEN HAS MORE GUTS THAN YOU OR YOUR STUPID BANDIT MASK EVER HAD. NOW DOG UP!
UH, MAX? DID YOU GET A LOOK AT FLUFFY?
IS IT TOO LATE FOR ME TO BACK OUT OF MY REPROOF AND FORGE A SUICIDE PACT?
YES
CARP

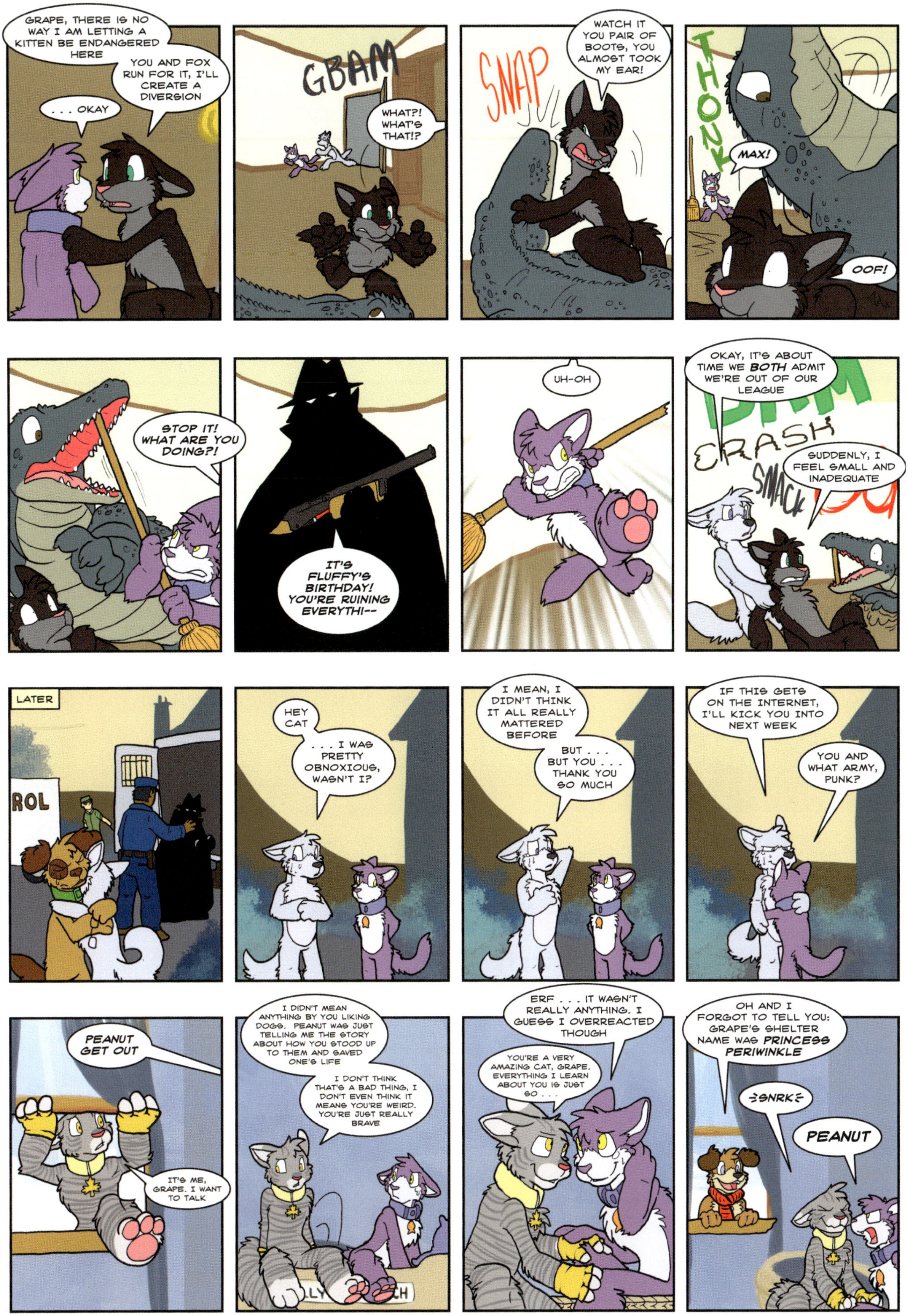

GRAPE, THERE IS NO WAY I AM LETTING A KITTEN BE ENDANGERED HERE
YOU AND FOX RUN FOR IT, I'LL CREATE A DIVERSION
. . . OKAY
GBAM
WHAT?! WHAT'S THAT!?
SNAP
WATCH IT YOU PAIR OF BOOTS, YOU ALMOST TOOK MY EAR!
THONK
MAX!
OOF!
STOP IT! WHAT ARE YOU DOING?!
IT'S FLUFFY'S BIRTHDAY! YOU'RE RUINING EVERYTHI--
UH-OH
OKAY, IT'S ABOUT TIME WE BOTH ADMIT WE'RE OUT OF OUR LEAGUE
CRASH
SMACK
SUDDENLY, I FEEL SMALL AND INADEQUATE
LATER
HEY CAT
. . . I WAS PRETTY OBNOXIOUS, WASN'T I?
I MEAN, I DIDN'T THINK IT ALL REALLY MATTERED BEFORE
BUT . . . BUT YOU . . . THANK YOU SO MUCH
IF THIS GETS ON THE INTERNET, I'LL KICK YOU INTO NEXT WEEK
YOU AND WHAT ARMY, PUNK?
PEANUT GET OUT
IT'S ME, GRAPE. I WANT TO TALK
I DIDN'T MEAN ANYTHING BY YOU LIKING DOGS. PEANUT WAS JUST TELLING ME THE STORY ABOUT HOW YOU STOOD UP TO THEM AND SAVED ONE'S LIFE
I DON'T THINK THAT'S A BAD THING, I DON'T EVEN THINK IT MEANS YOU'RE WEIRD. YOU'RE JUST REALLY BRAVE
ERF . . . IT WASN'T REALLY ANYTHING. I GUESS I OVERREACTED THOUGH
YOU'RE A VERY AMAZING CAT, GRAPE. EVERYTHING I LEARN ABOUT YOU IS JUST SO . . .
OH AND I FORGOT TO TELL YOU: GRAPE'S SHELTER NAME WAS PRINCESS PERIWINKLE
SNRK
PEANUT

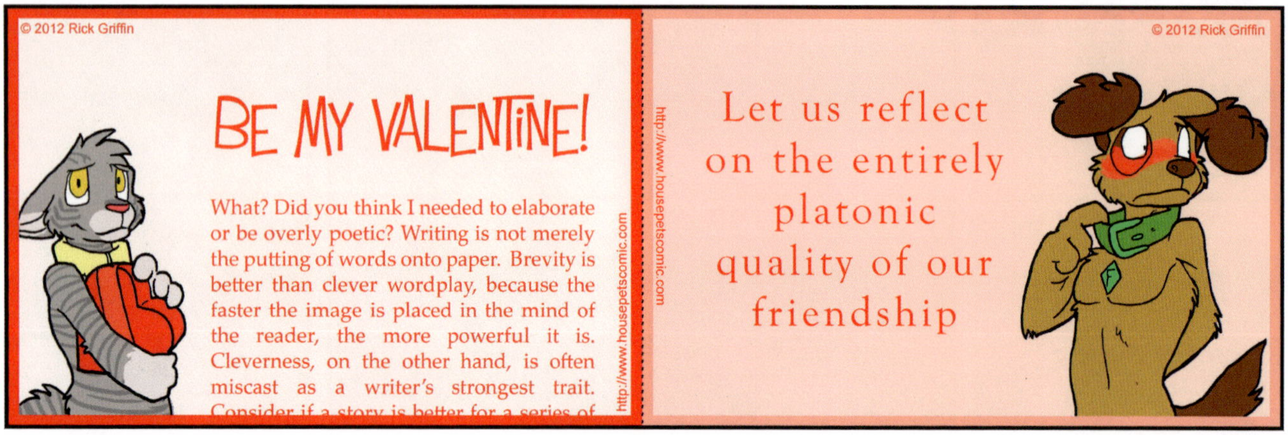
© 2012 Rick Griffin
BE MY VALENTINE!
What? Did you think I needed to elaborate or be overly poetic? Writing is not merely the putting of words onto paper. Brevity is better than clever wordplay, because the faster the image is placed in the mind of the reader, the more powerful it is. Cleverness, on the other hand, is often miscast as a writer's strongest trait.
http://www.housepetscomic.com
© 2012 Rick Griffin
Let us reflect on the entirely platonic quality of our friendship
http://www.housepetscomic.com

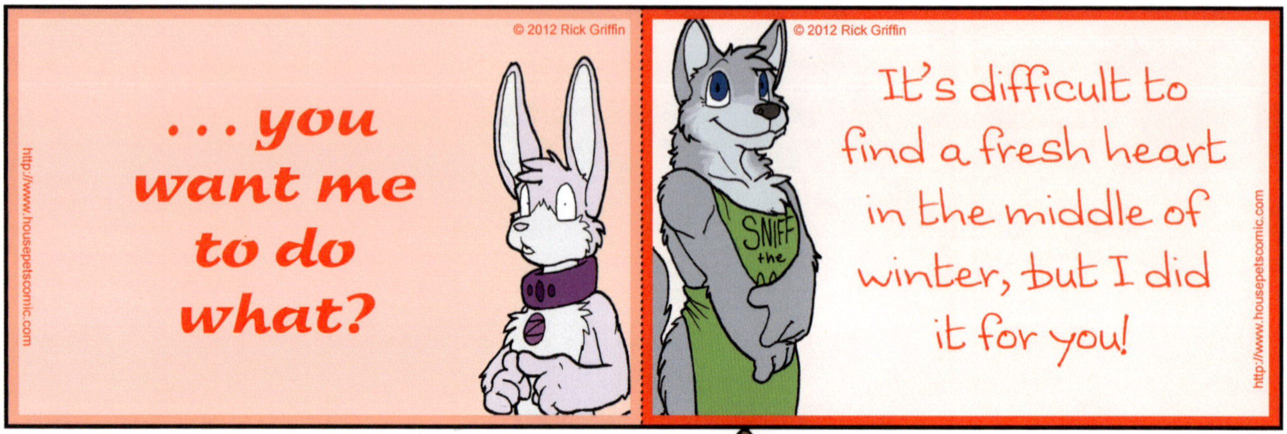
© 2012 Rick Griffin
. . . you want me to do what?
http://www.housepetscomic.com
© 2012 Rick Griffin
It's difficult to find a fresh heart in the middle of winter, but I did it for you!
SNIFF the
http://www.housepetscomic.com

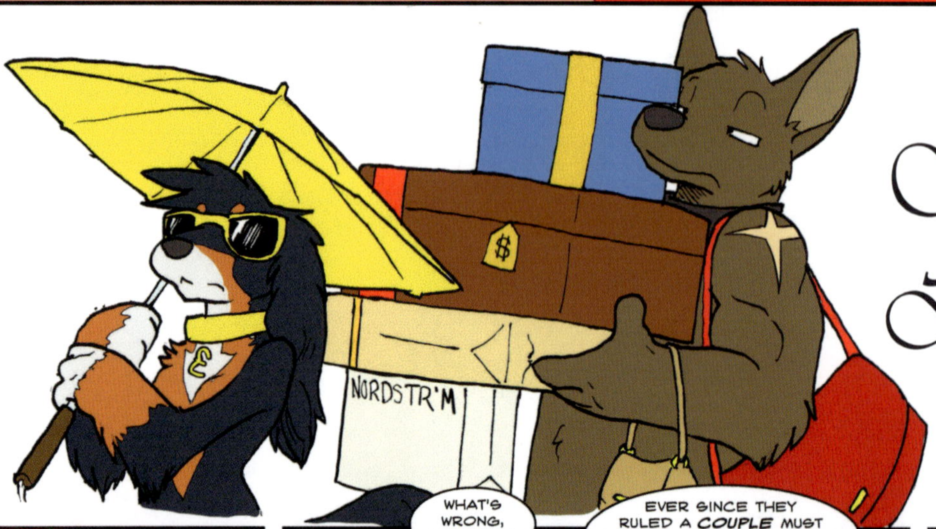
NORDSTR'M

Show Business

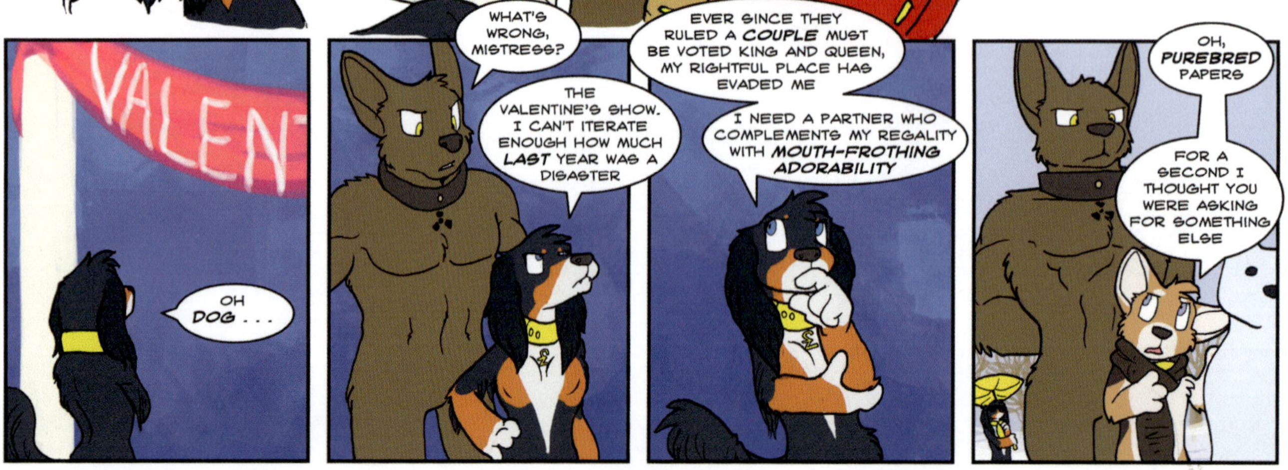
VALENT
OH DOG . . .
WHAT'S WRONG, MISTRESS?
THE VALENTINE'S SHOW. I CAN'T ITERATE ENOUGH HOW MUCH LAST YEAR WAS A DISASTER
EVER SINCE THEY RULED A COUPLE MUST BE VOTED KING AND QUEEN, MY RIGHTFUL PLACE HAS EVADED ME
I NEED A PARTNER WHO COMPLEMENTS MY REGALITY WITH MOUTH-FROTHING ADORABILITY
OH, PUREBRED PAPERS
FOR A SECOND I THOUGHT YOU WERE ASKING FOR SOMETHING ELSE

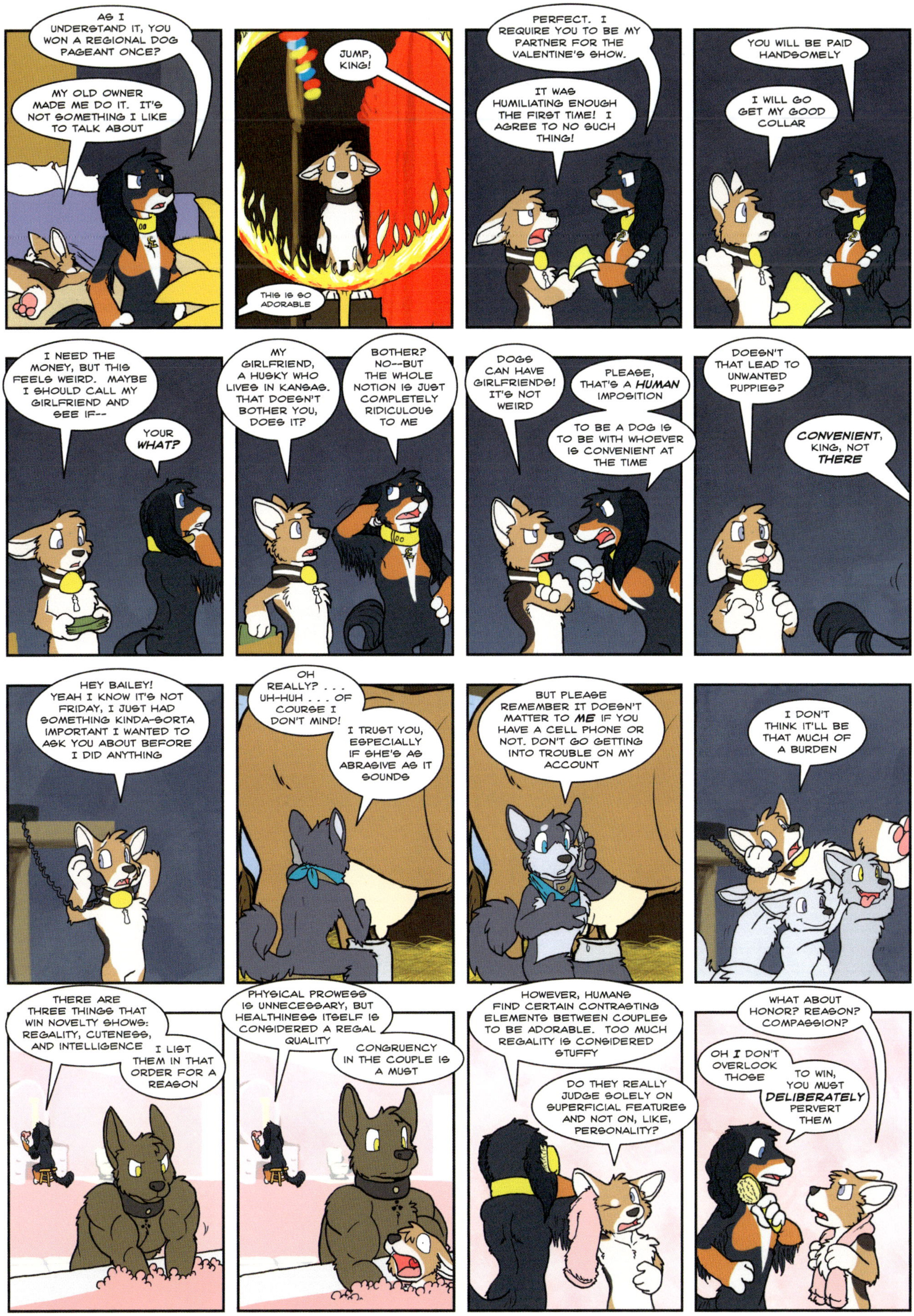
AS I UNDERSTAND IT, YOU WON A REGIONAL DOG PAGEANT ONCE?
MY OLD OWNER MADE ME DO IT. IT'S NOT SOMETHING I LIKE TO TALK ABOUT
JUMP, KING!
THIS IS SO ADORABLE
PERFECT. I REQUIRE YOU TO BE MY PARTNER FOR THE VALENTINE'S SHOW.
IT WAS HUMILIATING ENOUGH THE FIRST TIME! I AGREE TO NO SUCH THING!
YOU WILL BE PAID HANDSOMELY
I WILL GO GET MY GOOD COLLAR
I NEED THE MONEY, BUT THIS FEELS WEIRD. MAYBE I SHOULD CALL MY GIRLFRIEND AND SEE IF--
YOUR *WHAT?*
MY GIRLFRIEND, A HUSKY WHO LIVES IN KANSAS. THAT DOESN'T BOTHER YOU, DOES IT?
BOTHER? NO--BUT THE WHOLE NOTION IS JUST COMPLETELY RIDICULOUS TO ME
DOGS CAN HAVE GIRLFRIENDS! IT'S NOT WEIRD
PLEASE, THAT'S A ***HUMAN*** IMPOSITION
TO BE A DOG IS TO BE WITH WHOEVER IS CONVENIENT AT THE TIME
DOESN'T THAT LEAD TO UNWANTED PUPPIES?
CONVENIENT, KING, NOT ***THERE***
HEY BAILEY! YEAH I KNOW IT'S NOT FRIDAY, I JUST HAD SOMETHING KINDA-SORTA IMPORTANT I WANTED TO ASK YOU ABOUT BEFORE I DID ANYTHING
OH REALLY? . . . UH-HUH . . . OF COURSE I DON'T MIND!
I TRUST YOU, ESPECIALLY IF SHE'S AS ABRASIVE AS IT SOUNDS
BUT PLEASE REMEMBER IT DOESN'T MATTER TO ***ME*** IF YOU HAVE A CELL PHONE OR NOT. DON'T GO GETTING INTO TROUBLE ON MY ACCOUNT
I DON'T THINK IT'LL BE THAT MUCH OF A BURDEN
THERE ARE THREE THINGS THAT WIN NOVELTY SHOWS: REGALITY, CUTENESS, AND INTELLIGENCE
I LIST THEM IN THAT ORDER FOR A REASON
PHYSICAL PROWESS IS UNNECESSARY, BUT HEALTHINESS ITSELF IS CONSIDERED A REGAL QUALITY
CONGRUENCY IN THE COUPLE IS A MUST
HOWEVER, HUMANS FIND CERTAIN CONTRASTING ELEMENTS BETWEEN COUPLES TO BE ADORABLE. TOO MUCH REGALITY IS CONSIDERED STUFFY
DO THEY REALLY JUDGE SOLELY ON SUPERFICIAL FEATURES AND NOT ON, LIKE, PERSONALITY?
WHAT ABOUT HONOR? REASON? COMPASSION?
OH ***I*** DON'T OVERLOOK THOSE
TO WIN, YOU MUST ***DELIBERATELY*** PERVERT THEM

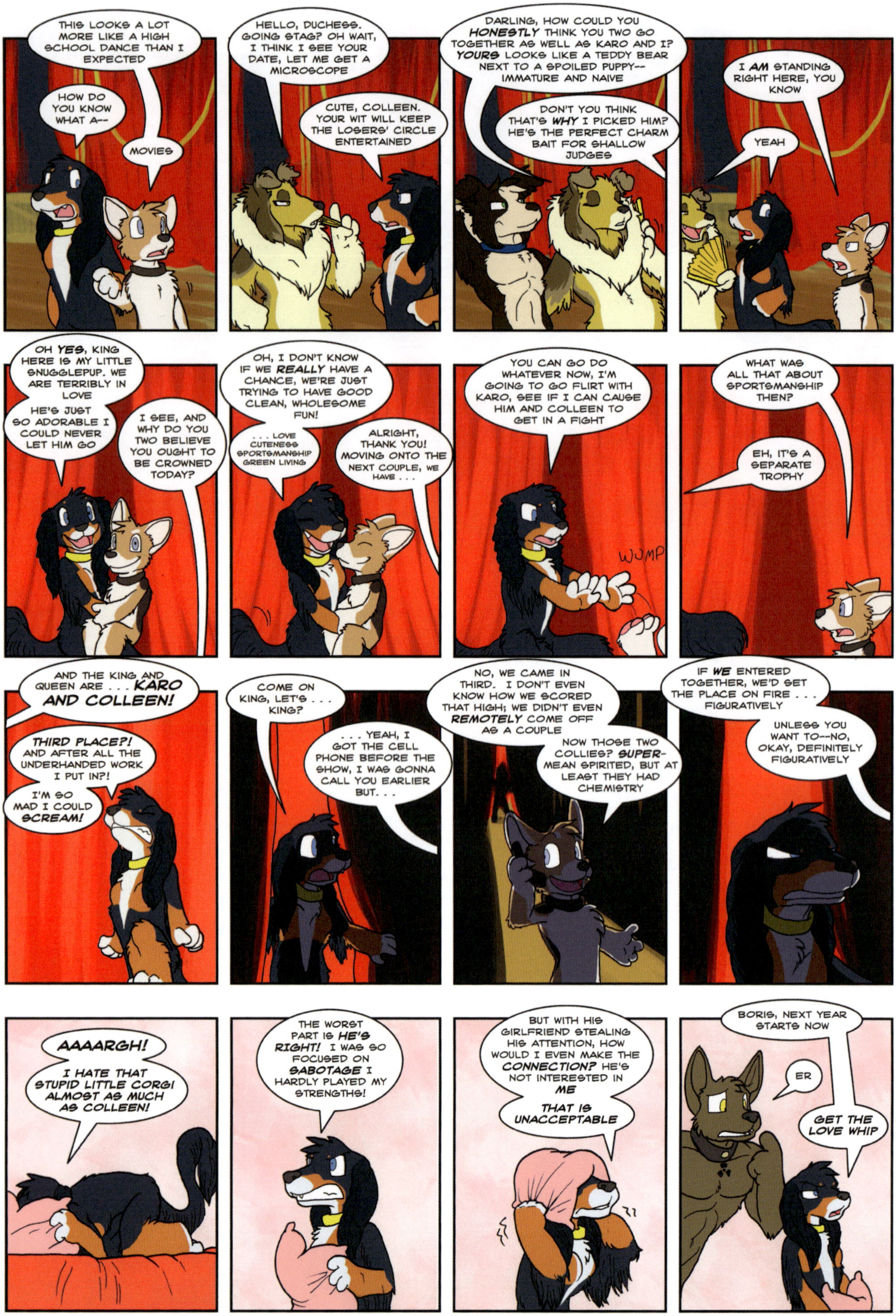

THIS LOOKS A LOT MORE LIKE A HIGH SCHOOL DANCE THAN I EXPECTED
HOW DO YOU KNOW WHAT A--
MOVIES
HELLO, DUCHESS. GOING STAG? OH WAIT, I THINK I SEE YOUR DATE, LET ME GET A MICROSCOPE
CUTE, COLLEEN. YOUR WIT WILL KEEP THE LOSERS' CIRCLE ENTERTAINED
DARLING, HOW COULD YOU HONESTLY THINK YOU TWO GO TOGETHER AS WELL AS KARO AND I? YOURS LOOKS LIKE A TEDDY BEAR NEXT TO A SPOILED PUPPY-- IMMATURE AND NAIVE
DON'T YOU THINK THAT'S WHY I PICKED HIM? HE'S THE PERFECT CHARM BAIT FOR SHALLOW JUDGES
I AM STANDING RIGHT HERE, YOU KNOW
YEAH
OH YES, KING HERE IS MY LITTLE SNUGGLEPUP. WE ARE TERRIBLY IN LOVE
HE'S JUST SO ADORABLE I COULD NEVER LET HIM GO
I SEE, AND WHY DO YOU TWO BELIEVE YOU OUGHT TO BE CROWNED TODAY?
OH, I DON'T KNOW IF WE REALLY HAVE A CHANCE, WE'RE JUST TRYING TO HAVE GOOD CLEAN, WHOLESOME FUN!
. . . LOVE CUTENESS SPORTSMANSHIP GREEN LIVING
ALRIGHT, THANK YOU! MOVING ONTO THE NEXT COUPLE, WE HAVE . . .
YOU CAN GO DO WHATEVER NOW, I'M GOING TO GO FLIRT WITH KARO, SEE IF I CAN CAUSE HIM AND COLLEEN TO GET IN A FIGHT
WUMP
WHAT WAS ALL THAT ABOUT SPORTSMANSHIP THEN?
EH, IT'S A SEPARATE TROPHY
AND THE KING AND QUEEN ARE . . . KARO AND COLLEEN!
THIRD PLACE?! AND AFTER ALL THE UNDERHANDED WORK I PUT IN?!
I'M SO MAD I COULD SCREAM!
COME ON KING, LET'S . . . KING?
. . . YEAH, I GOT THE CELL PHONE BEFORE THE SHOW, I WAS GONNA CALL YOU EARLIER BUT. . .
NO, WE CAME IN THIRD. I DON'T EVEN KNOW HOW WE SCORED THAT HIGH; WE DIDN'T EVEN REMOTELY COME OFF AS A COUPLE
NOW THOSE TWO COLLIES? SUPER-MEAN SPIRITED, BUT AT LEAST THEY HAD CHEMISTRY
IF WE ENTERED TOGETHER, WE'D SET THE PLACE ON FIRE . . . FIGURATIVELY
UNLESS YOU WANT TO--NO, OKAY, DEFINITELY FIGURATIVELY
AAAARGH!
I HATE THAT STUPID LITTLE CORGI ALMOST AS MUCH AS COLLEEN!
THE WORST PART IS HE'S RIGHT! I WAS SO FOCUSED ON SABOTAGE I HARDLY PLAYED MY STRENGTHS!
BUT WITH HIS GIRLFRIEND STEALING HIS ATTENTION, HOW WOULD I EVEN MAKE THE CONNECTION? HE'S NOT INTERESTED IN ME
THAT IS UNACCEPTABLE
BORIS, NEXT YEAR STARTS NOW
ER
GET THE LOVE WHIP

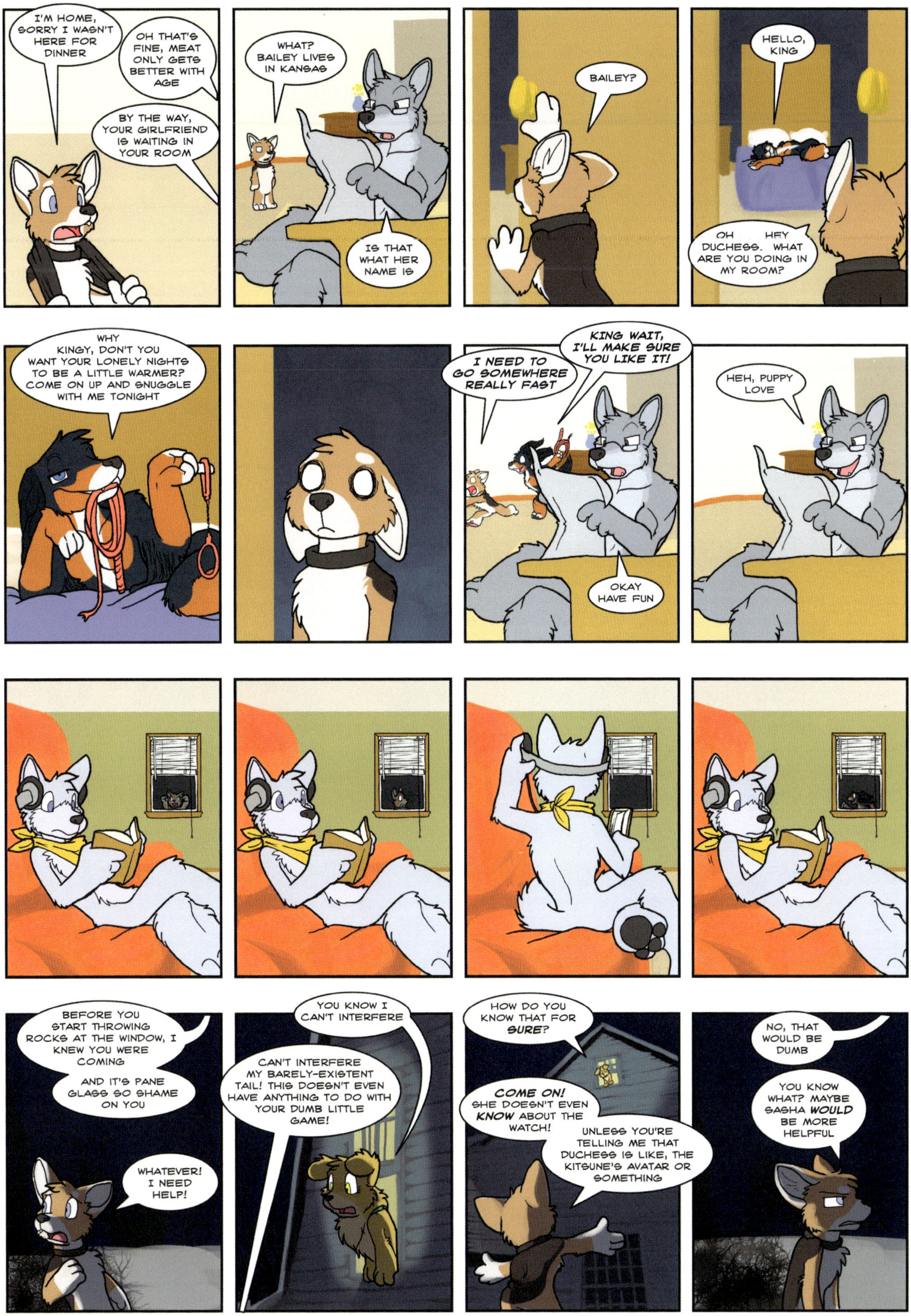
I'M HOME, SORRY I WASN'T HERE FOR DINNER
OH THAT'S FINE, MEAT ONLY GETS BETTER WITH AGE
BY THE WAY, YOUR GIRLFRIEND IS WAITING IN YOUR ROOM
WHAT? BAILEY LIVES IN KANSAS
IS THAT WHAT HER NAME IS
BAILEY?
HELLO, KING
OH HEY DUCHESS. WHAT ARE YOU DOING IN MY ROOM?
WHY KINGY, DON'T YOU WANT YOUR LONELY NIGHTS TO BE A LITTLE WARMER? COME ON UP AND SNUGGLE WITH ME TONIGHT
I NEED TO GO SOMEWHERE REALLY FAST
KING WAIT, I'LL MAKE SURE YOU LIKE IT!
OKAY HAVE FUN
HEH, PUPPY LOVE
BEFORE YOU START THROWING ROCKS AT THE WINDOW, I KNEW YOU WERE COMING
AND IT'S PANE GLASS SO SHAME ON YOU
WHATEVER! I NEED HELP!
YOU KNOW I CAN'T INTERFERE
CAN'T INTERFERE MY BARELY-EXISTENT TAIL! THIS DOESN'T EVEN HAVE ANYTHING TO DO WITH YOUR DUMB LITTLE GAME!
HOW DO YOU KNOW THAT FOR SURE?
COME ON! SHE DOESN'T EVEN KNOW ABOUT THE WATCH!
UNLESS YOU'RE TELLING ME THAT DUCHESS IS LIKE, THE KITSUNE'S AVATAR OR SOMETHING
NO, THAT WOULD BE DUMB
YOU KNOW WHAT? MAYBE SASHA WOULD BE MORE HELPFUL

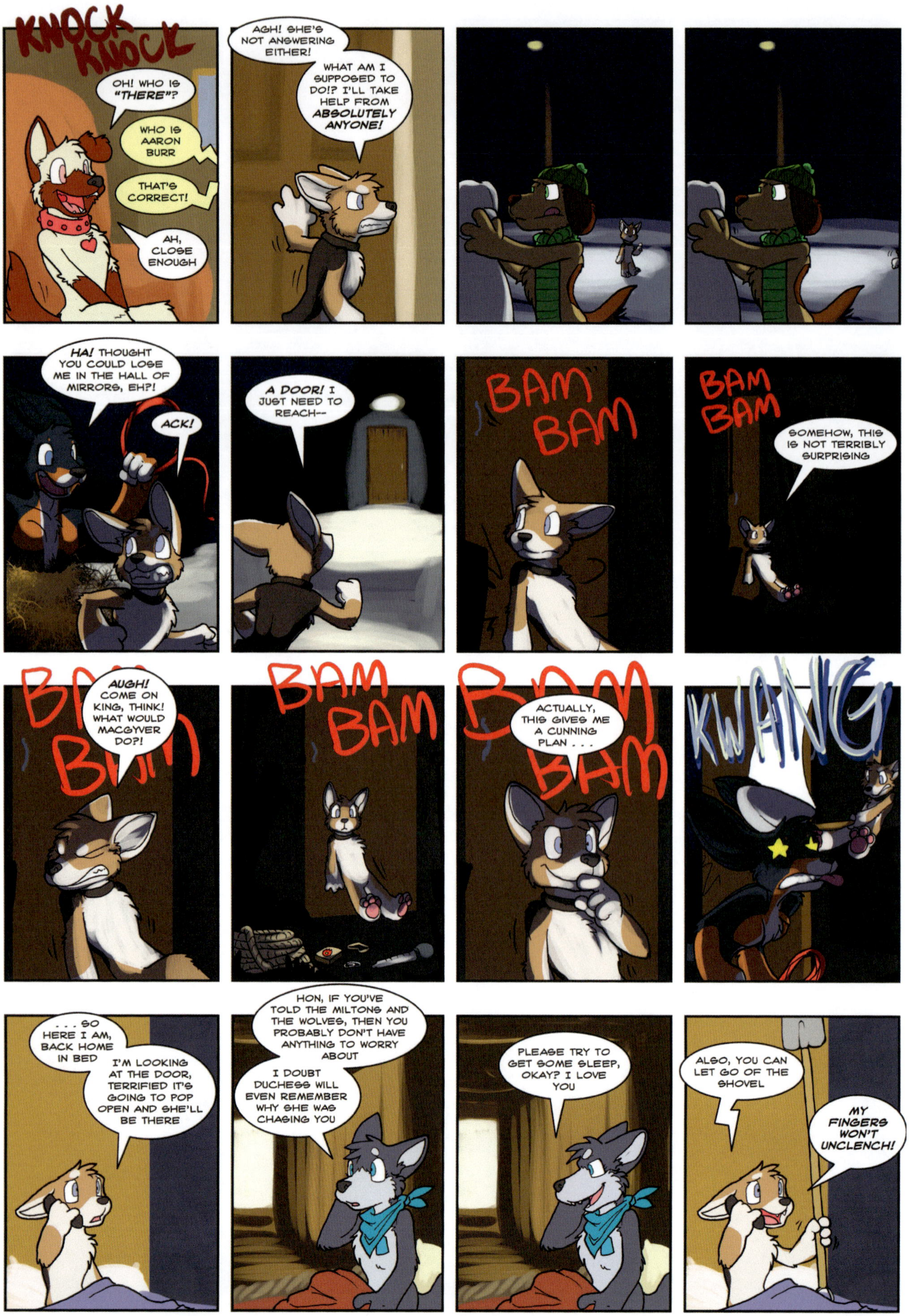
KNOCK KNOCK
OH! WHO IS "THERE"?
WHO IS AARON BURR
THAT'S CORRECT!
AH, CLOSE ENOUGH
AGH! SHE'S NOT ANSWERING EITHER!
WHAT AM I SUPPOSED TO DO!? I'LL TAKE HELP FROM ABSOLUTELY ANYONE!
HA! THOUGHT YOU COULD LOSE ME IN THE HALL OF MIRRORS, EH?!
ACK!
A DOOR! I JUST NEED TO REACH--
BAM BAM
BAM BAM
SOMEHOW, THIS IS NOT TERRIBLY SURPRISING
BAM BAM
AUGH! COME ON KING, THINK! WHAT WOULD MACGYVER DO?!
BAM BAM
BAM BAM
ACTUALLY, THIS GIVES ME A CUNNING PLAN . . .
KWANG
. . . SO HERE I AM, BACK HOME IN BED
I'M LOOKING AT THE DOOR, TERRIFIED IT'S GOING TO POP OPEN AND SHE'LL BE THERE
HON, IF YOU'VE TOLD THE MILTONS AND THE WOLVES, THEN YOU PROBABLY DON'T HAVE ANYTHING TO WORRY ABOUT
I DOUBT DUCHESS WILL EVEN REMEMBER WHY SHE WAS CHASING YOU
PLEASE TRY TO GET SOME SLEEP, OKAY? I LOVE YOU
ALSO, YOU CAN LET GO OF THE SHOVEL
MY FINGERS WON'T UNCLENCH!

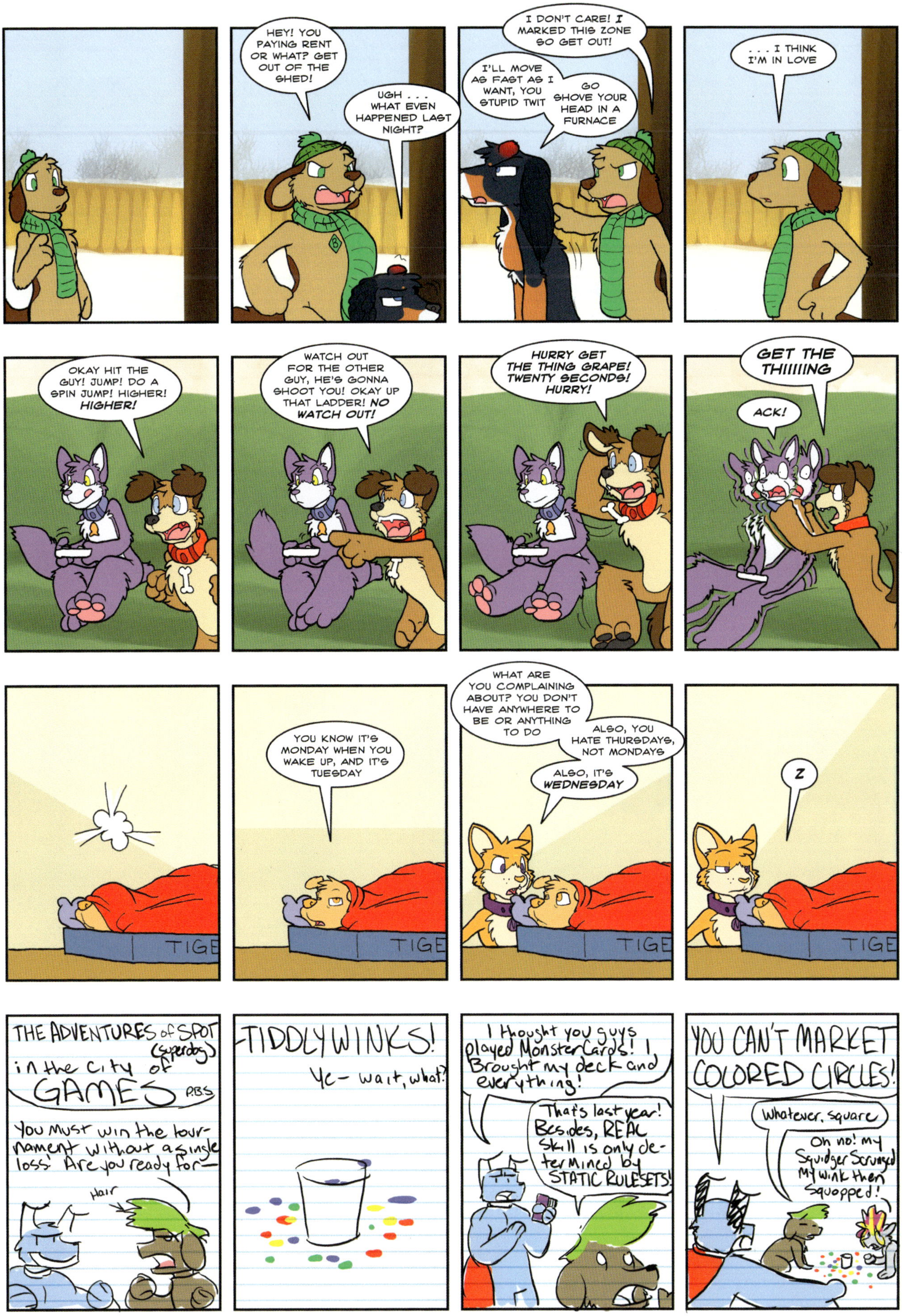
HEY! YOU PAYING RENT OR WHAT? GET OUT OF THE SHED!
UGH . . . WHAT EVEN HAPPENED LAST NIGHT?
I DON'T CARE! I MARKED THIS ZONE SO GET OUT!
I'LL MOVE AS FAST AS I WANT, YOU STUPID TWIT
GO SHOVE YOUR HEAD IN A FURNACE
. . . I THINK I'M IN LOVE
OKAY HIT THE GUY! JUMP! DO A SPIN JUMP! HIGHER! HIGHER!
WATCH OUT FOR THE OTHER GUY, HE'S GONNA SHOOT YOU! OKAY UP THAT LADDER! NO WATCH OUT!
HURRY GET THE THING GRAPE! TWENTY SECONDS! HURRY!
GET THE THIIIIING
ACK!
YOU KNOW IT'S MONDAY WHEN YOU WAKE UP, AND IT'S TUESDAY
WHAT ARE YOU COMPLAINING ABOUT? YOU DON'T HAVE ANYWHERE TO BE OR ANYTHING TO DO
ALSO, YOU HATE THURSDAYS, NOT MONDAYS
ALSO, IT'S WEDNESDAY
TIGE
Z
THE ADVENTURES of SPOT (superdog) in the city of GAMES
P.B.S.
You must win the tournament without a single loss! Are you ready for—
Hair
TIDDLYWINKS!
Ye— wait, what?
I thought you guys played MonsterCards! I brought my deck and everything!
That's last year! Besides, REAL skill is only determined by STATIC RULESETS!
YOU CAN'T MARKET COLORED CIRCLES!
Whatever, square
Oh no! my Squidger Scrunged my wink then Squopped!

what money buys

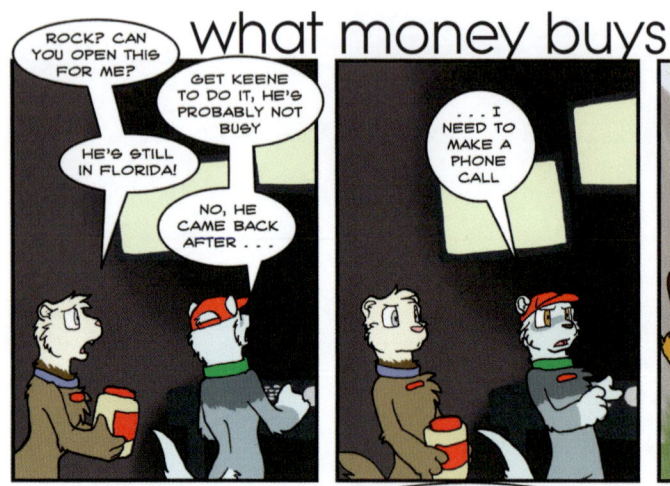

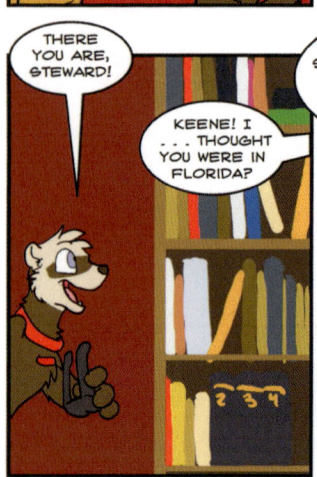

Panel 1:
- ROCK? CAN YOU OPEN THIS FOR ME?
- GET KEENE TO DO IT, HE'S PROBABLY NOT BUSY
- HE'S STILL IN FLORIDA!
- NO, HE CAME BACK AFTER . . .

Panel 2:
- . . . I NEED TO MAKE A PHONE CALL

Panel 3:
- HELLO! PLEASE HOLD
- YES I'D LIKE EXTRA SAUSAGE AND ANCHOVIES, AND IF YOU COULD DANGLE IT OVER THE ALLIGATOR PIT THAT WOULD BE LOVELY, THANK YOU!

Panel 4:
- HIS PHONE IS AT THE ZOO FOR SOME REASON
- FIELD TRIP!

Panel 5:
- WE'D LIKE TO SPEAK WITH ONE KARISHAD FOX OVER AN INCIDENT AFTER THANKSGIVING
- YOU'RE GOING TO TAKE HIM AWAY!?
- CERTAINLY NOT! JUST TALK WITH HIM
- OH . . . =SIGH= OKAY

Panel 6:
- ROCK! I FOUND HIM! HE'S INSIDE THE BLACK-FOOTED FERRET PEN, TOSSING A BEANBAG TO HIMSELF AND MUTTERING
- I DON'T THINK MR. STEWARD'S GOING TO BE VERY HAPPY
- IT'S NOT MR. STEWARD YOU SHOULD WORRY ABOUT . . .

Panel 7:
- I AM GOING TO *GET* THAT FOX . . .
- KEENE . . . YOU'RE SAFE NOW SO THERE'S NO NEED FOR DRASTIC ACTION--

Panel 8:
- . . . TO WORK FOR ME!
- . . . OKAY, THAT'S THE DIAMETRIC OPPOSITE OF WHAT I EXPECTED, BUT MY POINT STANDS

Panel 9:
- GREETINGS, FOX. KNOW THAT I DESPISE YOU AND WHATEVER IT IS YOU STAND FOR
- FIRE ANTS. SOMETIMES, THEY MAKE ME DO A LITTLE DANCE, TOO

Panel 10:
- LET ME BE FRANK
- YES, FRANKIE BABY?
- I HAVE NO IDEA WHAT YOU'RE TRYING TO PULL OR WHO YOU ANSWER TO OTHER THAN AGENTS OF CHAOS
- BUT I THINK I NEED YOU

Panel 11:
- PLEASE! WE HAVEN'T EVEN DATED!
- . . . IS IT *REMOTELY* POSSIBLE YOU CAN BE SERIOUS? FOR *HALF A SECOND?*

Panel 12:
- WELL IF *YOU'RE* SERIOUS, I SUPPOSE WE COULD START WITH DINNER AND A MOVIE . . .
- I WOULD SAY I WALKED RIGHT INTO THAT, BUT I'M SURE YOU REROUTED ALL POSSIBLE PATHS

Panel 13:
- THERE YOU ARE, STEWARD!
- KEENE! I . . . THOUGHT YOU WERE IN FLORIDA?

Panel 14:
- I HAD A LITTLE DETOUR! FORTUNATELY SOMEONE NOTICED THAT I WASN'T WHERE I WAS SUPPOSED TO BE, AND BROUGHT ME BACK!
- THE QUESTION IS, MR. STEWARD, WHY WAS THAT PERSON NOT YOU, FOUR MONTHS AGO?

Panel 15:
(silent)

Panel 16:
- THIS SMILE IS COMPLETELY ARTIFICIAL, BY THE WAY
- I GOT THAT

42

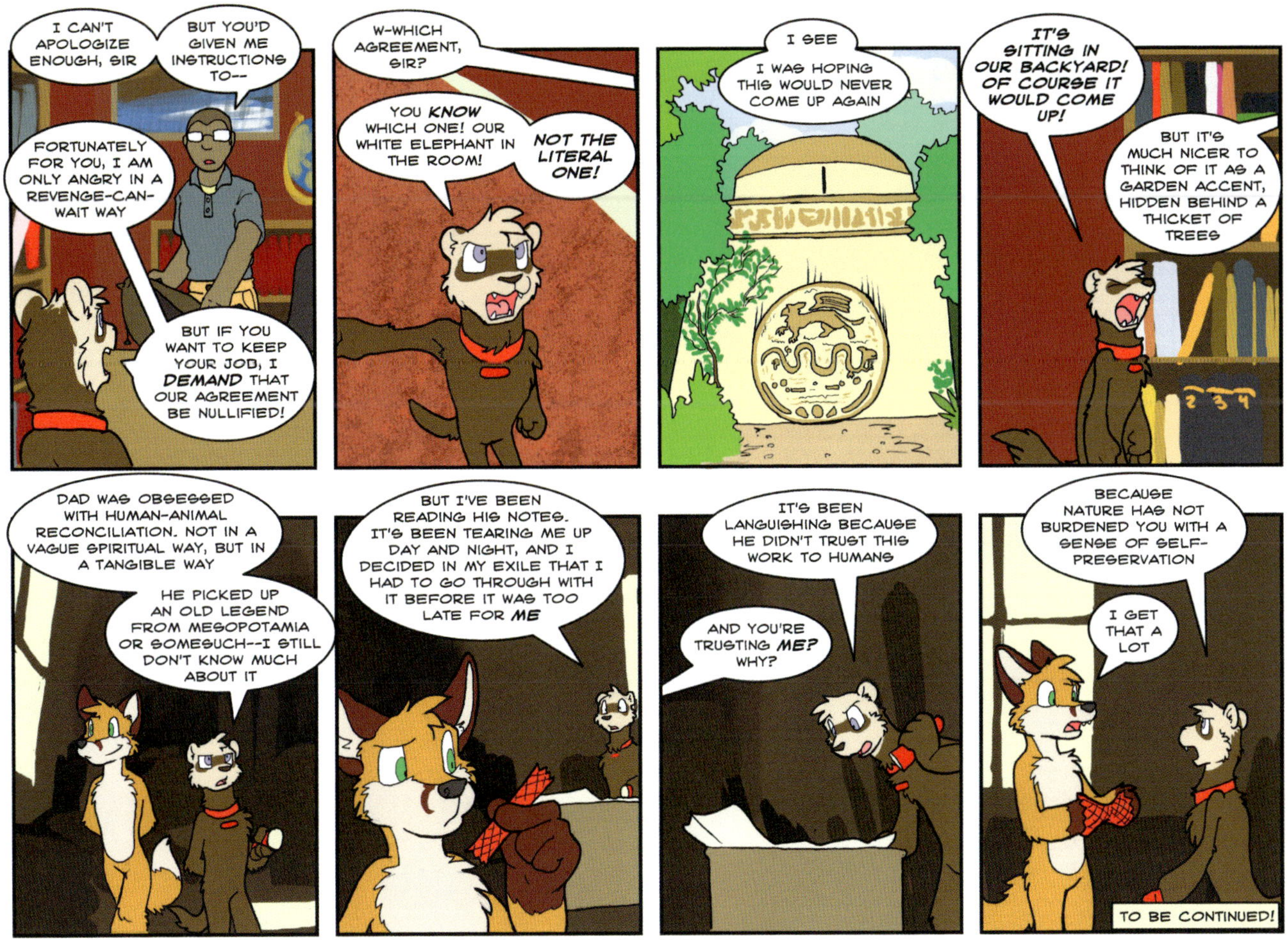
I CAN'T APOLOGIZE ENOUGH, SIR
BUT YOU'D GIVEN ME INSTRUCTIONS TO--
FORTUNATELY FOR YOU, I AM ONLY ANGRY IN A REVENGE-CAN-WAIT WAY
BUT IF YOU WANT TO KEEP YOUR JOB, I **DEMAND** THAT OUR AGREEMENT BE NULLIFIED!
W-WHICH AGREEMENT, SIR?
YOU **KNOW** WHICH ONE! OUR WHITE ELEPHANT IN THE ROOM!
NOT THE LITERAL ONE!
I SEE
I WAS HOPING THIS WOULD NEVER COME UP AGAIN
IT'S SITTING IN OUR BACKYARD! OF COURSE IT WOULD COME UP!
BUT IT'S MUCH NICER TO THINK OF IT AS A GARDEN ACCENT, HIDDEN BEHIND A THICKET OF TREES
DAD WAS OBSESSED WITH HUMAN-ANIMAL RECONCILIATION. NOT IN A VAGUE SPIRITUAL WAY, BUT IN A TANGIBLE WAY
HE PICKED UP AN OLD LEGEND FROM MESOPOTAMIA OR SOMESUCH--I STILL DON'T KNOW MUCH ABOUT IT
BUT I'VE BEEN READING HIS NOTES. IT'S BEEN TEARING ME UP DAY AND NIGHT, AND I DECIDED IN MY EXILE THAT I HAD TO GO THROUGH WITH IT BEFORE IT WAS TOO LATE FOR **ME**
IT'S BEEN LANGUISHING BECAUSE HE DIDN'T TRUST THIS WORK TO HUMANS
AND YOU'RE TRUSTING **ME?** WHY?
BECAUSE NATURE HAS NOT BURDENED YOU WITH A SENSE OF SELF-PRESERVATION
I GET THAT A LOT
TO BE CONTINUED!

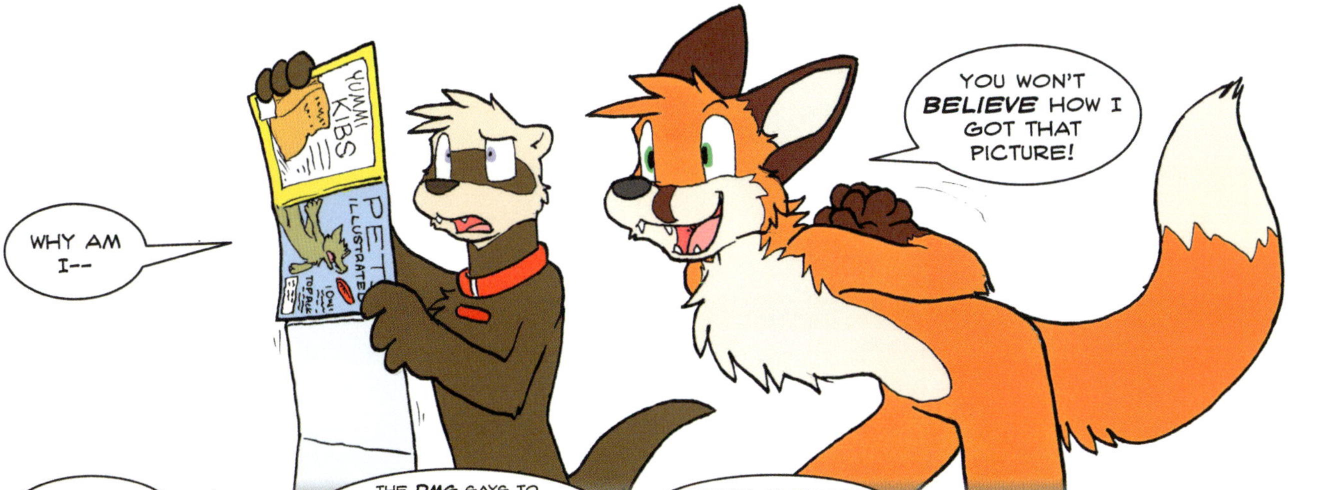
YUMMI KIBS
PET ILLUSTRATED
WHY AM I--
YOU WON'T **BELIEVE** HOW I GOT THAT PICTURE!

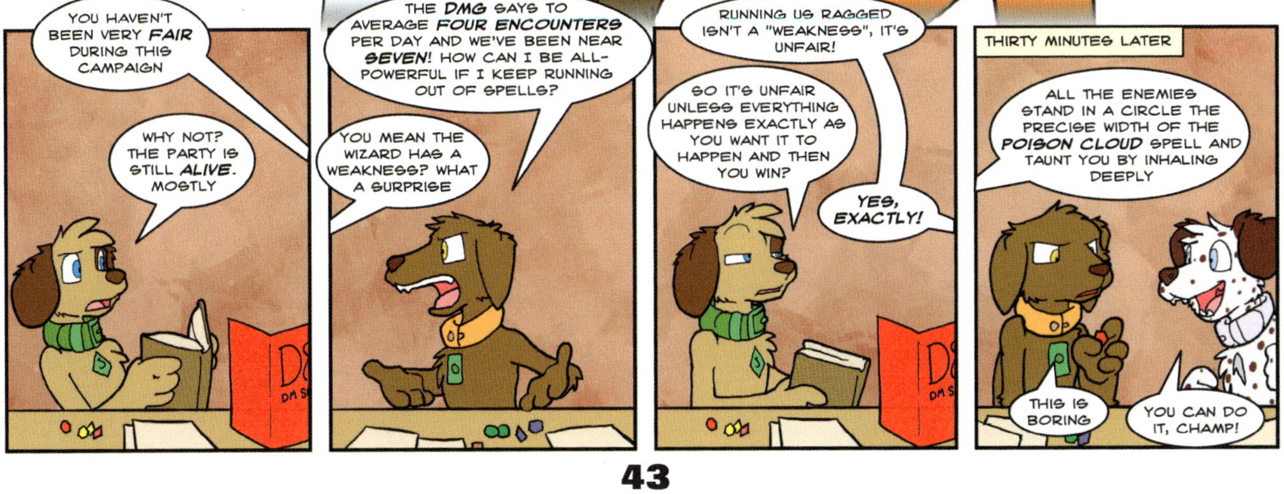
YOU HAVEN'T BEEN VERY **FAIR** DURING THIS CAMPAIGN
WHY NOT? THE PARTY IS STILL **ALIVE**. MOSTLY
THE **DMG** SAYS TO AVERAGE **FOUR ENCOUNTERS** PER DAY AND WE'VE BEEN NEAR **SEVEN**! HOW CAN I BE ALL-POWERFUL IF I KEEP RUNNING OUT OF SPELLS?
YOU MEAN THE WIZARD HAS A WEAKNESS? WHAT A SURPRISE
RUNNING US RAGGED ISN'T A "WEAKNESS", IT'S UNFAIR!
SO IT'S UNFAIR UNLESS EVERYTHING HAPPENS EXACTLY AS YOU WANT IT TO HAPPEN AND THEN YOU WIN?
YES, EXACTLY!
THIRTY MINUTES LATER
ALL THE ENEMIES STAND IN A CIRCLE THE PRECISE WIDTH OF THE **POISON CLOUD** SPELL AND TAUNT YOU BY INHALING DEEPLY
THIS IS BORING
YOU CAN DO IT, CHAMP!

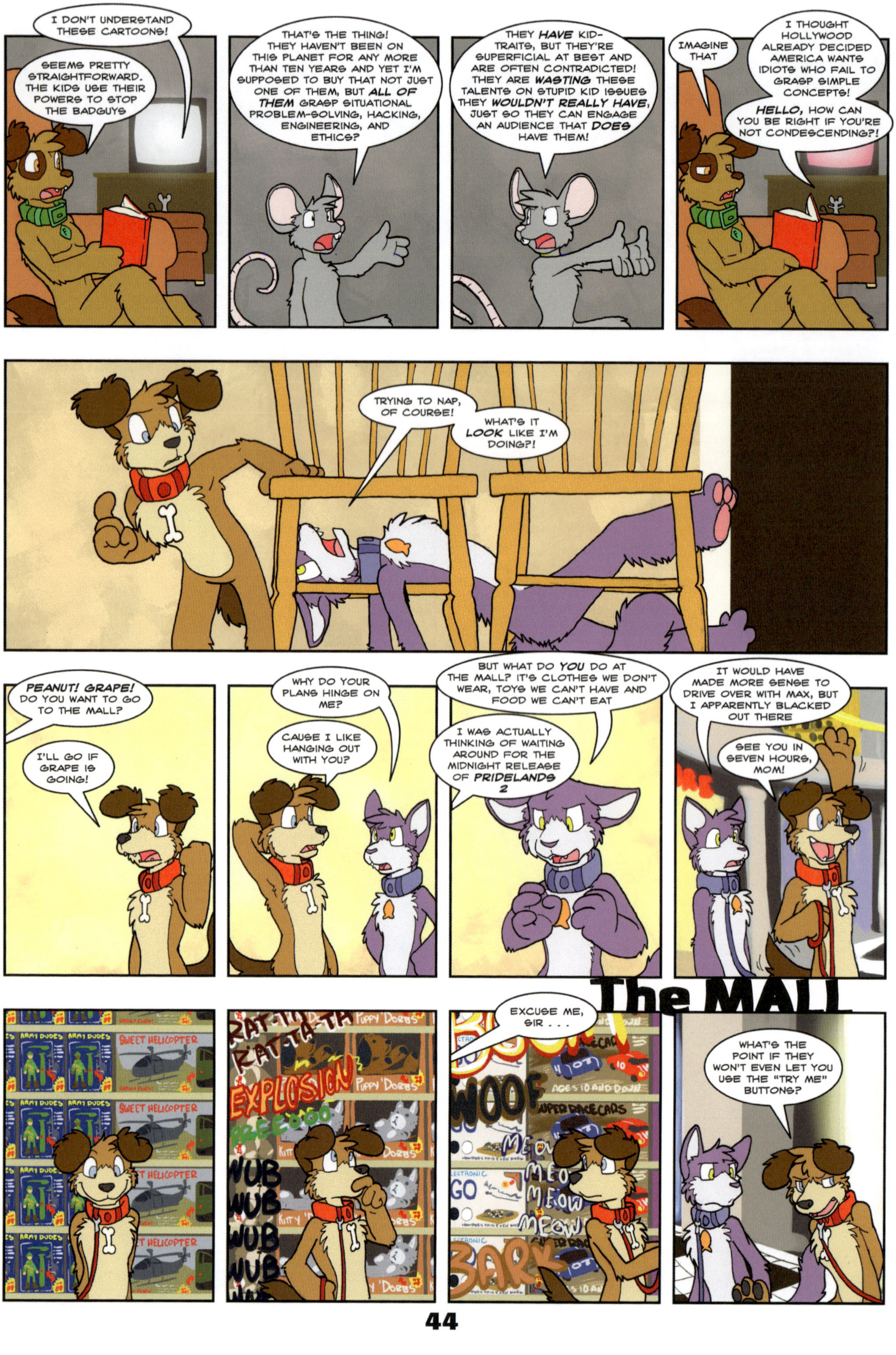
I DON'T UNDERSTAND THESE CARTOONS!
SEEMS PRETTY STRAIGHTFORWARD. THE KIDS USE THEIR POWERS TO STOP THE BADGUYS
THAT'S THE THING! THEY HAVEN'T BEEN ON THIS PLANET FOR ANY MORE THAN TEN YEARS AND YET I'M SUPPOSED TO BUY THAT NOT JUST ONE OF THEM, BUT ALL OF THEM GRASP SITUATIONAL PROBLEM-SOLVING, HACKING, ENGINEERING, AND ETHICS?
THEY HAVE KID-TRAITS, BUT THEY'RE SUPERFICIAL AT BEST AND ARE OFTEN CONTRADICTED! THEY ARE WASTING THESE TALENTS ON STUPID KID ISSUES THEY WOULDN'T REALLY HAVE, JUST SO THEY CAN ENGAGE AN AUDIENCE THAT DOES HAVE THEM!
IMAGINE THAT
I THOUGHT HOLLYWOOD ALREADY DECIDED AMERICA WANTS IDIOTS WHO FAIL TO GRASP SIMPLE CONCEPTS!
HELLO, HOW CAN YOU BE RIGHT IF YOU'RE NOT CONDESCENDING?!
TRYING TO NAP, OF COURSE!
WHAT'S IT LOOK LIKE I'M DOING?!
PEANUT! GRAPE! DO YOU WANT TO GO TO THE MALL?
I'LL GO IF GRAPE IS GOING!
WHY DO YOUR PLANS HINGE ON ME?
CAUSE I LIKE HANGING OUT WITH YOU?
BUT WHAT DO YOU DO AT THE MALL? IT'S CLOTHES WE DON'T WEAR, TOYS WE CAN'T HAVE AND FOOD WE CAN'T EAT
I WAS ACTUALLY THINKING OF WAITING AROUND FOR THE MIDNIGHT RELEASE OF PRIDELANDS 2
IT WOULD HAVE MADE MORE SENSE TO DRIVE OVER WITH MAX, BUT I APPARENTLY BLACKED OUT THERE
SEE YOU IN SEVEN HOURS, MOM!
The MALL
ARMY DUDES
SWEET HELICOPTER
RAT-TA-TA
RAT-TA-TA
PUPPY 'DOBBS
EXPLOSION
WUB
WUB
WUB
WUB
EXCUSE ME, SIR . . .
WOOF
SUPER RACECARS
MEOW
MEOW
MEOW
BARK
ELECTRONIC
GO
WHAT'S THE POINT IF THEY WON'T EVEN LET YOU USE THE "TRY ME" BUTTONS?

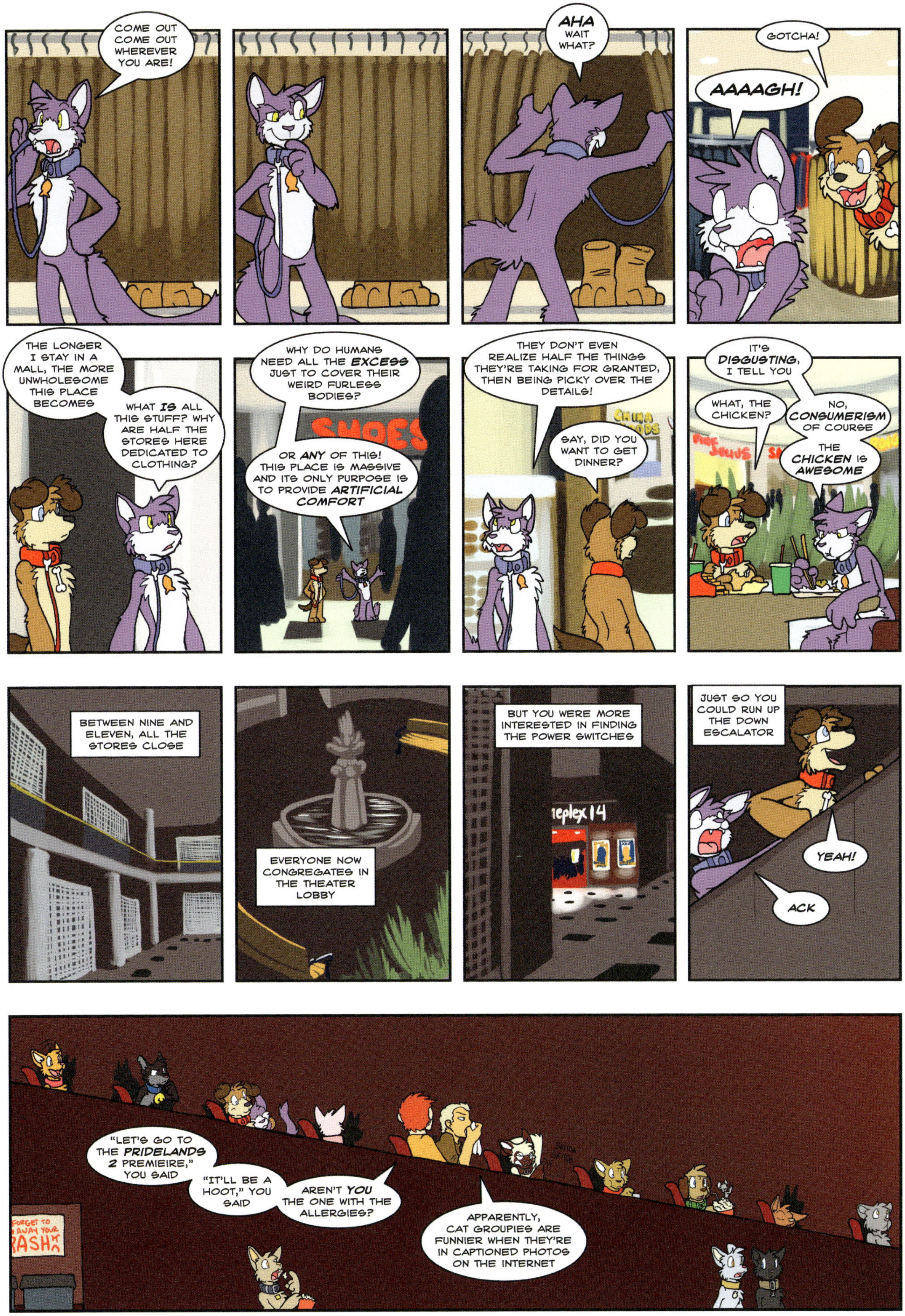
COME OUT COME OUT WHEREVER YOU ARE!
AHA
WAIT WHAT?
GOTCHA!
AAAAGH!
THE LONGER I STAY IN A MALL, THE MORE UNWHOLESOME THIS PLACE BECOMES
WHAT IS ALL THIS STUFF? WHY ARE HALF THE STORES HERE DEDICATED TO CLOTHING?
WHY DO HUMANS NEED ALL THE EXCESS JUST TO COVER THEIR WEIRD FURLESS BODIES?
SHOES
OR ANY OF THIS! THIS PLACE IS MASSIVE AND ITS ONLY PURPOSE IS TO PROVIDE ARTIFICIAL COMFORT
THEY DON'T EVEN REALIZE HALF THE THINGS THEY'RE TAKING FOR GRANTED, THEN BEING PICKY OVER THE DETAILS!
SAY, DID YOU WANT TO GET DINNER?
IT'S DISGUSTING, I TELL YOU
WHAT, THE CHICKEN?
NO, CONSUMERISM OF COURSE
THE CHICKEN IS AWESOME
BETWEEN NINE AND ELEVEN, ALL THE STORES CLOSE
EVERYONE NOW CONGREGATES IN THE THEATER LOBBY
BUT YOU WERE MORE INTERESTED IN FINDING THE POWER SWITCHES
JUST SO YOU COULD RUN UP THE DOWN ESCALATOR
YEAH!
ACK
"LET'S GO TO THE PRIDELANDS 2 PREMIEIRE," YOU SAID
"IT'LL BE A HOOT," YOU SAID
AREN'T YOU THE ONE WITH THE ALLERGIES?
APPARENTLY, CAT GROUPIES ARE FUNNIER WHEN THEY'RE IN CAPTIONED PHOTOS ON THE INTERNET

The Critical Review of Spot

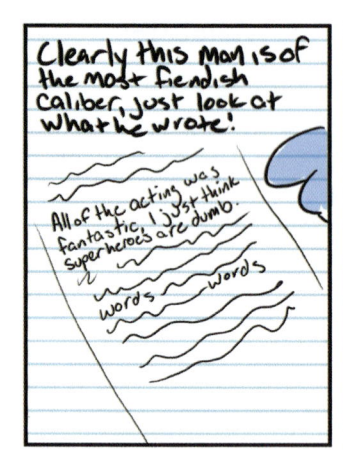

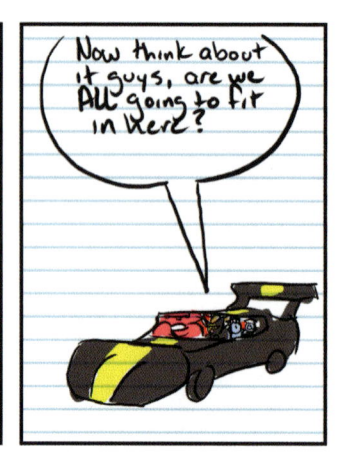

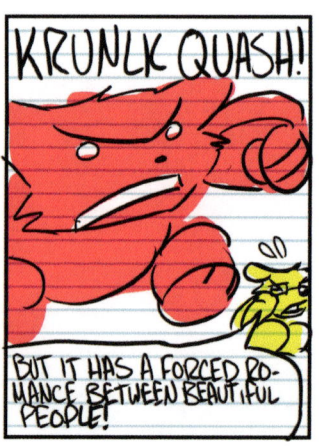

Panel 1: THE ADVENTURES OF SPOT (superdog) p.b.s. THE MOVIE — "AWESOME, AS CHARGED" -critic

Panel 2: "Gentlemen, our movie has received high praise! The Bland Tomatoes score is at a 99%!" "Only 99?"

Panel 3: "Yes, it appears someone has written a NEGATIVE REVIEW!"

Panel 4: *gasp!* (They are off-panel)

Panel 5: "Clearly this man is of the most fiendish caliber, just look at what he wrote!" — "All of the acting was fantastic, I just think superheroes are dumb. words words"

Panel 6: "He think we dumb?! That not valid criticism! He dumb!" "And more importantly, wrong!"

Panel 7: "I for one cannot abide this libel! In order to restore the honor of our movie, we must squelch the dissenting opinion! To the Bat-Bat Mobile-Mobile!"

Panel 8: "Now think about it guys, are we ALL going to fit in here?"

Panel 9: MEANWHILE — "Muahahaha! It is I, the Critic, and by giving a poor review to a critically acclaimed movie, I will draw all that sweet, sweet attention to me! M-mmm!"

Panel 10: "Yeah that's totally what it looks like"

Panel 11: "Our heroes convene on the critic's house" "Okay buster, time to pay for your crime, which doesn't pay!"

Panel 12: "What's your deal! I can have an opinion!" "Wait, did you just bring a half a dozen superheros to my door and threaten to beat me up for what I said?"

Panel 13: "Well yeah" "Okay, I surrender. I guess I'll have to give up my job and let my kids starve"

Panel 14: "Oh come on, don't make us the bad guys here! Just remove your bias from your critical review! Can you do that?" "Well I guess— there was ONE superhero movie I liked"

Panel 15: "Now we're getting somewhere! What was it?" "'The Green Lamp'"

Panel 16: KRUNK QUASH! "BUT IT HAS A FORCED ROMANCE BETWEEN BEAUTIFUL PEOPLE!"

46

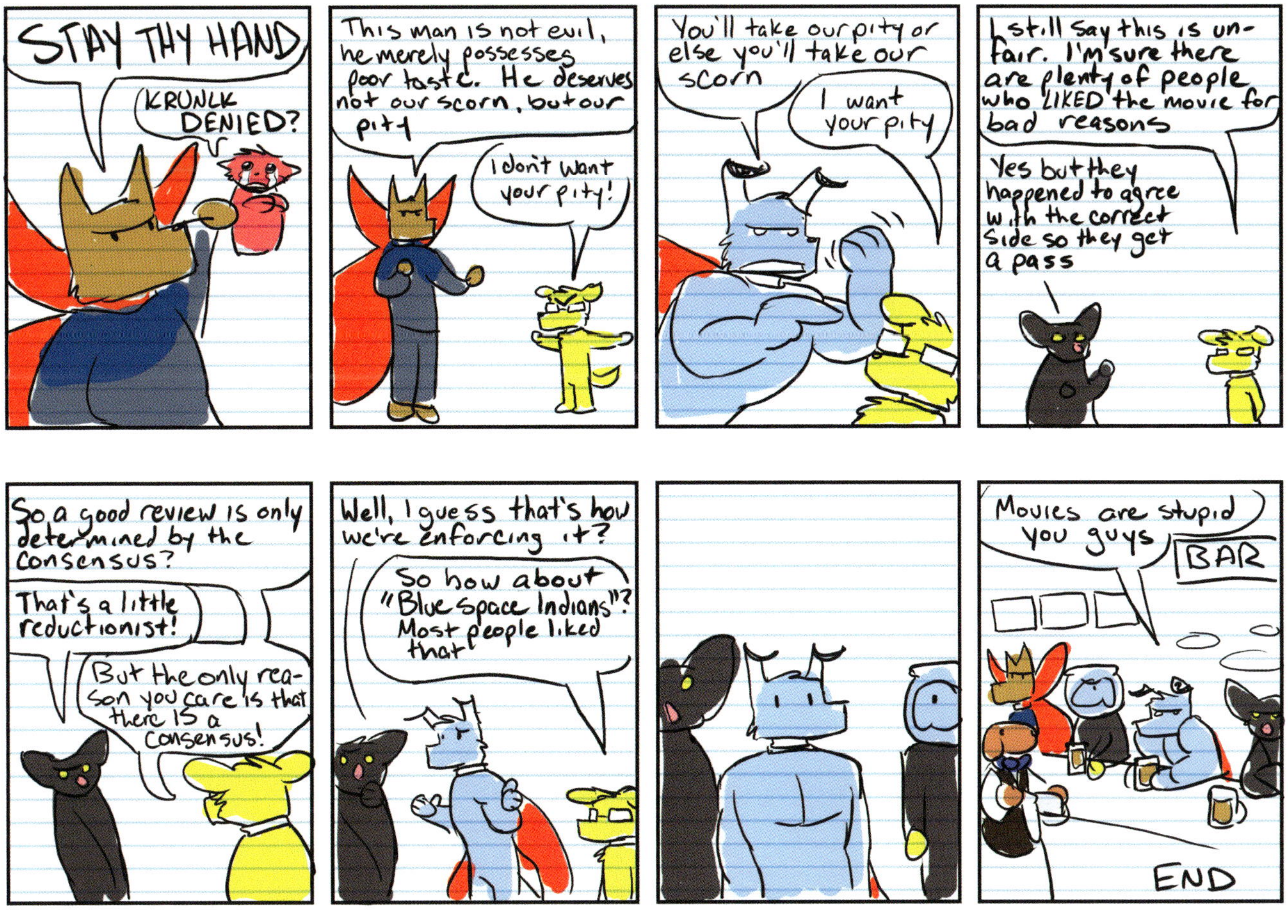
STAY THY HAND
KRUNLK DENIED?
This man is not evil, he merely possesses poor taste. He deserves not our scorn, but our pity
I don't want your pity!
You'll take our pity or else you'll take our scorn
I want your pity
I still say this is unfair. I'm sure there are plenty of people who LIKED the movie for bad reasons
Yes but they happened to agree with the correct side so they get a pass
So a good review is only determined by the consensus?
That's a little reductionist!
But the only reason you care is that there IS a consensus!
Well, I guess that's how we're enforcing it?
So how about "Blue space Indians"? Most people liked that
Movies are stupid you guys
BAR
END

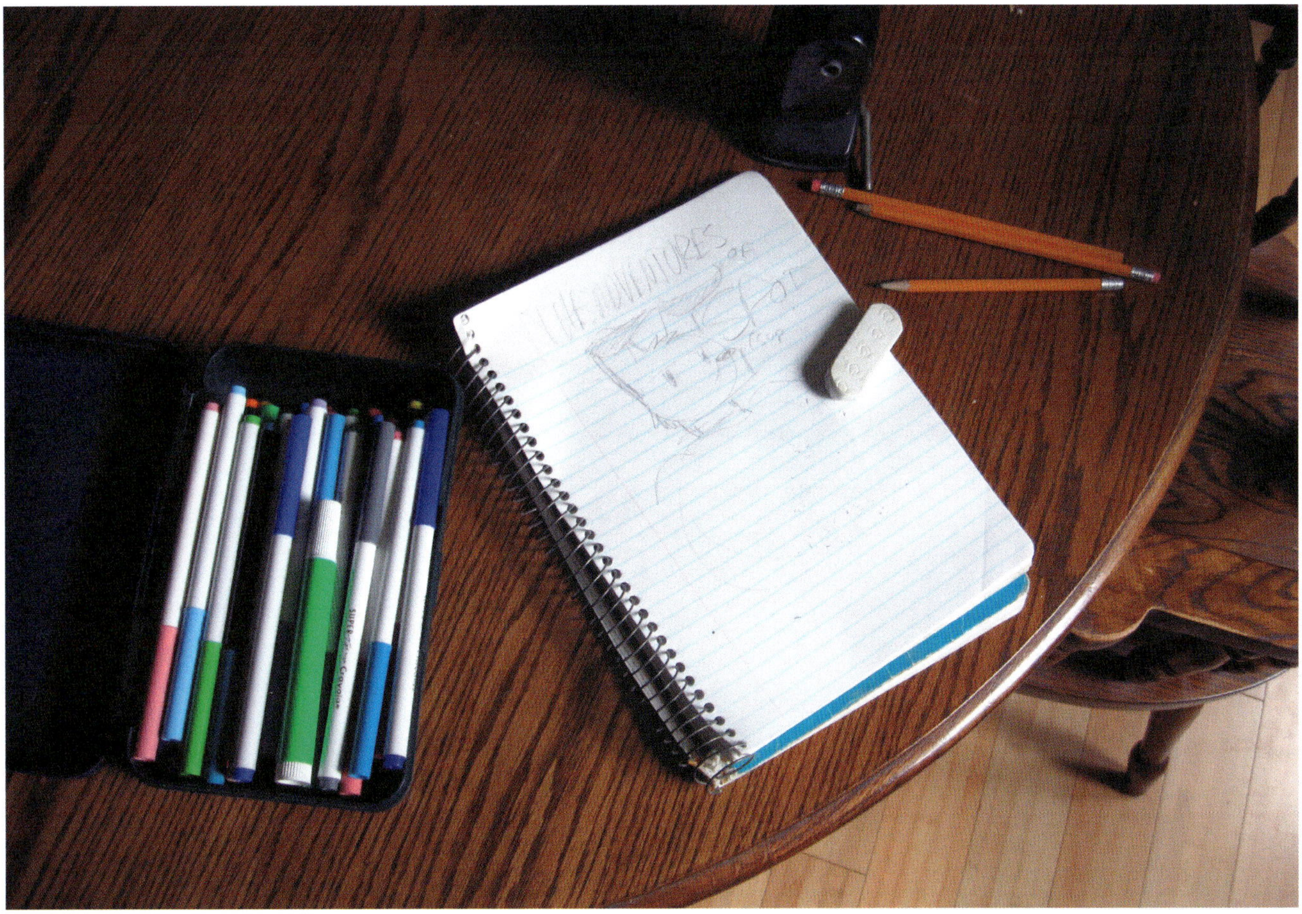

Peanut's Workspace

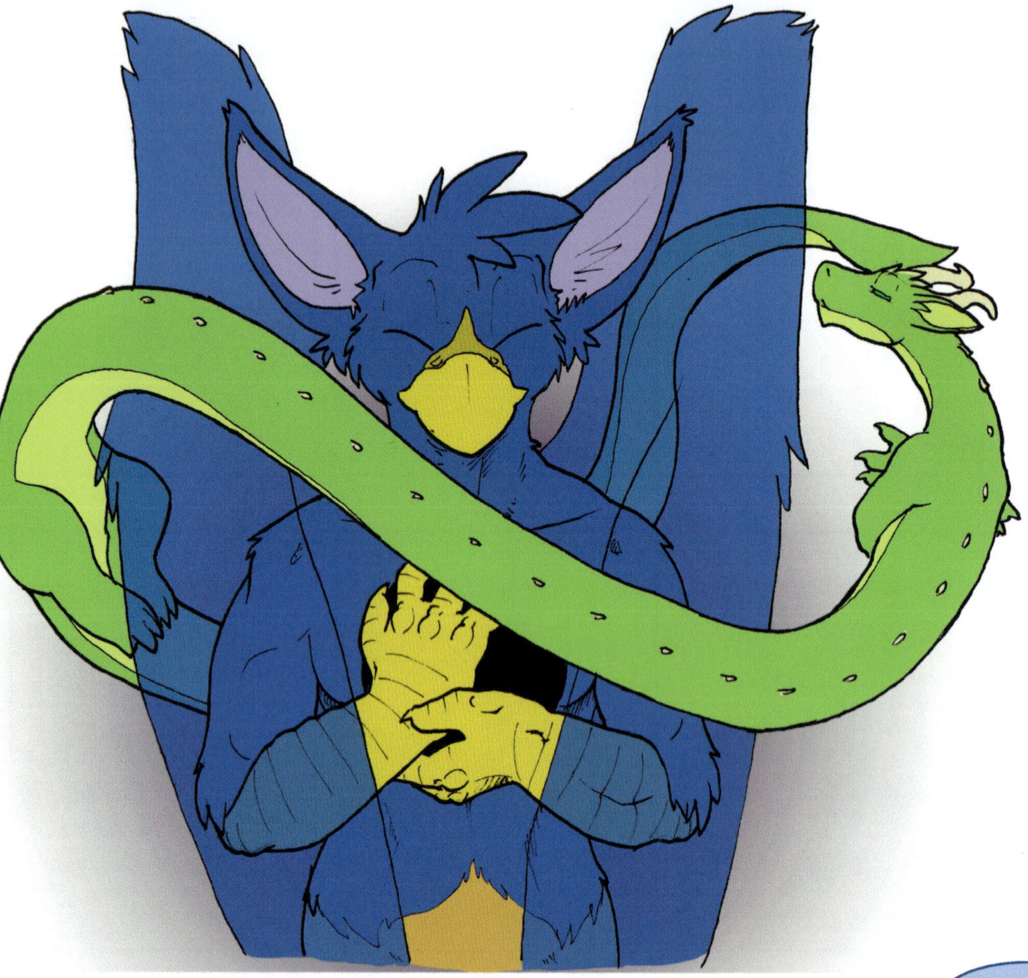

The Trial In Heaven

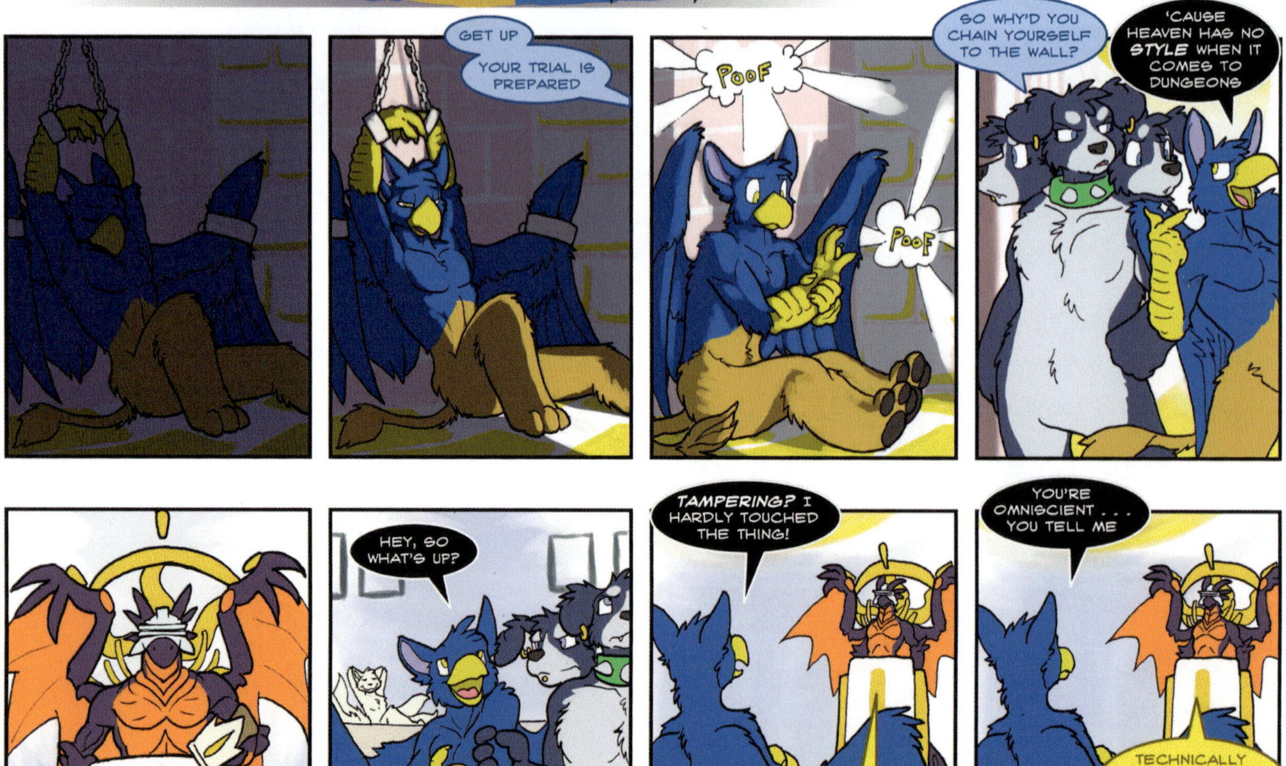

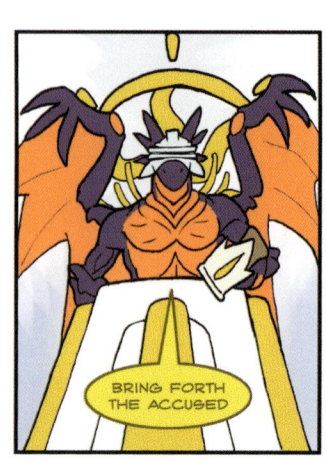

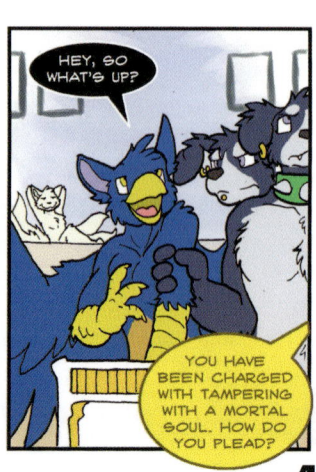

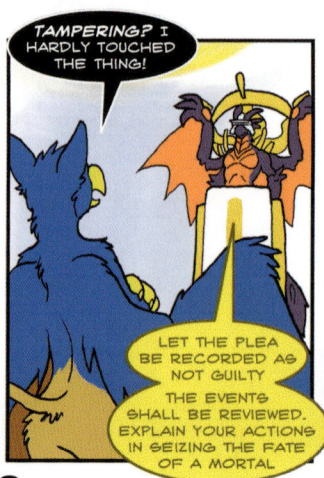

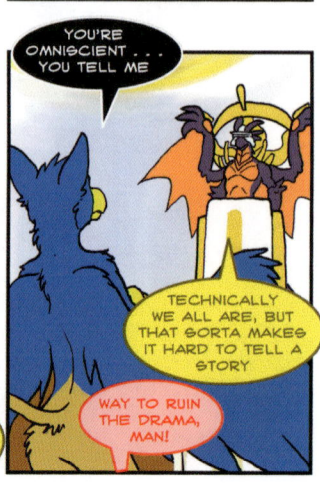

GET UP
YOUR TRIAL IS PREPARED
POOF
POOF
SO WHY'D YOU CHAIN YOURSELF TO THE WALL?
'CAUSE HEAVEN HAS NO STYLE WHEN IT COMES TO DUNGEONS
BRING FORTH THE ACCUSED
HEY, SO WHAT'S UP?
YOU HAVE BEEN CHARGED WITH TAMPERING WITH A MORTAL SOUL. HOW DO YOU PLEAD?
TAMPERING? I HARDLY TOUCHED THE THING!
LET THE PLEA BE RECORDED AS NOT GUILTY
THE EVENTS SHALL BE REVIEWED. EXPLAIN YOUR ACTIONS IN SEIZING THE FATE OF A MORTAL
YOU'RE OMNISCIENT . . . YOU TELL ME
TECHNICALLY WE ALL ARE, BUT THAT SORTA MAKES IT HARD TO TELL A STORY
WAY TO RUIN THE DRAMA, MAN!

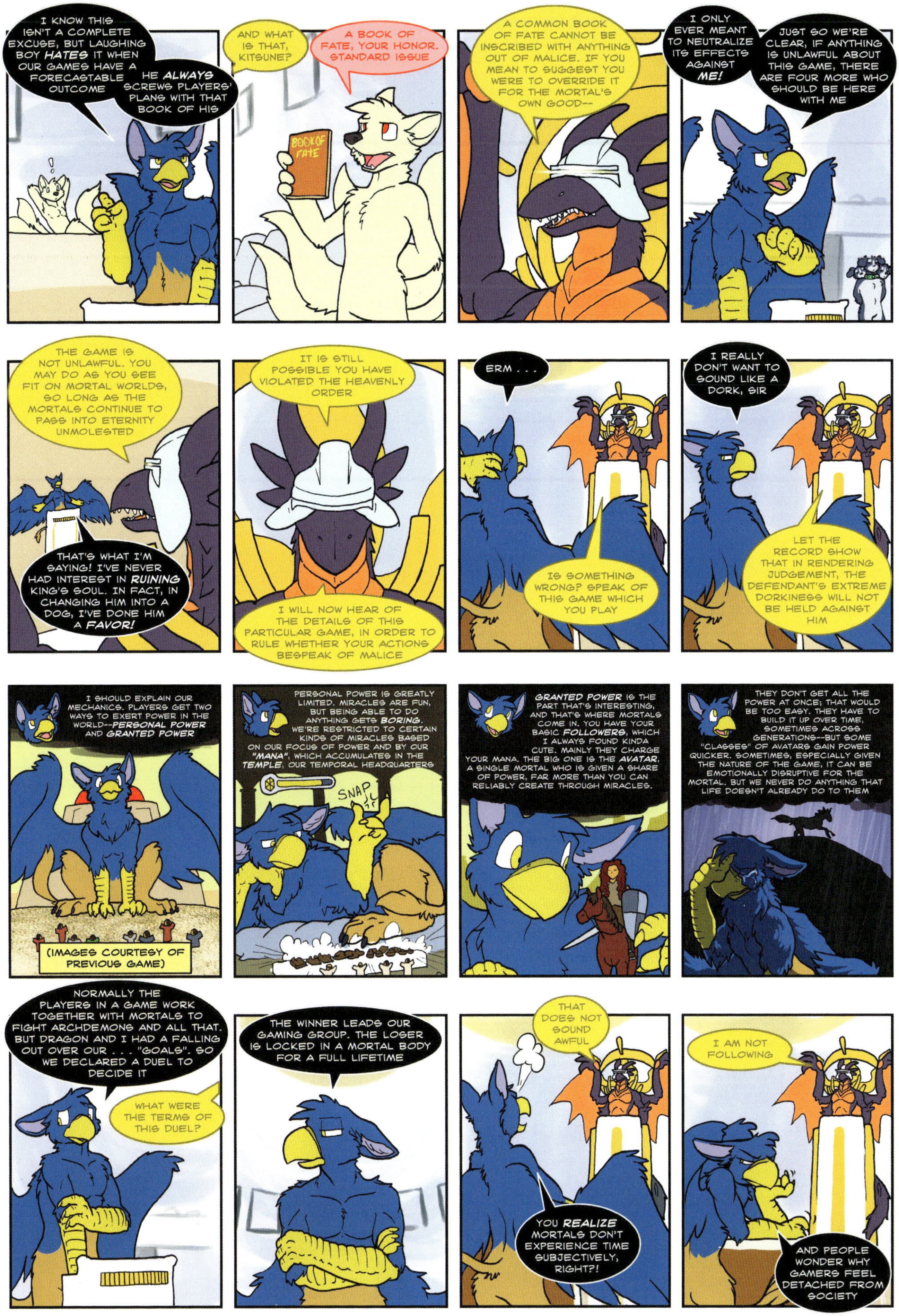

I KNOW THIS ISN'T A COMPLETE EXCUSE, BUT LAUGHING BOY ***HATES*** IT WHEN OUR GAMES HAVE A FORECASTABLE OUTCOME
HE ***ALWAYS*** SCREWS PLAYERS' PLANS WITH THAT BOOK OF HIS
AND WHAT IS THAT, KITSUNE?
A BOOK OF FATE, YOUR HONOR. STANDARD ISSUE
BOOK OF FATE
A COMMON BOOK OF FATE CANNOT BE INSCRIBED WITH ANYTHING OUT OF MALICE. IF YOU MEAN TO SUGGEST YOU WERE TO OVERRIDE IT FOR THE MORTAL'S OWN GOOD--
I ONLY EVER MEANT TO NEUTRALIZE ITS EFFECTS AGAINST ***ME!***
JUST SO WE'RE CLEAR, IF ANYTHING IS UNLAWFUL ABOUT THIS GAME, THERE ARE FOUR MORE WHO SHOULD BE HERE WITH ME
THE GAME IS NOT UNLAWFUL. YOU MAY DO AS YOU SEE FIT ON MORTAL WORLDS, SO LONG AS THE MORTALS CONTINUE TO PASS INTO ETERNITY UNMOLESTED
THAT'S WHAT I'M SAYING! I'VE NEVER HAD INTEREST IN ***RUINING*** KING'S SOUL. IN FACT, IN CHANGING HIM INTO A DOG, I'VE DONE HIM A ***FAVOR!***
IT IS STILL POSSIBLE YOU HAVE VIOLATED THE HEAVENLY ORDER
I WILL NOW HEAR OF THE DETAILS OF THIS PARTICULAR GAME, IN ORDER TO RULE WHETHER YOUR ACTIONS BESPEAK OF MALICE
ERM . . .
IS SOMETHING WRONG? SPEAK OF THIS GAME WHICH YOU PLAY
I REALLY DON'T WANT TO SOUND LIKE A DORK, SIR
LET THE RECORD SHOW THAT IN RENDERING JUDGEMENT, THE DEFENDANT'S EXTREME DORKINESS WILL NOT BE HELD AGAINST HIM
I SHOULD EXPLAIN OUR MECHANICS. PLAYERS GET TWO WAYS TO EXERT POWER IN THE WORLD--***PERSONAL POWER*** AND ***GRANTED POWER***
(IMAGES COURTESY OF PREVIOUS GAME)
PERSONAL POWER IS GREATLY LIMITED. MIRACLES ARE FUN, BUT BEING ABLE TO DO ANYTHING GETS ***BORING***. WE'RE RESTRICTED TO CERTAIN KINDS OF MIRACLES BASED ON OUR FOCUS OF POWER AND BY OUR ***"MANA"***, WHICH ACCUMULATES IN THE ***TEMPLE***, OUR TEMPORAL HEADQUARTERS
SNAP
GRANTED POWER IS THE PART THAT'S INTERESTING, AND THAT'S WHERE MORTALS COME IN. YOU HAVE YOUR BASIC ***FOLLOWERS***, WHICH I ALWAYS FOUND KINDA CUTE. MAINLY THEY CHARGE YOUR MANA. THE BIG ONE IS THE ***AVATAR***, A SINGLE MORTAL WHO IS GIVEN A SHARE OF POWER, FAR MORE THAN YOU CAN RELIABLY CREATE THROUGH MIRACLES.
THEY DON'T GET ALL THE POWER AT ONCE; THAT WOULD BE TOO EASY. THEY HAVE TO BUILD IT UP OVER TIME, SOMETIMES ACROSS GENERATIONS--BUT SOME "CLASSES" OF AVATARS GAIN POWER QUICKER. SOMETIMES, ESPECIALLY GIVEN THE NATURE OF THE GAME, IT CAN BE EMOTIONALLY DISRUPTIVE FOR THE MORTAL. BUT WE NEVER DO ANYTHING THAT LIFE DOESN'T ALREADY DO TO THEM
NORMALLY THE PLAYERS IN A GAME WORK TOGETHER WITH MORTALS TO FIGHT ARCHDEMONS AND ALL THAT. BUT DRAGON AND I HAD A FALLING OUT OVER OUR . . . "GOALS". SO WE DECLARED A DUEL TO DECIDE IT
WHAT WERE THE TERMS OF THIS DUEL?
THE WINNER LEADS OUR GAMING GROUP. THE LOSER IS LOCKED IN A MORTAL BODY FOR A FULL LIFETIME
THAT DOES NOT SOUND AWFUL
YOU ***REALIZE*** MORTALS DON'T EXPERIENCE TIME SUBJECTIVELY, RIGHT?!
I AM NOT FOLLOWING
AND PEOPLE WONDER WHY GAMERS FEEL DETACHED FROM SOCIETY

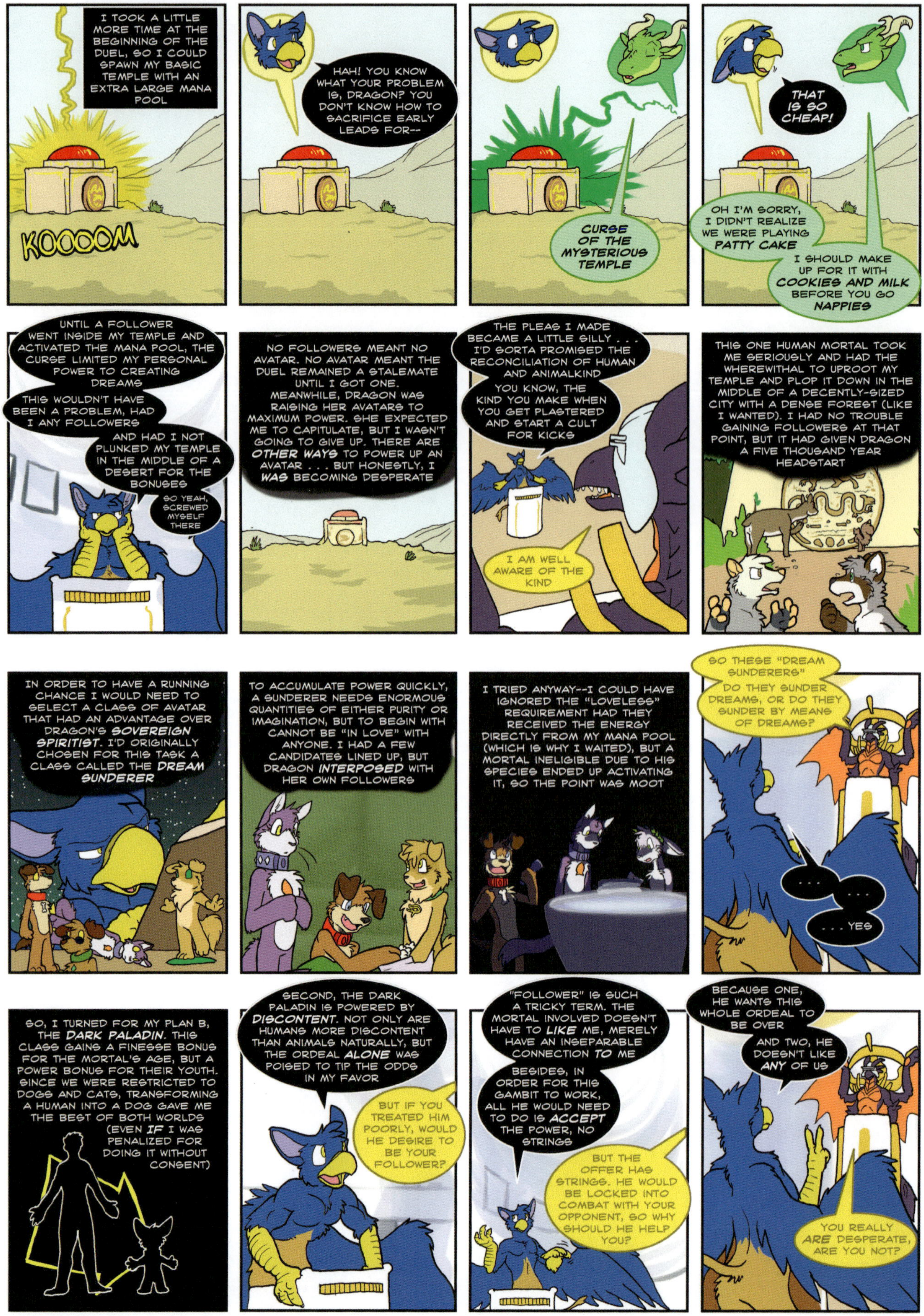
I TOOK A LITTLE MORE TIME AT THE BEGINNING OF THE DUEL, SO I COULD SPAWN MY BASIC TEMPLE WITH AN EXTRA LARGE MANA POOL
KOOOOM
HAH! YOU KNOW WHAT YOUR PROBLEM IS, DRAGON? YOU DON'T KNOW HOW TO SACRIFICE EARLY LEADS FOR--
CURSE OF THE MYSTERIOUS TEMPLE
THAT IS SO CHEAP!
OH I'M SORRY, I DIDN'T REALIZE WE WERE PLAYING PATTY CAKE
I SHOULD MAKE UP FOR IT WITH COOKIES AND MILK BEFORE YOU GO NAPPIES
UNTIL A FOLLOWER WENT INSIDE MY TEMPLE AND ACTIVATED THE MANA POOL, THE CURSE LIMITED MY PERSONAL POWER TO CREATING DREAMS
THIS WOULDN'T HAVE BEEN A PROBLEM, HAD I ANY FOLLOWERS
AND HAD I NOT PLUNKED MY TEMPLE IN THE MIDDLE OF A DESERT FOR THE BONUSES
SO YEAH, SCREWED MYSELF THERE
NO FOLLOWERS MEANT NO AVATAR. NO AVATAR MEANT THE DUEL REMAINED A STALEMATE UNTIL I GOT ONE. MEANWHILE, DRAGON WAS RAISING HER AVATARS TO MAXIMUM POWER. SHE EXPECTED ME TO CAPITULATE, BUT I WASN'T GOING TO GIVE UP. THERE ARE OTHER WAYS TO POWER UP AN AVATAR . . . BUT HONESTLY, I WAS BECOMING DESPERATE
THE PLEAS I MADE BECAME A LITTLE SILLY . . . I'D SORTA PROMISED THE RECONCILIATION OF HUMAN AND ANIMALKIND
YOU KNOW, THE KIND YOU MAKE WHEN YOU GET PLASTERED AND START A CULT FOR KICKS
I AM WELL AWARE OF THE KIND
THIS ONE HUMAN MORTAL TOOK ME SERIOUSLY AND HAD THE WHEREWITHAL TO UPROOT MY TEMPLE AND PLOP IT DOWN IN THE MIDDLE OF A DECENTLY-SIZED CITY WITH A DENSE FOREST (LIKE I WANTED). I HAD NO TROUBLE GAINING FOLLOWERS AT THAT POINT, BUT IT HAD GIVEN DRAGON A FIVE THOUSAND YEAR HEADSTART
IN ORDER TO HAVE A RUNNING CHANCE I WOULD NEED TO SELECT A CLASS OF AVATAR THAT HAD AN ADVANTAGE OVER DRAGON'S SOVEREIGN SPIRITIST. I'D ORIGINALLY CHOSEN FOR THIS TASK A CLASS CALLED THE DREAM SUNDERER
TO ACCUMULATE POWER QUICKLY, A SUNDERER NEEDS ENORMOUS QUANTITIES OF EITHER PURITY OR IMAGINATION, BUT TO BEGIN WITH CANNOT BE "IN LOVE" WITH ANYONE. I HAD A FEW CANDIDATES LINED UP, BUT DRAGON INTERPOSED WITH HER OWN FOLLOWERS
I TRIED ANYWAY--I COULD HAVE IGNORED THE "LOVELESS" REQUIREMENT HAD THEY RECEIVED THE ENERGY DIRECTLY FROM MY MANA POOL (WHICH IS WHY I WAITED), BUT A MORTAL INELIGIBLE DUE TO HIS SPECIES ENDED UP ACTIVATING IT, SO THE POINT WAS MOOT
SO THESE "DREAM SUNDERERS"
DO THEY SUNDER DREAMS, OR DO THEY SUNDER BY MEANS OF DREAMS?
. . .
. . .
. . . YES
SO, I TURNED FOR MY PLAN B, THE DARK PALADIN. THIS CLASS GAINS A FINESSE BONUS FOR THE MORTAL'S AGE, BUT A POWER BONUS FOR THEIR YOUTH. SINCE WE WERE RESTRICTED TO DOGS AND CATS, TRANSFORMING A HUMAN INTO A DOG GAVE ME THE BEST OF BOTH WORLDS
(EVEN IF I WAS PENALIZED FOR DOING IT WITHOUT CONSENT)
SECOND, THE DARK PALADIN IS POWERED BY DISCONTENT. NOT ONLY ARE HUMANS MORE DISCONTENT THAN ANIMALS NATURALLY, BUT THE ORDEAL ALONE WAS POISED TO TIP THE ODDS IN MY FAVOR
BUT IF YOU TREATED HIM POORLY, WOULD HE DESIRE TO BE YOUR FOLLOWER?
"FOLLOWER" IS SUCH A TRICKY TERM. THE MORTAL INVOLVED DOESN'T HAVE TO LIKE ME, MERELY HAVE AN INSEPARABLE CONNECTION TO ME
BESIDES, IN ORDER FOR THIS GAMBIT TO WORK, ALL HE WOULD NEED TO DO IS ACCEPT THE POWER, NO STRINGS
BUT THE OFFER HAS STRINGS. HE WOULD BE LOCKED INTO COMBAT WITH YOUR OPPONENT, SO WHY SHOULD HE HELP YOU?
BECAUSE ONE, HE WANTS THIS WHOLE ORDEAL TO BE OVER
AND TWO, HE DOESN'T LIKE ANY OF US
YOU REALLY ARE DESPERATE, ARE YOU NOT?

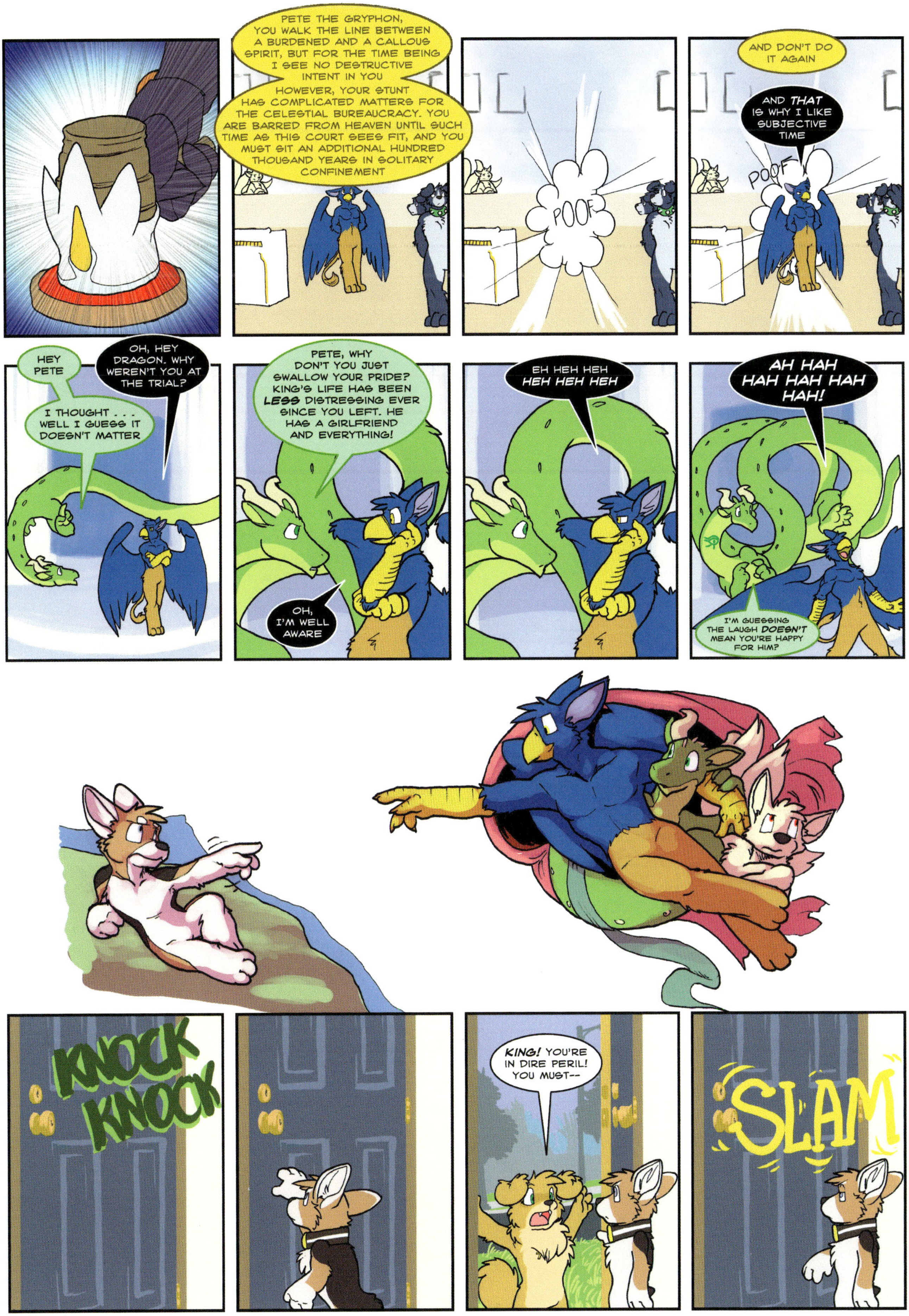
PETE THE GRYPHON, YOU WALK THE LINE BETWEEN A BURDENED AND A CALLOUS SPIRIT, BUT FOR THE TIME BEING I SEE NO DESTRUCTIVE INTENT IN YOU
HOWEVER, YOUR STUNT HAS COMPLICATED MATTERS FOR THE CELESTIAL BUREAUCRACY. YOU ARE BARRED FROM HEAVEN UNTIL SUCH TIME AS THIS COURT SEES FIT, AND YOU MUST SIT AN ADDITIONAL HUNDRED THOUSAND YEARS IN SOLITARY CONFINEMENT
POOF
AND DON'T DO IT AGAIN
AND THAT IS WHY I LIKE SUBJECTIVE TIME
POOF
HEY PETE
OH, HEY DRAGON. WHY WEREN'T YOU AT THE TRIAL?
I THOUGHT . . . WELL I GUESS IT DOESN'T MATTER
PETE, WHY DON'T YOU JUST SWALLOW YOUR PRIDE? KING'S LIFE HAS BEEN LESS DISTRESSING EVER SINCE YOU LEFT. HE HAS A GIRLFRIEND AND EVERYTHING!
OH, I'M WELL AWARE
EH HEH HEH HEH HEH HEH
AH HAH HAH HAH HAH HAH!
I'M GUESSING THE LAUGH DOESN'T MEAN YOU'RE HAPPY FOR HIM?
KNOCK KNOCK
KING! YOU'RE IN DIRE PERIL! YOU MUST--
SLAM

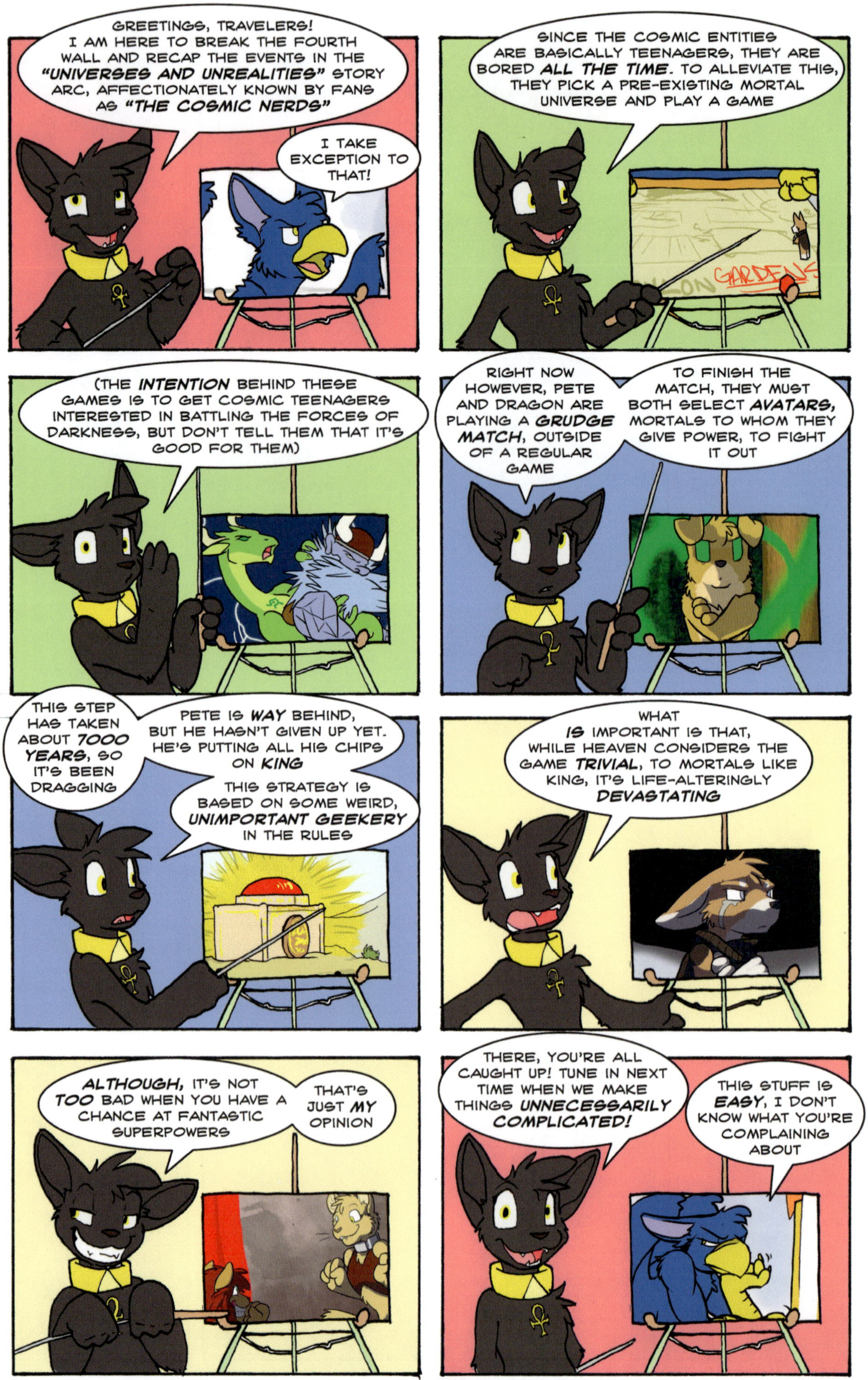
GREETINGS, TRAVELERS! I AM HERE TO BREAK THE FOURTH WALL AND RECAP THE EVENTS IN THE "UNIVERSES AND UNREALITIES" STORY ARC, AFFECTIONATELY KNOWN BY FANS AS "THE COSMIC NERDS"
I TAKE EXCEPTION TO THAT!
SINCE THE COSMIC ENTITIES ARE BASICALLY TEENAGERS, THEY ARE BORED ALL THE TIME. TO ALLEVIATE THIS, THEY PICK A PRE-EXISTING MORTAL UNIVERSE AND PLAY A GAME
(THE INTENTION BEHIND THESE GAMES IS TO GET COSMIC TEENAGERS INTERESTED IN BATTLING THE FORCES OF DARKNESS, BUT DON'T TELL THEM THAT IT'S GOOD FOR THEM)
RIGHT NOW HOWEVER, PETE AND DRAGON ARE PLAYING A GRUDGE MATCH, OUTSIDE OF A REGULAR GAME
TO FINISH THE MATCH, THEY MUST BOTH SELECT AVATARS, MORTALS TO WHOM THEY GIVE POWER, TO FIGHT IT OUT
THIS STEP HAS TAKEN ABOUT 7000 YEARS, SO IT'S BEEN DRAGGING
PETE IS WAY BEHIND, BUT HE HASN'T GIVEN UP YET. HE'S PUTTING ALL HIS CHIPS ON KING
THIS STRATEGY IS BASED ON SOME WEIRD, UNIMPORTANT GEEKERY IN THE RULES
WHAT IS IMPORTANT IS THAT, WHILE HEAVEN CONSIDERS THE GAME TRIVIAL, TO MORTALS LIKE KING, IT'S LIFE-ALTERINGLY DEVASTATING
ALTHOUGH, IT'S NOT TOO BAD WHEN YOU HAVE A CHANCE AT FANTASTIC SUPERPOWERS
THAT'S JUST MY OPINION
THERE, YOU'RE ALL CAUGHT UP! TUNE IN NEXT TIME WHEN WE MAKE THINGS UNNECESSARILY COMPLICATED!
THIS STUFF IS EASY, I DON'T KNOW WHAT YOU'RE COMPLAINING ABOUT

Next time, on

Housepets!

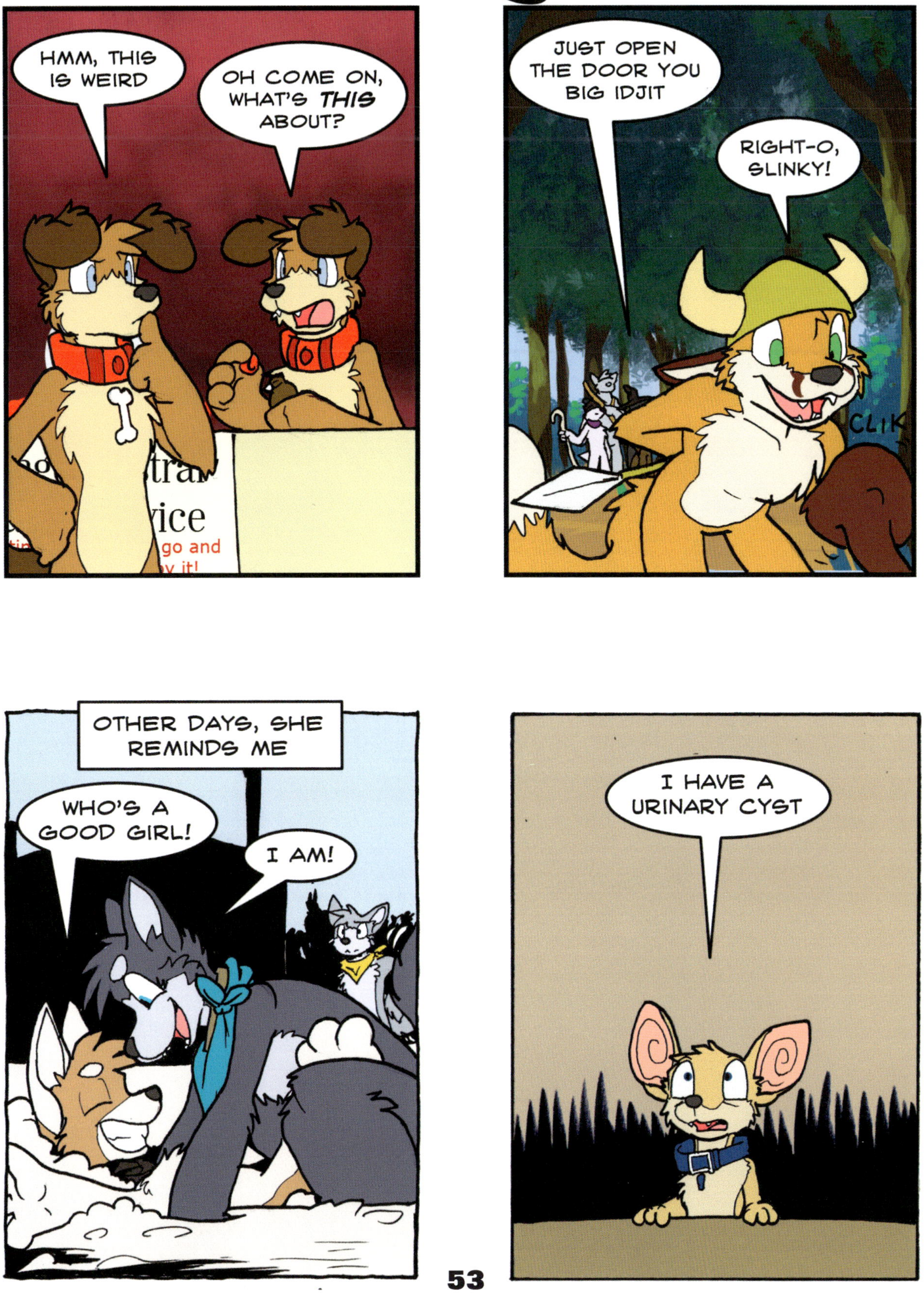
HMM, THIS IS WEIRD
OH COME ON, WHAT'S *THIS* ABOUT?
JUST OPEN THE DOOR YOU BIG IDJIT
RIGHT-O, SLINKY!
CLIK
OTHER DAYS, SHE REMINDS ME
WHO'S A GOOD GIRL!
I AM!
I HAVE A URINARY CYST